MORE THAN A *Story*

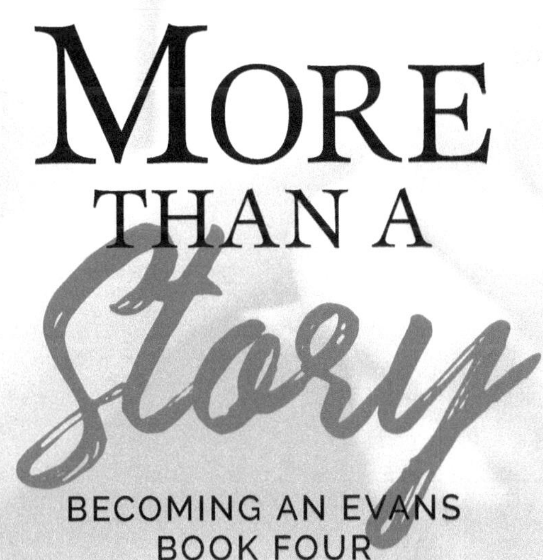

JENNI BARA

Point Publishing

More Than A Hero
Becoming an Evans Book Four

Edits by Jennifer Galan Mistic Edits
Line, Copy and Proofreading by Beth Lawton VB Edits
Interior formatting by Alt 19 Creative
Cover by Kari March Designs

ISBN: 978-1-7375600-6-7 (ebook)
ISBN: 978-1-7375600-7-4 (paperback)

Jennibara.com

*For everyone with a plan who
had to learn to pivot; I promise,
even when it seems like the end
of the world, it works out.*

1

"GET SOME GLASSES, jackass—I'll donate to the cause." The man's shouts caused Taran to wince, and not only because of the volume.

New York fans were obnoxious, but they also tended to be *wrong*. That was a good call. The ball was so low it almost hit the dirt. Not even close to the strike zone.

"Guy's got it out for us. He might as wella'be wearing purple the way he's calling for the Rockies," another fan added as Taran worked not to roll her eyes.

The ridiculous part of it was, the game was all but over: two outs, top of the ninth, Metros by three. Nobody was on base for the Rockies. The fans might be screaming, but all they needed was one more strike, and the game was done.

"Strike," the man behind the plate called as the ball smacked into the leather mitt. Cheers sounded across the stadium, and the music played. Check the box for another NY Metros win, putting them at the top of the AL East.

Even with the screaming crowd, the entire game had been a disappointment. Taran needed a story for her sports gossip blog, and typically, a Saturday night at the ballpark brought something out.

But not tonight.

It was like everyone fun stayed home. Not one gossip-worthy person had shown up. No politician eating a hot dog, no Grammy winner singing the National Anthem, no star-studded boxes for a photo op of Hollywood's elite. Not even former players watching their team; just an average game.

She pushed off the armrests and stood before heading up the concrete steps that led away from the *Sports Illustrated* box seats behind the home team dugout. Although the tickets were up for grabs for any of the reporters on staff, she used them more than anyone else. Sneaking between the people, she weaved toward the tunnels beneath the seats that housed forty thousand fans for every game day.

"Hey, kid," security called out as she rounded the corner out of the crowd and into the back tunnels. "Hey—*kid.*"

Taran turned. Being four-eleven, she dealt with this a lot. Especially when she dressed to blend in. Not being noticed was the key to getting a story.

"Not a kid, not lost, don't need to find mom or dad." She pulled her lanyard out from under her shirt and flashed her press pass.

"She's good," Grey announced from farther down the tunnel. He was normally the security doorman, and Taran knew him well. The middle-aged man smirked as she got closer. "Might have even confused me today, Taran. Really working the young kid look."

She shrugged. It was easier if everyone ignored her. And everyone usually ignored a kid. Her image required her to blend in.

"Got something juicy?" he asked, waiting for a funny story she'd usually spill without effort, but she shook her head.

"Not today. It's like fun had an allergy to the game tonight."

"It *was* quiet. We didn't even kick anyone out. But the Rockies suck this year, so it's not shocking. I expected a blowout."

Taran nodded, but her phone buzzed in her pocket before she could add more. The second buzz told her it was a call, not a text, meaning it was her family or her boss. She wasn't sure which was worse. Either way, she was in for a lecture.

"Have a good night," Taran said to Grey before heading farther down the tunnel. She pulled her phone out, frowning at the name before accepting the call. "Hey."

"How was it? Get anything?" her boss said without even a hello.

Taran sighed. "Wayne, my blog is not your problem."

"Your blog helps drive our hard copy sales. It's linked on our website, and if you keep up the stories, people keep reading your full-length articles. And for the last few weeks, its sucked."

Taran scratched at the coffee stain on her T-shirt above the words: *It's okay if you don't like baseball. It's kind of a smart person sport.* It was impossible to say he was being unfair because her blog had been dragging for a while. It was April, and her clicks had been down since mid-March. She knew why. Like she expected, March had been a rough month, and finding gossip wasn't high on her list of priorities. If she wanted to take the easy way out, she could have explained why she was dragging. But she was tired of the sympathy.

"I'll find something," she assured him.

"Or create it." His statement was flippant.

Taran sucked in hard. "We work for *Sports Illustrated*, not the *National Inquirer.*"

"It's a blog, for God's sake. Get the clicks, then retract it tomorrow. No one cares."

Her fingers tightened on the phone, pressing the metal into her palm. There were hard lines she didn't cross.

"That's not who I am." Even if she was currently a gossip reporter, she wasn't willing to outright lie in any story. Man, she was amazed that they even needed to have this conversation. Five years ago, she never would have believed she'd work for this type of man. But over these last few years, everything about her life had taken a hard left turn.

"Yeah, you and your *principles*. Anyway, how about next month's article?"

"I have until Monday to find someone."

She wrote full-length feature articles for the monthly magazine. Her stories were more color than fact and focused hard on the players' lives outside of sports.

"Have you contacted any of my big five?"

Wayne had a list of athletes he wanted her to feature before the end of the calendar year. Although he deemed it a reasonable list, she knew better. The first was the hottest rookie baseball player of the year, and everyone was after him. The second one was a soccer star living in Guatemala. She'd reached out to his agent twice already but hadn't even gotten a call back. The next two were on a media hiatus, and the last one—the elusive white whale—had never in his entire career done a color interview. He was good at answering questions about his game, even when he was playing poorly, but if anyone dared to ask about his personal life, the interview ended.

"You're in the same building as Corey Matthews. Make an attempt."

The white whale himself. It wasn't shocking that Wayne demanded she go after him first. But unless the stars aligned and luck suddenly had her back, she wasn't going to get Corey Matthews to agree to anything. He *hated* gossip reporters.

"Do you hear me?"

"Yeah." She glanced down at her clothes. She'd stand out like a sore thumb if she went into the locker room looking like a kid. There was a change of clothes in her car, so she'd have to head out to the parking garage and hope Matthews didn't leave before she got back. But everyone knew the pitcher bounced out as quickly as possible after a game.

"Yeah, what?" he asked. "Do I need to take care of locking down articles for you? Try to keep up with the big boys, princess."

Wayne had never wanted to hire her. He was old, crotchety, and a full-blown sexist. He thought the only place women belonged in sports reporting was in front of the camera where they could look cute. She fantasized about stabbing him with a fork, but that was about as likely as her getting an interview with the elusive Matthews. Still, she needed this job. Any chance of her dream job had ended in disaster two years ago.

"I'll get one of the five by Monday." She made the impossible promise to get him off the phone and hung up, having no earthly idea how the hell she was going to do it.

2

TONIGHT, COREY DIDN'T quite hate the Captain America nickname like he normally did.

"We're heading to Poison. Want to come?" Ryan Daily, the second pitcher in the Metros' rotation, walked out of the locker room behind him. The guys on the team went to that bar after home games, and everyone in New York knew this. It was a great place to get media attention or a quick hookup, but it wasn't the spot to relax after a game. At least not for Corey.

"Thanks, but I'll pass," Corey said.

His baseball team was starting out the season at the top of the division, and Corey had pitched another great game. Including preseason, it was his twelfth in a row. A record for the man whose head game caused his pitching to be about as consistent as the spring weather. Even if that was the only thing going well in life, that should be enough, but it wasn't.

"Blowing us off for a hot date?" Daily asked.

Corey just smirked.

Daily smiled as they fist-bumped. "Have fun, Cap. Bet she'll love that your ugly mug is about to be all over," Daily said as he walked away.

Sideline was finally thinking about replacing the face of their multinational sportswear brand. And since their current brand ambassador, Marc Demoda, and Corey were tight, they'd talked Sideline into a campaign using both men to transition from Marc to Corey.

He'd *good old boyed* the media after the game, and not one of the eight men in the locker room had mentioned his third inning. Even the harsh New York media had nothing bad to say about Corey these days.

"Good game, Captain," another teammate called before he made it out of the locker room but he smiled. No one was being sarcastic when they called him Captain America today.

His phone beeped in his pocket and he wondered which of the many Evans siblings was texting him.

He was surprised to see Clayton's name on the screen.

Call me.

He was grateful that was all it said.

Corey flicked up and hit the call button.

"Dude," was the twenty-two-year-old's replacement for hello.

"Where's the fire?" Corey answered.

"It's official. They don't want me."

He sighed. Clayton was the youngest Evans sibling—more than ten years younger than Corey—and was currently at USC on a hot deadline with the NFL draft. All he wanted was to come home to New York with a contract to be the next QB for any tri-state area team. It hadn't looked promising since none of the teams needed a quarterback for a few more years, barring some devastating injury, and Clayton was too high priced for a team without the need.

"You're pouting about being one of the top three draft picks this year. You know that, right kid?" Corey asked.

"Fuck you. I called *you* because I thought you would get it," Clayton shot back.

Corey wouldn't correct him about who actually made the call, because the truth of it was that he knew exactly how Clayton felt. He, too, had wanted more than anything to come back to New York and pitch after college.

Corey cracked his neck left and right. He couldn't lie to Clayton and say he was good enough to play wherever he wanted.

Ten years ago, Corey, sporting an Olympic gold medal, had been one of the best pitchers to come into the MLB, and even that wasn't enough to get him back into the New York area. The Houston Astros had drafted him.

He stopped mid-step and shut his eyes, reliving that time of his life.

Looking back, Houston hadn't been *that* bad. The city itself was great, and the space he gained from all the drama in his life had been his saving grace. Plus, he'd had fun in Houston, and he'd grown up a lot.

"Hello?" Clayton demanded in his ear, and Corey wondered how long he'd been silent. He glanced around, realizing he couldn't stand here staring into space, and continued to the exit.

"Yes, I know how you feel, Clay, but tell me this. Do you really want to play football?" he asked, juggling the phone on his shoulder and searching for his keys in his gym bag. That's what it came down to—if he wanted to play, he'd go where they'd play him.

"*Yes.*" All of Clayton's frustration came through in that one word.

"Who wants ya?" Corey asked. He was going to sell the hell out of that team. Especially one that might, in the future, let Clayton go to a team that could pay more.

"Mostly Denver and Seattle."

"Ha, the hauntingly bad luck of going top three."

Clayton snorted.

"Joking aside, Seattle's got the first pick and Denver the third, right?"

"If you say I'm living every kid's dream, I'm hanging up."

He remembered people saying similar things to him when he was drafted out of Penn State. It had crushed him not to be in New York.

"It's either going to be the mile-high can't breathe capital of the world or the rainy dark cloud of the US," Clayton moaned.

"You really think both cities suck? Or you've decided not to give anyone but New York a chance?" he asked, as he started down the tunnel to the parking garage.

"Both cities suck. Suckety suck, suck, suck." Clayton sounded like a teenager.

"Don't be a pussy. Seattle—that city has potential. I know it means going number one, but the piano bars, the fish market, the docks, the underground, the club scene—all awesome. And it's more of a neighborhood than any other city. I'd go there." Corey nodded at another of his teammates as he opened the tunnel door into the parking garage. "I doubt you'll be lonely since we'll all visit you constantly."

"Just what I need, a bunch of people checking up on me. I hate the west coast," Clayton mumbled.

"Really?" Corey shook his head and hit the unlock button on his key fob. "You seem happy as a pig in shit every time I see you in Cali."

"I mean—" He couldn't finish the sentence because it was true.

"Look, Clay, you want to be home, but it's not time yet. I know exactly how you feel, but being away from everyone means you can put the time in to earn your stripes in Seattle." Corey leaned against the side of the red truck.

"I guess that's true. You guys would try to make me hang out all the time, especially Beth. I mean, I'm her favorite," Clayton joked about his sister and one of Corey's best friends.

"Horseshit. I'm her favorite. And besides, Seattle won't be able to afford you in three years, and you can force a trade back home then."

"Ya think?" Clayton sounded hopeful.

Corey switched his phone to the other hand and rolled his sore shoulder, causing the ice still taped to him to crack. "I'm sure. Denver could afford to keep you. Seattle can't. Ask your agent. He'll tell you the same thing. Go with Seattle."

"Thanks bro," Clayton said.

"Anytime, Clay, and don't melt in all that rain," Corey teased as he adjusted his shoulder again, and turned his head a bit, catching the movement of someone in the shadows. He narrowed his eyes. It looked like a ten or twelve-year-old boy hiding behind the pole several feet away. He didn't understand how he could have gotten into the parking garage, but the kid was definitely close enough to hear the conversation.

"Oh, by the way, that third inning—fuck—you sucked. Did you forget that the guys shouldn't be hitting the ball?" Clayton was laughing as Corey cursed him.

"You want a pep talk going into the draft? Don't mention that inning. I got out of it, so don't even start with the worst one of the season shit." Corey moved straight to the pole, heading after the kid. "I got to go, Clay."

The white stripes of the Yankee cap were easy to see moving in the dark between two SUVs. Corey guessed the route and quickly eased the other way around the big black Escalade, beating him to the back of the car. The kid was still looking over his shoulder, checking to see where he'd gone, when he smacked into Corey's chest and fell backward.

Corey caught his small arm before the poor kid hit the concrete. "Whatcha doing here, kid?"

The Yankees cap snapped up, and a pair of sea-mist-green eyes looked up at him. "My job," said a voice that was definitely *not* male.

He quickly released his hold on the thin arm, not wanting to be accused of assault, and the woman stumbled back again but righted herself.

Corey crossed his arms over his chest and stared down at the little woman. She couldn't have been more than five foot, and she was maybe a hundred pounds soaking wet. There was not a curve on her, at least not one he could see under her big white T-shirt and what looked like a ten-year-old boy's jeans. He rocked back on his heels.

"What exactly is your job?"

A small crease appeared between her green eyes. "You don't know who I am?"

Normally, that question came across snotty, but the way she said it was more incredulous. Like honest to God, he should know her. Corey wasn't one of those guys who forgot a woman, and he scanned her again—from the stupid Yankee hat riding low on her forehead, covering ink-black hair, to the coffee stain on the white shirt with a snarky saying, to the tips of the Nike sneakers with a hole in one toe.

"Nope," he said unapologetically.

"Well then, let's meet again for maybe the twelfth time." Her sarcastic tone set his teeth on edge.

"If I've met you twelve times, you clearly aren't memorable," Corey snapped back.

"Whatever you say." She rolled those sea-green eyes making a *you're an idiot* face.

"Who the hell are you?" he demanded.

"Taran. Murphy." Each syllable popped slowly out of her mouth as she raised a single thin eyebrow. It would have pissed him off if the name didn't send ice into his veins.

A breath hissed through his teeth. "*Sports Illustrated* gossip reporter."

Normally, he played the game of media darling with reporters. But not this one. This one traded in athlete gossip. She would exploit an athlete's personal life for a career boost. The kind he never gave a second glance. He didn't remember her because he'd probably never looked at her. Want to talk about his game, his team, his arm, his contracts, his agent? He'd give a reporter all the time in the world. Want to talk about his personal life? As far as he was concerned, the reporter didn't exist. But at the moment, her existence was glaring. He reran the conversation with Clayton through his mind. Seattle and Denver might both be off the table if any of what either man said was reported. Nobody wanted a whiney quarterback who didn't want to be part of the team. And Corey couldn't remember exactly what he had said aloud about Clayton's feelings.

"In Case You Didn't Know." She quoted the name of her monthly article.

"What did you hear?" Corey demanded.

"Enough." The cat that ate the canary smile she flashed had his hands fisting. "I think I've got this week's blog."

"Blog?" he asked, narrowing his eyes at her.

"It's when people write articles on a website," she said slowly, enunciating every word with a sugary sweet voice, implying he was a dumb fuck.

He knew what a damn blog was. He just hadn't realized she wrote one.

"What will it take for you to forget it?" he asked, but he sneered at being forced into a game he didn't want to play.

She paused and stared at him for a beat, and then a devilish smile slowly spread across her face. "The full interview for next month's article."

He snorted. "Clayton's not doing interviews. He's on a media hiatus."

It almost looked like he'd confused her, but before he could zero in on the look, it was gone, replaced by an arrogant, not-my-problem-stare. "I'm sure Clayton would do an interview with someone you said was okay."

"Yeah, right." Anyone who knew Corey knew he'd never trust the person who wrote "In Case You Didn't Know."

"I'm sure you could convince him if you needed to." Her shrug was nearly imperceptible in that ridiculously big stained shirt.

"What do you expect me to do—call you my girlfriend and ask him for a favor?" He snorted again at the idiocy of the idea.

But Taran just smiled. "That would work."

Now he laughed outright. "Sorry, I don't fuck trash reporters—even desperate ones."

Those sea-mist eyes turned hard as diamonds. "No interest on this end either."

He glanced at her again. She probably had no life of her own. That's why other people's personal lives interested her so much.

"However, I want an invite to the Demodas' place. I know you're going, and so am I if you don't want to read about your lovely phone call with Clayton on my blog tomorrow." She shot him an icy glare, daring him to balk. "Your choice."

Corey wasn't playing chicken with a reporter. He turned to walk away, but she called out.

"By the way, he's right about the third."

Corey froze. How the hell could she know what Clayton had said about that inning? There was no way she could have heard him unless she'd paired his phone. He whipped back around.

"What?" he demanded.

"You heard me." She looked as intimidating as a ten-year-old boy, yet those green eyes said, *I know your secrets.*

"Clone my phone?"

She crossed her arms under her nonexistent chest. "Even I know there are lines."

"Blackmail isn't one of them?" he sneered.

"It's not blackmail. It's bribery since you're the one trying to buy your way out of my blog," she said. He didn't want to consider whether she had a point. He couldn't be the reason another trashy reporter ruined someone he cared about.

"Get in the car," he demanded, and didn't turn back to see whether she followed.

3

COREY WAS FUMING. He started the truck and backed out before he'd given her a chance to close the passenger door.

"Jesus," Taran snapped as the door smacked shut, but he ignored her, turning up the radio. "Country?"

"Three years in Houston," was his only reply.

Neither of them said another word.

Bringing her was a terrible idea, but he didn't know what else to do, and he refused to read about Clayton on every news outlet tomorrow. His stomach bottomed out at just the idea of that.

Hot Shots, Corey and Clayton's all-in-one agent, publicist, and financial adviser firm, had made the right call when they told Clayton to stay away from the media. He was already a big name, so Hot Shots suggested driving his brand up by not being available. But it had made the media crazy for anything to do with Clay. A story focused on him whining about hating the teams that wanted him would blow up the twenty-four-hour news cycle and kill a top draft pick for him. The story would be a big deal, so Taran Murphy had left him between a rock and a hard place, and the bitch knew it.

He stewed as he drove, getting angrier by the minute. It had been stupid to leave the tunnel's safety on the phone. But conversations with the Evanses weren't usually filled with newsworthy information, so he hadn't considered someone overhearing.

He slammed the truck into park as soon as he stopped in Beth and Marc's driveway and turned to the silent woman next to him.

"I get final say in the article about Clayton—I see it and approve it before you publish anything," he demanded.

She shrugged.

"Is that a yes? Because I can't tell with that ugly ass shirt you're wearing."

"Okay, whatever." Her indifference wasn't comforting.

"No, I want it in writing. *Now.*" He pushed her back into the seat and reached into the glove compartment. He pulled out the first thing he saw and thrust it at her.

"Is this an RSVP card?" Taran asked, distracting Corey from searching through the center console for a pen. "Mel Holly's wedding?"

Shit.

"Give me that." He yanked the ivory card back from Taran. The last thing he wanted to talk about with a reporter was his famous ex-girlfriend's upcoming wedding. Hell, neither Mel nor he had ever officially confirmed their almost two-year relationship to anyone in the media, and he wasn't starting with Miss "In Case You Didn't Know."

"Hmm."

But before she could say more, he flung a different piece of paper at her along with a pen before folding and pocketing the RSVP card.

"What do you want me to do with this insurance card?" she asked, raising a thin black eyebrow at him.

"Flip it over and take dictation. I, Taran Murphy, promise to give Corey Matthews the final say in any articles, blogs, tweets, stories, or anything publicly viewed that I write about the Evans or Demoda families. And then sign it." His tone was ice, one that he almost never used, but he was pissed—no one messed with the closest thing he had to family.

She shrugged again, wrote something, signed it and handed it back to him. "There."

She'd written exactly what he'd said in big bubbly writing, and she'd even signed her name with a heart after the *y*. He sneered at it. She sure had cutesy handwriting for a woman who looked like a homeless preteen boy.

"Fine, let's go," he said, knowing that had been almost too easy. But he got out of his car and headed inside without looking back.

The commotion of a crowd came from the kitchen at the back of the house. He knew Nick, Grant, and Clayton weren't in town, but the other four Evans brothers might be there, considering how loud it was. It was odd to hear music, but the laughter wasn't out of place.

"Is there a bathroom?" Taran asked.

Corey pointed to the door to their left before leaving the stupid woman. It was a relief to have a few minutes to enjoy the Evanses before he had to explain her. He cracked his neck, forcing himself to relax, and smiled as he sauntered into the kitchen.

"The hero has arrived," he said, and Beth looked away from the commotion going on across the room.

"We all saw the third," she said pointedly as she stood at the counter, her blond curls surrounding her tired face. He was sure she'd rather be in bed, but she'd never kick them out.

"You wrecked it again, Luke," Danny complained from across the room.

What the hell were these two up to now?

Danny and Luke both stood shirtless on top of Marc's stone coffee table while Morgan, their oldest brother Nick's fiancée, held a phone playing a clip of "I'll be Missing You" over and over again.

"No, that was you. I shook on beat; you looked like you were having a seizure." Luke crossed his arms.

"Oh my God, guys, look at this one. I'm going to wet my pants." Morgan laughed.

"It's supposed to be hot, not funny," Danny snapped.

"Well, if you'd go for more *Magic Mike*, and less ER patient, it might be." Luke threw his hands into the air as Morgan laughed again.

"Idiots," Beth mumbled and rolled her eyes at her brothers and their antics.

"Are they trying to beat Clayton?" Corey asked as Luke and Danny started a ridiculous dance. This was exactly why Beth and Marc's house was where he came to relax. After two minutes here, his anger had melted away.

"Yup, Clayton's newest TikTok just passed two million views, so now these two have to shirtless dance their way past him," former Metros star pitcher Marc Demoda said from the table with a headshake and a small chuckle. "God forbid the youngest might win at something. You going to join them?"

"Hard pass," Corey answered. "You doing this?" Corey asked Will, who was sitting next to Marc.

"Does that seem like me? Nick and his guys at work dueted Clayton already though. Apparently they're bored today," Will scoffed.

"Of course they did. I'm sure Wyatt was driving that truck," Corey teased happily as he grabbed the plate of enchiladas Beth handed him. "Have I told you lately that I love you?"

"Only every time I give you food," she replied flatly and yawned.

"Tired?" Corey asked her, but he was moving to Morgan, who had finally shut off the song. "Hey, beautiful," he said, bending down to give her a quick cheek kiss.

"Hey, Cor. Let's take a break, guys. It's getting worse, not better," Morgan said.

"Woman's always tired these days," Danny complained, giving Beth a teasing smirk as he headed to the kitchen table. "Tired or cranky. It's like PMS on crack, and chocolate doesn't help."

Luke chuckled as he sat down, and Morgan whacked him.

"*She made two people.* She gets flowers and back rubs and should be told repeatedly how awesome she is, not laughed at," Morgan schooled them. The guys groaned.

"Yeah, we get it. My wife is amazing. But this baby girl… Her brother's good. But this little devil," Marc said, smiling down at his daughter in his arms, "doesn't sleep."

Corey noticed for the first time the dark circles under Marc's eyes. Beth moved to the table with a few cold beers, which she dropped in the center.

"Give me my goddaughter." Corey smiled. "I can eat and hold the gorgeous baby. I got skills," he said and took the pink bundle from Marc. He smiled down at the baby; she truly was a perfect combination of two beautiful people. Those green eyes of Beth's smiled up at him, wide awake.

"Take a picture to send to Glory. She thinks she's cornered the market on being a good godparent. If I have to hear about how awesome she is one more time, I'm going to puke," Danny demanded.

"Why are you talking to my sister? Her focus is supposed to be on finishing her last semester of college, not messing around with you." Marc frowned.

Corey chuckled. Danny had a hard-on for Marc's sister, which Marc hated. The thing Corey wasn't sure about was if Glory hated it or not.

Someone cleared their throat from the kitchen doorway, and everyone turned. Taran had taken off the awful Yankee's cap, and her ink-black hair was knotted on the top of her head with whisps of bangs hanging around her face. Instead of the stained T-shirt, she wore an oversized sweater that might as well have been a tent dress over black leggings. Corey scowled; he wasn't sure if this was worse or better than the last outfit, but he *had* momentarily forgotten about her.

Everyone looked at Corey.

Shit.

"Well, it seems I brought…that," he said and nodded her way.

Beth's eyebrows shot up, and Marc's gaze narrowed momentarily before his mouth fell open in surprise.

"*Oh*—hey, Taran," he said.

Corey wasn't sure what to make of the look Marc shot him. Taran, however, flashed a smile at Marc. "It's been forever."

"That's because I'm still mad at you," Marc reminded her.

Corey watched Taran laugh, and for the first time, he saw her look feminine. The way the smile danced on her face made her look…almost cute. If he didn't hate her for what she did and what she was currently doing *to him*, he might say, in that moment, she was sort of hot. And even though he was mad, he was staring.

"For saying you were decent?" she asked and raised an eyebrow at Marc while a smirk played on her pink lips.

Marc shrugged. "At that point, I wasn't big on people knowing that fact, and your article made me sound like a nice guy."

Hmm. Corey hadn't realized Taran had written about Marc.

"I was doing my job." Taran didn't seem at all sorry as she flashed a white-toothed smile at Marc that again had Corey staring.

"Oh," Beth said from across the table. "Are you doing an 'In Case You Didn't Know'?"

Taran turned her gaze from Marc to Beth. "Sorry. Since Corey doesn't seem inclined, I'll introduce myself. Taran Murphy. I write for *Sports Illustrated,* but tonight's not work. I'm just here with Corey."

Yeah, right. Corey's jaw tightened. Will, who'd become one of Corey's best friends, glanced across the table at him, but Corey just shook his head. It took him a moment to realize everyone was waiting for him to say something.

"Blindly accept this, or we'll go," he replied to the shocked *hello you've said nothing about dating someone* expressions around the room.

"I can leave," Taran offered. "You were right, Corey. This was a bad idea. No matter the reason, a reporter will never be welcome here."

As soon as the words came out of her mouth, Corey frowned; he knew what the response to that would be.

Like he expected, Beth was on her feet before Taran could take one step. "Taran, I'm *so sorry.* I'm exhausted and cranky. *Any* friend of Corey's is welcome here, reporter or not."

Marc wrapped his arms around his wife's waist and pulled her close. "I was teasing, Taran; you did right by me. I know I've given you crap about the article, but you told the truth. And I'm pretty sure my agent approved it."

Taran smiled.

"I didn't know to save dinner, but do you want a beer?" Beth asked.

Luke hopped up from his seat next to Corey and went for another chair so Taran would have a seat, and Danny struck up a conversation with her. They all stepped up for him. And that felt like lead in his stomach because she *was* here for a story, so he grabbed the last beer off the table for himself.

"If you want a beer, get it yourself. I pitched seven innings while you sat and did nothing," Corey told her.

Danny blinked at him before turning to Taran. "Well, doll, I'll get you a beer and then tell you all the ways you can thank me." He directed his lady-killer smile at Taran as he got up.

"She's not pretty enough to be your type," Corey asserted before he thought better of it. Morgan sucked in a breath, but Taran stared indifferently.

"It really galls him that I'm not a baseball bunny. I offered a makeover, but he said I wouldn't be around long enough for that. Right?" Those green eyes full of challenge turned his way, and he was lost. He heard a few chuckles around the table. "I'm not Danny's type either, huh?"

"Taran," Danny called from the fridge, and she turned away from Corey. "You have two *x*'s, right?"

Taran clearly didn't understand.

"Chromosomes," Corey explained.

"Yeah," she hedged.

"Then you are most definitely my type, and," Danny said, leaning down to put her drink on the table and linger over her shoulder, "I don't know if anyone has ever told you this, but you have dirty eyes, and I love that."

The smile Danny sent her made her laugh out loud. But damn, that was it; when she smiled, she did have dirty eyes.

"I've definitely heard it. It's why I keep ending up with men so far out of my league." Taran sent Danny a sly smile as she leaned back in her chair. "And you look like a bag of fun."

It was Danny's turn to laugh. "Too bad you didn't meet me first."

"Shut up, Danny," Corey hissed automatically.

The older Danny got, the more he looked and acted like his older brother, Bob, who was Beth's first husband, and it always put Corey on edge. He reached for another beer that Danny had brought over, and Marc looked at him quizzically before taking back his daughter. Probably a good idea because Corey was getting his drunk on.

4

COREY STOOD ON the front stoop of a cute townhouse only a few blocks from his own apartment. His head was pounding, and his mouth felt like cotton, but he'd had Will drop him here to get his damn truck. He didn't know what had possessed him to let the woman steal his car keys, but he'd stayed at Marc's last night and begged for a ride to her place this morning. And now this stupid woman wasn't answering her door. He'd been knocking for at least five minutes, so he pounded again, louder this time, causing another throb in his head. Still no answer. When he was about to break a window, the red wooden door finally swung open to reveal a hot little body in black fitted Sideline shorts and a teeny tiny crop tank top.

"What the hell?" she asked, and he realized this hot body actually belonged to his little car thief.

He tipped up his sunglasses to get a better view, but winced at the sunlight. Taran was definitely small everywhere, but the fitted clothes showed off her hour-glass curves. The two inches of tan skin between her tank and shorts revealed a toned waist, and the scoop of the neck showed a small handful of boob. He was hungover, but not dead.

"If you look like that, why do you cover it up with crap?"

She didn't react, just tipped her head and stared at him.

He pushed his glasses onto his head and walked past her inside. "This looks like a girl's place," he said, taking in her space.

Wallpaper, glass tables with brass edging, flowers and framed photos, one of those princess crystal chandeliers, a white and tan area rug, and a gray button sofa with too many pink throw pillows. It was tasteful, very tasteful, but feminine and not what he'd expected from Taran.

She ran her hand through her straight midnight hair, flipping it out of her eyes. "Should we have the two x's conversation again?" Not that they needed to when she crossed her arms, pushing up her boobs, and stared at him with those sex eyes.

He turned to her as he leaned on the distressed white fireplace mantle. "Are you wearing a bra?"

She frowned and stretched. "I'm not a morning person. Are we flirting or fighting?"

It was his turn to frown—he wasn't sure either. "Neither. I just need my keys you stole."

"Dude, it's not theft if they're forced on you—I said no multiple times." She yawned. That cute little ass, the one that five minutes ago, he didn't know she had, wandered out of the room, returning a few moments later with a bottle of water and keys. His keys, which she didn't return, stayed in her hand as she glared at him. "When is the next date?"

"If you think this is dating, you need to get out more." Corey shook his head, causing another ache; he wasn't sure if he was flirting again or not. He needed some aspirin.

"I meant a date with the Evanses, although I'd happily be your plus one to Mel Holly's wedding," she said, handing him the water bottle.

He gritted his teeth. His ex's wedding wasn't a topic he was hashing out with her, nor were there enough threats in the world to get him to take the "In Case You Didn't Know" queen to Mel's wedding.

She stared at him, waiting, with the water bottle extended, so he finally took it, along with the four Advil she had in her palm.

"What's this?" *Was this woman a freaking mind reader?*

"Are you going to tell me you're not hungover? Because you were drunk as heck last night." That thin eyebrow arched up, daring him to deny it.

He didn't bother. At least he hadn't said anything stupid that she might use in her blog.

"Thanks," he replied and let the water cure his cottonmouth in one long chug.

"I would have joined you, but it would kill my image to say I hate beer, so nursing a beer was the best I could do," she said and flopped on the sofa, still holding his keys, and folded her legs under her.

"Nosy ass reporters have to drink beer?" he asked.

"Yup, must like beer and must keep ourselves separate from what we're reporting on. The two commandments," she agreed but clearly didn't mean it.

Her head was resting on the sofa and her eyes were closed, but Corey could hear the eye roll in her tone. His gaze danced across her petite features and smooth skin. When her eyes were removed from the mix, she looked delicate. Even her ears were small and cute. Corey shook his head, annoyed with himself. He didn't like this woman.

"No issue stealing my car though—that's not crossing a line," Corey grumbled, feeling off-kilter after the last twelve hours.

"Again, you *forced* me to take it so Danny wouldn't drive me home," she said. When he growled, Taran had the nerve to chuckle. "Don't be jealous. No female could resist that boy."

"Who said I was jealous?" His teeth were on edge. That was the last thing he wanted to hear. Yet what did he care about what she did? Or who she did it with?

"Danny—I think four times?"

"Shut up," Corey snapped, but her lips twisted into a smirk as if she was purposely annoying him. "Danny would have gotten you something besides beer if you asked."

"Probably, but like I said, I needed to fit in with the guys," Taran reminded him.

"Free advice," Corey said, flopping into one of those dainty winged armchairs that only a woman would choose. "If you don't want to seem girly, don't decorate your house like Princess Kate's sitting room and don't sign your name with bubble letters and hearts." He also closed his eyes.

"Normally," her tone packed a bit of a punch, "the only people I let in my house know me."

"I'm just the exception?" he asked with a grin and wondered if she was really a girly girl, although that didn't seem to fit her.

"I didn't invite you over. Your annoying ass barged in," she replied, and he lost the grin. "How did you find my house anyway?"

"My agent. Resourceful guy, and he should be. I pay him enough," Corey responded.

"Hot Shots," she mumbled. "Hate those guys. They make my life crap. I've had to promise my firstborn, my left arm and my right one to them multiple times to get access to their athletes."

"Reporters, I hate them," Corey mumbled—because it was true.

"Only the females," she corrected, not getting riled. "With the guys, you're their best bud."

"No, I don't mind the ones who report about the game. The other crap is no one's business." Corey glared at her, although she couldn't see because her eyes were still closed.

"I get it," she said, and it didn't even sound sarcastic.

"Really?" How could she say that? Her entire career had been built on telling the world about athletes' lives outside of the game.

"Yes." Those sea-green eyes opened and really looked at him. He could see honest remorse in her eyes and maybe even pity, which put his teeth on edge. "At a very young age, your privacy was grossly and inappropriately violated—repeatedly. You were traumatized. Understandably, you get cold feet about color interviews."

He didn't want pity, nor did he want her understanding. He wanted her to shut up about it. "You do the same thing every day and get paid for it."

She sighed. "Have you read any of my articles?"

He scoffed. "I don't read trash."

"Maybe read one or talk to someone I wrote about before you write me off, because I don't write trash." She stood up and handed him his keys.

He frowned as the keys fell into his palm.

"Get out of my house," she said.

"Huh?" Corey asked. He thought she wanted another "date" with the Evanses. "Is that supposed to be a punishment because I didn't want to hang out with you? You were the one blackmailing me."

"*Get. Out.*"

She scowled at him, so he stood and walked out, shocked when the door slammed hard behind him.

5

TARAN SIGHED AND leaned against the closed door. The smell of Obsession for Men floated across her entry way, leaving a hint of Corey Matthews behind. Nothing was working out the way she wanted. And she was done with it.

Last night, it had seemed like a great idea to bluff her way into some time with the great Corey Matthews. This morning, it was clear it was a bad idea. Taran had no idea what he'd been talking to Clayton about on the phone. She had only caught the tail end of the conversation—something about rain, and then Corey cursing Clayton out for making fun of his bad third inning. Truthfully, she didn't know what Clayton had said about the third when she agreed with it. But she saw an opportunity, and she'd taken it.

She'd hoped Corey would take her home with him, and when Marc said she'd done a great job on her article about him, Marc would suggest she do one about Corey. Corey Matthews would listen to his trusted friends and end his long protest about any personal interviews. He'd let her do an article since she was a reporter the family trusted. That's what she'd thought would happen because she saw what everyone else in the country saw in their favorite pitcher. The agreeable good old boy, the sweet *awe shucks* boy of baseball.

However, a few minutes with Corey Matthews told her he was neither agreeable nor trusting. He might play good old boy with the public, but he had a darker side. A depth she could see forming behind that shiny exterior. Not that the shiny exterior was anything to turn her nose up at. A body of steel, a mane of gorgeous dark blond hair set off by deep brown eyes slightly lighter in the center, and a chiseled jaw covered with a sexy scruff.

There was no denying Matthews was a mouth-watering piece of male perfection. But she had always known that about him. But she hadn't realized he wasn't boy-next-door sweet like he portrayed himself in every public thing he did. In fact, he was an asshole. And now that she knew, she couldn't see the true man agreeing to an article. And the fact that her boss was demanding she do one this season sucked even harder.

At least she had her blog piece done. Danny and Luke were perfectly willing to let her blog about their TikTok "war" with their brothers. The piece would be a hit, linking all three videos, plus an extra idea from Marc. He was willing to donate a dollar for every like to his wife's charity, Helping Hands. Everyone was on board. Nick and Clayton had both been called and had both okayed the entire thing. But she still needed an article for next month to get her boss off her ass.

She sighed and knocked her head against her door a few times. Taran had to tell Wayne who her feature would be about by tomorrow. At this point, she'd have to go with Clayton Evans, which would make him happy since he was one of Wayne's top five. But that meant dealing with Hot Shots, because regardless of what Corey thought, she wasn't using him for that. She circled back to the phone call she'd have to make to tell off Hot Shots' founding partner, Sean Taylor.

He had given out her private address. He *owed* her.

She went back up to her room, searching for her cell and craving her bed because she hated to be up before noon. After a quick scroll through her contacts, she crawled back under the covers to make the call.

"No." Sean's jovial voice on the other end of the phone answered before she could even ask anything.

"You should just put that on your voicemail as the greeting," Taran replied sarcastically.

"I'd need two numbers." The smile was obvious in his voice.

"Does that mean you actually say yes to some people?" Although Taran didn't believe that was true.

"My real clients—I say yes to every stupid thing they want from me."

"Yes, your clients." Taran frowned. "Exactly why I called."

"Which one? Because it's still probably no." Sean was so full of it. Half his clients would love to have a feature article in any print, and they'd sell their mothers for one in the magazine she worked for.

"Which one did you give my private address to?" Taran asked.

He laughed on the other end of the line. "Did you really steal his car?"

"People tend to forget what they've given away when they're trashed and acting like assholes." With that statement she knew she'd have his full attention.

"What?" It was a whisper of a word before he recovered and used the business tone she rarely got from him. "No way. Matthews is my best-behaved client. And the jackals would have eaten that story up, especially with his mom. Taran, you cannot tell this story."

Listening to the clicks of typing in the background, she could picture the agent to the stars at his desk, fingers flying over the keyboard to find where Corey had been last night. Jackals—the paparazzi, as most people knew them—hadn't seen one very drunk Corey Matthews last night. She had. And he was more ornery when he was drunk than he was sober.

"You're making a few too many assumptions, Sean." Taran had him eating out of her hand now.

"What do you mean?" he demanded.

"Your client brought me with him to the Demodas' last night, for umm, what do they call it?" Taran paused for dramatic effect. "Beer night? I think that's what Corey said."

"Horseshit!"

"I don't think your client's quite that bad." She laughed.

"Cut the crap. What are you doing with Corey Matthews, Taran? I can't imagine he agreed to an 'In Case You Didn't Know,' so what's the deal?" Sean was serious now.

Nothing was the correct answer, because she was done with him. He'd never agree to an article, and she refused to hang out with someone who insulted her at every turn. Still, she didn't tell him that.

"I guess you'll have to wait to find out," she answered coyly before turning serious. "However, give out my private address to *anyone* again, and my blogs will hit *all* your guys right where it counts. That's a line you know better than to cross, Sean."

It was a threat no agent wanted to get. The media and sports agencies had a love-hate relationship because they depended on each other.

Sean sighed. "Maybe, but since it was Matthews, I figured you wouldn't mind. I can't see many sports writers being unhappy about a few minutes alone with him. Not to mention I doubt any woman would turn him away if he showed up at their doorstep."

Taran tensed. She hated that about the business. The assumption that women always wanted to sleep with the star player, or if they were pretty enough, the star wanted to sleep with them. She, however, fit into neither of those categories. And she intended to keep it that way. She was a respected reporter across every sport, and staying that way meant she wouldn't let even a joking rumor get anywhere.

"I've never slept with anyone to get a story. You know me way better than that," she snapped. "Give out my private address again, and *hell* will rain down on you."

There was silence on the other end. Sean had to realize he'd crossed a line. "Does this mean you're not bringing the brisket tonight? Because Erin will kill me if I piss you off," Sean said finally.

Taran tried to stay mad, but she failed. "No, I'll come. I just have to figure out my car situation because it's still at the stadium."

There was another pause. "How about as an *I'm sorry for being an asshat,* I use my magic agent skills to get that car situation worked out?"

"Deal." Taran smiled. This was exactly what she wanted—with the hope that she could talk Sean into letting her feature Clayton. But the slight tingle in the back of her mind said to never trust a lawyer.

6

"WHAT'S UP?" COREY asked as soon as his truck connected Sean's call.

"You got plans today?" his agent asked.

It was an off day for the team, and Corey wouldn't pitch again for another five. But during the season, it was rare for him to be completely free.

"On my way in to throw a few now, then full team meeting at two thirty. Should be done around four, why?" Corey asked. "Wait—you get the contracts from Sideline?"

The Sideline endorsement deal was a big one. Corey's biggest to date, and he wanted it locked in.

"No, but they should be in soon." Sean didn't add anything, and Corey tensed, guessing what this call might be about.

"If this is about the award show, it's not until September. I already told you I'd think about it." Corey cracked his neck and ran his hand along the rough hair on his jaw.

"I know you don't like to drag out your parents' drama, but a lifetime achievement award at the Tonys is a huge deal. Your mother isn't around to accept it, so they would really like you to do it."

"I'm well aware." Corey's jaw ached, and he worked to stop gritting his teeth. From the day he was born to the world-renowned pitcher and the superstar, he'd dealt with their drama. His life front page news. His parents' toxic relationship had been like crack to the press, so Corey'd had to live out the drama both at home and on the front page of every magazine most of his life. It had been a relief when both of his parents died. His dad died from a heart attack five years ago, his mother from liver failure only two. Although it made him a crappy son, his life was easier now that they were gone. And it made boundaries with the press a lot more doable.

"Look, I know you don't want drama, but with Beth and Mel both in good places—"

"*Stop*," Corey interrupted, his hands gripping the wheel. "I said I'd think about accepting my mother's award in her place. I said I'd consider making an appearance at Mel's wedding. And Beth is perfectly settled. So there is no reason to drag *her* into *anything*."

"Right," Sean said quickly. "I didn't mean to imply." He sighed, and Corey relaxed, knowing Sean was stepping back. "I actually called because the wife's having some people over for a barbeque-type thing tonight. Interested?"

Corey opened his mouth but wasn't sure how to respond. It wasn't just the abrupt change in topics that threw him. He and Sean got along—well enough. But they didn't talk outside of work, so Corey had to double check.

"You're inviting me over—to *your* place?" He hadn't meant for it to sound like it was an asinine request, but shit—he'd never been to Sean's house. Sean and his partner Austin hung out with Beth and Marc a lot, but he hadn't ever gone with them. "Did Marc ask you to invite me or something?" Corey asked when Sean didn't respond. He knew he'd been off late-ly, and the Evanses had all been worried, but he didn't think Marc would talk to Sean about it.

"No—no," Sean said. His agent was usually one of those silver-tongued guys who could sell a lion a cage, but Sean didn't sound like himself. And it was making Corey nervous. "It's okay if you don't want to, just thought you might."

Well, shit, it wasn't that Corey didn't want to go—he didn't want Sean to think that.

"I mean." Corey swallowed. "I guess."

"Great. Can you grab Taran on the way here?" Sean rushed out.

"*Taran*?" What the actual fuck? But before he could say more, Sean went on.

"Yeah. I had her car sent here by accident, and my wife is bitching about me going to get her, so since you're right there anyway…"

Corey sighed.

"I guess." The *what the hell* didn't leave his tone, but Sean ignored it.

"Great. See you at five."

Corey glanced down at his phone to make sure Sean had really hung up. That conversation was completely out of char-acter for his agent. Corey wasn't sure what was weirder: that Sean had asked him to come hang out or that he asked him to pick up Taran Murphy. Well, at least now Corey could make sure she didn't write the stupid Clayton blog.

She wouldn't have told Sean about that conversation, would she? He didn't think so. She didn't seem as gossip hungry as some of the press he'd dealt with. But she *was* bribing him for a story. He couldn't figure the girl out. However, he had no time to try now because he needed his full focus to be on baseball. He was not messing up his win streak, and he was stiff and still hungover—things his pitching coach would not appreciate. He was about to get chewed out.

Six hours later, he was back over the bridge at the townhouse where he'd started his day, now tasked with picking up Taran. And since he was pounding repeatedly on the door without an answer again, he was certain she hadn't been told the plan.

The door flung open. "Jeez, give me a freaking minute. They pay you by the hour, right?"

That didn't seem like a greeting meant for him, yet Taran had disappeared. The door sat halfway open, and an open door seemed like an invitation to enter.

The second he stepped into the room, the smell of something just this side of heaven hit his nose—sweet yet spicy. They were supposed to go to Sean's for dinner, so he wasn't sure why she'd be cooking, but if it tasted half as good as it smelled, he'd eat it every day from now until forever.

He would have asked, but Taran was talking to someone who clearly wasn't him because she just said, "kill the big one first."

He walked into the family room he'd been in only hours ago, and there stood Taran with a PS4 remote in her hand, staring at the screen and talking into a headset. Above the fireplace mantel hung a television that had looked like a mirror this morning. Corey chuckled. *Diablo.* He didn't know many women who played. Especially ones who stood in princess living rooms and dressed like teenagers.

Taran's cut-off jean shorts and oversized hoodie hid the body he'd gotten a peek at this morning. He couldn't see much now except a pair of short legs that ended in tiny black Converse sneakers. She looked about fifteen today, which aged her five years from yesterday, when he thought she was a ten-year-old boy.

He shook his head. He couldn't peg this woman. "What level are you?"

"Seventy paragon two," she answered without looking.

Huh, impressive. Seventy was a max level. It meant he could find her online and play with her. A quick glance at her screen name, T-cup2009, and he committed it to his memory for future reference. He liked to play with people all the time, especially when they had no idea it was him. Then he watched quietly until she got to the checkpoint and told the people on the other end of her headset she had to go. Her character ported to town, and she finally turned.

"What the hell are *you* doing here?"

He had no idea who she was expecting, and the pay by the hour thing added another level of confusion. The only people he could think that someone might let in and pay by the hour were hookers.

"I'm your ride. Who were you expecting?"

"God damn it to all hell," she said to no one and then turned those fired-up sex eyes to him. "Never trust a lawyer."

"What the hell is that supposed to mean?" Corey asked.

"That you're my ride." She said it like it was clear, but he still didn't get it. She ignored his obvious confusion, simply crossing her arms over her chest. "Have you ever been to one of Erin's dinners?"

"Who?" he asked before remembering his agent's wife's name.

"Never mind." She dismissed the conversation with a wave of her hand.

Corey glanced down and smirked as he read her hoodie. "'Just pretend I'm not here. That's what I'm doing.' Antisocial?"

She nodded, and the black knot of hair bounced on her head. "I've heard that about you, yes."

He scoffed, but she just left the room.

Corey assumed she'd be back eventually and flopped into one of those stupid, uncomfortable chairs while he waited. She must have gone to change because she didn't look dressed to go out. His gaze wandered back to the image of T-cup2009, a wizard wearing some nice gear. He didn't have the time for hard core games, but *Diablo* was the perfect alternative for him because he liked the role play fantasy. His character was a demon hunter, which would work nicely with a wizard. The screen name was a curious choice though; maybe she collected cups or something.

He chuckled.

"What?" Taran demanded, having reappeared in the room.

"What's that?" Corey asked, tipping his chin toward the large pan in her hands. She hadn't spent the last five minutes changing. She was still wearing the same crappy outfit, but she'd retrieved the dish containing the smell that he'd just about die to eat.

"Dinner. Do you have manners? Maybe you want to be a gentleman and grab it for me. It's thirty pounds of meat," she said as she struggled along.

"It weighs, what, ten pounds more than you?" Corey stood up. Not many people questioned his manners.

"Yeah, being four-eleven, I've never heard the *I'm small* jokes before. If you call me a midget, I swear to God, I will punch you." Her eyes flashed, daring him. Normally he wouldn't call someone a midget because he didn't want to disrespect anyone, but the way she said it made it a challenge. And one he couldn't ignore.

She didn't look impressed, even after he grabbed the chafing dish from her.

"What is this?' He sniffed, and this time the question sounded more like a plea leaving his lips.

"My family's famous brisket—beef barbeque brisket," she answered, and his mouth watered. "Put it in the car and don't spill it—everyone will be pissed if there is no food."

"Spill?" His eyes narrowed. "Is this shit going to spill in my truck?"

She shot him a withering look. "Are you really one of *those* guys?"

"What do you mean?" he demanded.

"Your truck is your best friend, the love of your life, your firstborn child, and an addition to your package all rolled into one." Her eyebrow cocked.

Oh, was she trying to egg him on? She was all about throwing down the gauntlet, but the thing she needed to learn was that he had no problem doing it.

"My package doesn't need an addition. Trust me, *midget*." He smiled at her when her eyes flashed at the term. Yeah, this was fun. "Want me to bend down a bit so you can punch me?"

"After dinner," she promised. Although the smirk she wiped off her face as fast as it had appeared implied she was having fun. "I don't want to explain to your agent why you have a broken nose." She turned to the front door. "Come on. Out of my house that once again I *didn't* invite you to."

He took the silver dish out to his truck. She was on his tail, and when she stopped to lock the door behind her, he couldn't help but ask. "Aren't you going to change?"

A small line puckered between her eyes as her gaze washed over him. "Why would I change? You're the one who's overdressed."

Corey glanced down at his khaki pants and polo shirt and back to her jean shorts and snarky hoodie, which now had two barbecue stains on it. "Meaning I don't look like I got my clothes out of a dumpster?"

Taran flashed him one of those smiles that left him staring. "Target; it's the Saks Fifth Avenue of dumpsters."

Cheeky.

As she opened the passenger door, he asked. "Do you need a boost, or can you climb in like a big girl, shorty?"

"I think I can manage."

The tiny waif of a girl hoisted herself into the lifted truck like it was nothing. He refused to be impressed as the door slammed shut behind her. Watching Taran flip her bangs out of her eyes as he walked around the hood made him realize he liked this woman and had no idea why.

Taran was by no means beautiful. She looked like a train wreck. She was rude, and she hassled him. She didn't like him, and he wondered if she'd give him the time of day if he didn't know Clayton. He should have been turned off by her occupation, but he kept forgetting she was a reporter because she didn't act like one.

Taran hadn't asked him any personal questions since they had met, and she made no effort to get any information out of him. Right now, she seemed annoyed that she had to deal with him, which was strange since she was blackmailing him to hang out with her—right?

And yet, as he started his truck, he decided he was going to find T-cup2009 on *Diablo,* and he was going to find another reason to see her in person. He laughed at himself. He was such a male—all pheromones and bad decisions.

"Why are you laughing now?" She sent him a sideways glance.

"Why do men do anything?" Corey responded, because the answer was obvious. Her. With men, it was always a *her*.

"Because they're asshats? At least that's what it always seems like to me."

Corey glanced over, but she was staring out the window. He couldn't tell if she was making a comment or giving away a piece of herself. "Bad experiences?" he asked since she didn't seem inclined to elaborate.

"No one left me at the altar, cheated on me with my best friend, or stood me up for prom, but I grew up with a brother, and I'm close to my sister's husband. Then my two best friends' husbands; those two—talk about *asshats*." She hit that last word hard. "Boy, are they on my list."

"One of three?" he asked, feeling jealous of another woman with a big family.

"Youngest," she answered.

He chuckled as he thought of Clayton. "The spoiled baby."

"Asshat," she grumbled.

He changed the subject to something he hoped would make her a little less hostile. "How do you know Sean? And don't tell me through your dealings with Hot Shots because I know that's a lie before you even say it."

The way she talked about going to Erin's dinners told him this wasn't her first, and Sean didn't mix business and pleasure. He had a feeling being invited tonight had more to do with the woman in his passenger seat than anything else.

She turned her misty green gaze his way. "You're going to make such a big deal over this."

"What?" he asked.

She sighed like he was grating on her last nerve. "Those two best friends I was talking about a second ago? Erin and Sid."

He paused, sucked in a breath, and then tried not to make a big deal out of it. "The asshats are Sean Taylor, my agent, and Austin Jensen, my financial advisor—the founding partners of *Hot Shots*?"

He failed.

"They have a third partner now. We dated. Not much of a spark, but he's not too bad," she said simply.

Corey was sure his eyes were bugging out of his head. "How old are you?" he demanded.

"Twenty-eight."

He wasn't sure he believed that. When he looked at her closer, she looked maybe twenty-two?

"Why? How old did you think I was?"

"Yesterday? Ten," he answered honestly.

She glared and then rolled her eyes. "I'm just going to thank you."

"What?"

"Apparently, you think I'm a child prodigy who started writing feature articles at seven."

Corey hadn't thought about her career, and it was weird again to have it pointed out that she was a reporter. "Twenty-five is still impressive to start features," he said begrudgingly, because it was. Even if her career choice left something to be desired.

She ignored his comment completely. "Second house on the left. Brick with the fence," she said, nodding her head toward the house she pointed out.

"What?"

"GPS you're using tells me you've never been here," she said simply and hopped out when he parked. She moved quickly to get the tray of brisket—which had his car smelling like heaven on earth—out herself. "Don't worry, your *baby's* safe. It didn't spill," she said and disappeared with the tray, heading to the front door.

He followed, intending to help, but didn't get a chance because Sean's front door opened.

About a year ago, Hot Shots had reorganized into three divisions, headed by the three men. Sean did all the contracts and deals. Austin took care of investing and money management. And the new guy did publicity and damage control. Something Corey never really needed. Still, Corey'd met the guy, but what the hell was his name?

"Mike, I hate your partner." She frowned at the guy she claimed to have dated, but let him lean down and give her a quick kiss on the cheek before passing him the dish.

This curly-haired skinny clown had dated Taran? She needed someone with more backbone than this guy. She tucked her bangs behind her ear, then her finger trailed along her neck. Corey itched to let his lips follow the same trail before sucking at the soft skin at the base of her throat. Would she taste sweet? Or would she be as tart as her personality?

"Let me guess. Asshat of the year?" Mike asked, interrupting his thoughts.

But Taran rolled her eyes and wrote the idiot off in one look.

This woman needed someone who could turn those sea-green eyes hot and put that pint-sized pistol in her place. Maybe tie her down and let her beg for release, and not from the ropes.

He blinked.

Wow, *where had that come from*? He watched her saunter out of the room, thinking maybe it wasn't that strange an idea.

"That's a new look on you, and not one I want released to the press," Sean said from across the room. "What's up with you two?"

Corey smiled over his shoulder at the guy he paid to keep reporters like Taran away from him. "I guess we'll see, won't we?"

He walked into the kitchen in time to see Taran lean over the counter and grab something white and creamy on a fork before sucking it into her mouth. Her orgasmic smile and satisfied groan stopped him in his tracks. Damn, he needed to clear that counter and put a different kind of satisfied smile on her face right now.

He didn't know what was going on with him today. Maybe he just had sex on his brain because he hadn't gotten laid in so long. It *had* been a while; he didn't have a lot of time during the season because his head needed to stay in the game, and he wasn't much for random hookups. So in the year since he'd ended things with Mel, he'd had a longer than normal dry spell.

"Marc was right." Sean sighed behind him.

"About what?" Corey asked, but his focus was still on Taran as she took another bite.

"You two," Sean said but didn't elaborate. "Hi, Taran," he called, and Taran turned and glared at him.

"After our conversation about sending uninvited people to my house, I don't think we're on speaking terms." She spun, leaving her back to them.

"Corey." Sean's wife, Erin, stood across the room, warm skin and dark hair, as beautiful as ever. Although her usual smile was replaced with something that looked more…assessing? The slant of her almond eyes had him on edge.

"Thanks for inviting me," he replied, and she nodded somewhat coolly.

"Should the two of us maybe—talk?" Sean suggested.

"About?" Corey asked.

"Me," Taran called from across the room. "Can't you see no one wants us dating?"

He supposed that should have been clear, but Corey hadn't seen that coming. What was the problem with them dating? Apart from the fact that they weren't. It was clear they were friends with Taran, but he couldn't understand why these people would have an issue with them together.

"Are you going to tell them, or am I? Because I don't care, and you seem to have issues." Taran turned her green eyes back on him.

"What?" Corey asked. What issues did he have?

She rolled her eyes and sighed. "We are not dating. We are not *ever* going to be dating. I overheard him and Clayton talking yesterday, and I tried to bribe him into getting me an interview with Clayton."

Dead silence was the only response to her statement. Sean, Mike, and Erin looked from Taran, who had returned to the creamy sauce she was eating, to Corey, who was glaring at her because she didn't need to make it sound like she was disgusted with dating him.

"Let me get this straight," Sean finally snapped. Corey didn't need to turn to know Sean was glaring at him. "Without consulting me in any way, shape, or form, you let a reporter bribe you into something—something which just so happens to be an interview with one of your closest friends and my client?"

"Not to mention we haven't heard from Beth, Marc, or Clayton." It took Corey a second to remember the guy's name, although he'd just heard Taran call him Mike.

"They don't know," Corey said through gritted teeth. "The little piss ant didn't go blabbing her mouth to them, just you."

Corey instantly regretted the name-calling because everyone but the piss ant herself was now glaring at him.

Taran chuckled.

"The three of us have a date with my office," Sean demanded to Corey and Mike before turning his eyes on Taran, steadfastly ignoring them. "You and I will talk later."

As he walked out of the room, Corey heard Taran call, "I already told you we aren't on speaking terms—asshat!"

Corey didn't want to smile, but he couldn't help it.

"You think she's funny?" Sean demanded, slamming the office door behind them. "Because I don't find this at all funny, Matthews. If this only affected you, I'd say 'well, he did it to himself,' but you're letting her write about Clayton?"

The smile fell from Corey's face, and his jaw clenched. "She blackmailed me, but I'm the one getting a lecture right now?" He'd been trying to protect Clayton, and somehow this had all gotten turned around on him. He was pretty sure he could blame the green-eyed devil in Converses. This was exactly why he hated reporters; they always turned things around so shit got crazy.

"I'll get to her next, but you—you know better than this. You're normally the one I have no issue with—*zero*! So why is it I'm sitting here watching you smile like a dog in heat, while I heard from a reporter that you got wasted, gave her your keys, and let her bribe you into a story?"

Corey opened his mouth and closed it again. He stared at his agent. There was an explanation. He knew there was, but at the moment, he had no idea why he hadn't called them last night to do immediate damage control. But *this* was exactly what he paid them *to do*.

"Let's start this conversation over." Corey stared down his agent. "It's your job to handle my shit. So stop bitching and start handling it. You have tons more difficult clients than me, and I doubt you ever stood there lecturing any of them before the problem was solved." Corey stood up, towering over the six-foot man. "I think this has very little to do with me and everything to do with that pint-sized pound of trouble out in your kitchen."

Sean simply crossed his arms over his chest and glanced past Corey to Mike. The guy had been a partner in Sean's agency for over a year but Corey had never really dealt with him, and he wasn't sure why this asshole was even in the room.

"Got something to say, or are you just here to be nosey?" he asked Mike.

"I handle damage control. You don't normally deal with me because you don't usually create issues." Mike crossed his arms and frowned. "However, now we have an issue."

"And the idea of you dating Taran, well, you're a terrible match," Sean added.

"Why?" Corey asked. He knew it was a terrible idea, but it galled the hell out of him that they thought he wasn't good enough for their friend. His circle of trust was tight, and until this moment, he thought Sean was on the inside. "You know what? I don't want to know. You're fired. Both of you." He didn't wait for a response. He simply opened the door and left the office.

He walked back to the kitchen and straight up to the woman who'd caused the last twenty-four hours of crazy in his life. She looked at him in confusion, like she couldn't imagine what he needed from her. He hadn't even realized why he was coming to her until he stood in front of her. But he was fuming, and he needed a physical outlet.

Taran sat on the counter, her legs criss crossed in front of her, and yet he still had to lean down to be at her level. And lean down he did, grabbing the back of her neck and feeling the brush of soft hair on his hand as he pulled her to him. She put up no fight. In fact, she grabbed his shoulders and held on just as their lips met.

It might have been Corey's idea, but he wasn't prepared for the punch of lust he felt as soon as his mouth touched hers. Her lips were soft and tasted like southern deliciousness, something warm and creamy. He wanted a deeper taste. It took almost no coaxing to get her to open to his conquering tongue. From there, he dominated her mouth. She felt soft and pliant under his hands. Her legs fell from their crisscross to alongside him, and she molded herself to him, letting him have his way with her body, her tongue.

For a moment, he forgot he was standing in his newly fired agent's kitchen and let his pounding desire and frustration with the little creature in his arms lead the way. His body burned with a deep pulsing need he'd never in his life felt as Taran moaned against his mouth and twisted her fingers in his hair. Someone cleared their throat, and he remembered exactly where he was. He took one more moment of enjoyment before he forced himself to end what he'd started.

When he finally pulled away, he blinked at the woman sitting on the counter below him, her green eyes throwing sparks of passion back in return. He had no idea why he had just kissed her or why she'd kissed him back so thoroughly. He wasn't sure what to say or what he wanted from here. No, that was a lie. The burn in his gut told him exactly what his body wanted. But he didn't know whether he was willing to act on it. He wasn't sure of anything other than that in twenty-four hours, this tiny woman had turned his life upside down.

7

TARAN WATCHED COREY'S face mirror her own confusion before he walked away without a word, leaving her lips still wet from the shocking kiss he'd just given her.

What the hell was that?

Every molecule in her body still tingled, like somehow Corey had jump started her electrical system, leaving it charged and ready to go. She'd thought this part of her was forever broken; it had been years since she'd felt anything like this.

In all honesty, it had been years since she'd experienced feelings without effort. It took a focus on her part to engage. Silent chants of *today is a happy day: smile, laugh, joke.* Forcing herself to feel was sometimes exhausting. It was just easier not to. Except, with Corey, the playful banter came naturally; the smiles that pulled at her lips were real when he was around. And whatever just happened with that kiss.

She hadn't meant to respond.

At first, she had simply grabbed onto his shoulders so she wouldn't fall, but then once his lips had moved against hers, something inside her just took over. The brush of day-old scruff rough against her cheeks and chin, the feel of soft, strong lips dominating her own, the pressure of his calloused hand against her neck—her body had just reacted. Her heart sped up, her stomach flipped, and an ache rocked through her.

And *man alive*, who knew the asshole could kiss like that?

"What the Sam Hill was that?" Sydney asked from the doorway to the backyard. Taran had no idea how long her friend had been standing at the door. She and Erin had been sitting and chatting while Erin tossed the salad for dinner when Corey came in, and suddenly her entire body was abuzz with everything Matthews.

"I don't know." Taran doubted either woman would believe that because she had just finished telling Erin how there was absolutely nothing going on with her and the great Corey Matthews.

The knot that had long ago disappeared tightened her stomach. The burning ache locked her jaw, and once again, she felt shaky; she felt lost. And yet the urge to walk out the door and follow him was undeniable. Unwilling to process any of it, she pushed it aside, refusing to be thrown off by a stupid kiss.

Instead of questioning her further Sydney turned to Sean and Mike who stood at the opposite entrance to the kitchen. Sydney said nothing as she tucked her long blond hair over her shoulder and stared at the two men.

"He fired us." Sean answered her unasked question but he was still staring at the door Corey had just walked out of—like he was shocked he was gone. "Technically he didn't fire your husband. I think Austin's side of the business might be okay. Since our contracts are somewhat separate, we might be able to make it work. He's worth hundreds of millions. I don't think we can just let that go."

Taran shook her head. She never thought that making up one little lie about Clayton would turn into this, but it also confirmed what she'd always known about journalism. A reporter can't ever dance a line of integrity, because it never leads anywhere good. And she knew she had. Never in a million years would she actually blackmail someone for a story.

She sighed.

"I'm sorry, Sean. I didn't realize this stupid thing was going to blow up so bad." She hopped off the counter and headed out the front door after Corey. She would fix this.

Surprisingly, Corey was still outside. She walked up to his window and knocked twice. Corey startled before the window came down silently.

"You don't need to tell me that what happened between us was a huge mistake. I'm well aware," Corey said, glaring like she had done something wrong. Although she wasn't the one who'd initiated the kiss, she couldn't deny that once he'd gotten the ball rolling, she'd jumped on without any hesitation. Not that she could explain that.

Taran frowned. "I wasn't going to," she assured him, although she didn't entirely disagree either.

"Then what do you want?"

"Don't fire Hot Shots. It's not their fault that I made a stupid decision to go around them to get a story," Taran said. Leaving out that the story she was trying to get was actually about the man himself.

Corey's lips dropped into a tight line, and he cracked his neck left, then right. "Why do you think I fired them?" he finally asked.

"Sean didn't say, but I feel like it's my fault." She kicked her foot repeatedly, the white rubber of her Converse sending pebbles across the stone driveway. She glanced down until he spoke.

"Maybe indirectly, but why on God's green earth would I want to employ people to look out for my best interests and have my back when they don't even think I'm good enough to date their friend?" Corey's gaze cut straight through her, almost like he was challenging her to tell him he was wrong.

Taran cocked her head and paused. "Wait—what?"

"Taran, I fired them because they don't believe in me, or trust me, if they don't think I'm good enough to date you…" Corey sighed again. "Look, I don't know why I kissed you or why you jumped on it like you haven't gotten laid in *years*."

"Excuse me?" she spat.

"We were both there, Taran." Corey frowned at her.

Where did he get off? Every other sentence out of his mouth was offensive. And he intended them to be. She crossed her arms and glared. "You are such an asshat."

A dimple popped right above the scruff of dark blond beard. "Your go-to insult."

"You know what? I came out here to apologize and tell you that I had no idea what you and Clayton were talking about. That I was sorry I crossed a line I shouldn't have, but now I'm just going to tell you to take a long, long walk off a very short cliff."

Corey laughed again, and Taran had the urge to deliver the punch she'd promised him earlier. But a door opened and closed behind her, and there stood Austin. It only took one look to know that Sean's partner had been caught up on everything, and the good-looking older man had his game face on. Clearly, he didn't appreciate anything she'd done in the last twenty-four hours. As he approached, his sky-blue eyes cut her to pieces.

"Taran," he said, but as always with his accent, it sounded more like *Turn*. The southern accent that pressed hard into every word he spoke reminded her of her former fiancé, Jeremy. "I need a minute with my client."

"Do you have a problem with us dating?" Corey asked him before Taran could answer. They weren't dating, but that didn't seem to be an issue for Corey and the daggers shooting out of his eyes.

Austin turned to him. "If you want to date this pain in my ass, be my guest, but personally, I think you might find someone better." The *better* came out more like *bitter*.

It was Taran's turn to shoot a nasty look, and Austin was on the receiving end of it.

She walked away before she did something she'd regret and slammed back into the kitchen, where all eyes were on her. "What?" she asked them.

That was a stupid question. They either wanted to know what was going on between her and Corey or why he'd fired them. The first she couldn't answer, and the second, well, she understood Corey's point of view on that, and he was probably right. So instead, she turned her eyes on Sean.

"I want to write an 'In Case You Didn't Know' on Clayton Evans next month. I know he's on a media hiatus, but this is a good way to bring him back into the public eye, and I could probably pull strings and get him the cover. Wouldn't it be nice for your best draft pick to grace the *Sports Illustrated* cover two days after the draft?" She stared Sean down waiting for an answer.

He finally sighed. "I was actually going to suggest it to you before you started this whole mess."

"Great," she snapped. All she could think about was Corey's comment about not being laid in years. Where did he get off?

So what if she hadn't had sex in over two years? How was it his business? And she had only responded to his kiss. It wasn't like *she'd* walked into the room and randomly kissed *him*. Now Corey would be a roadblock to this story; she was certain he was on his way to at least one of the Evanses to drag her name through the mud. "Talk to Clayton today, and tell him I'll be on a flight out to spend the next two weeks with him."

That was how she did her stories. She didn't do interviews. She immersed herself in the life of her feature and learned what they were really like. Her stories weren't about image or status. They were about getting to know the subject. The real lives of the athletes America loved to love, or loved to hate.

"No need," Sean said.

"Sorry. I don't call stories in," she reminded him. And she frowned again as she thought about the way Corey had laughed when Austin called her a pain in the ass. She wasn't really. She was just tough, and she needed to be to keep her life together.

"I meant," Sean corrected, "Clayton will be in Jersey this week for Nick Evans's wedding."

"Even better," Taran lied. She'd go out to see him regardless. But his being here was worse because it meant immersing herself in the Evanses' world, and that meant more Corey Matthews.

The man who thought she couldn't get a guy to sleep with her.

"The good news is he's not moving his money. But he refuses to have us do his contracts or publicity." Austin walked back in and turned to his wife. "Hun." That was all it took. One word, and Sydney knew exactly what her husband wanted. She cleared the girls out of the room. As Taran followed her and Erin outside, she knew they were going to grill her. The problem was she had no idea what to say.

But Erin turned to her and said, "Why didn't you just ask Sean about Clayton? Seriously, Taran, for the last two weeks he's been saying he was going to ask you to do a story on Clayton. You know Sean trusts you."

She did know that. "I didn't want to write about Clayton. That was Corey's idea."

They both looked confused, so she told them how the whole thing had started and how they'd gotten where they were today. They were both laughing when she was done.

"My meddling husband. If he had just butted out, he wouldn't have these problems." Erin shook her head.

Sydney's face said she didn't totally agree with that statement. "Are you still after the Matthews story?"

Taran could lie, but she felt like she'd done enough of that in the last two days. "Until Wayne changes his mind, I'll probably always be after that story."

Sydney's blond hair bounced as she shook her head. "This is nothing but trouble."

8

"I FIRED HOT Shots," Corey said, barging into Will's family room uninvited. He hadn't intended to come here. He'd been driving around just letting off steam, and after a couple of hours he'd found himself in front of his best friend's house.

"Uh—you fired your agent?" Will picked up the remote from the coffee table and paused the show he'd been watching.

"Now I need a new one, and probably a publicist." Corey flopped next to him on the sectional. "I have contracts coming in—that I *cannot* read—and events coming up. It's mid-season. I don't have time for this shit. And I have no idea who to hire because Hot Shots are the best."

"Am I allowed to ask why?" Will scratched his head.

"Taran." Corey shook his head. He knew what he'd told Taran was both the truth and the right call, but it still pissed him off that it had to happen. "They didn't want me dating Taran."

"Hold up," Will said. He stood and walked into the kitchen, returning with two beers. Corey took one, and Will took a sip of the other. "I missed about twelve steps here because I swear you told me this morning that you two weren't really dating."

"We weren't dating; we aren't dating. I don't even want to date her." Corey frowned. He thought that was the truth. "It's more of a principle thing."

Will looked like he was going to say something but sank into the cushions of the sofa, then let out a small laugh. "Or an overreaction? Can I ask how this even came up with them?"

"I kissed her." Corey frowned and spun the beer between his hands absently, staring into space as he remembered the kiss.

"What?"

Corey got the impression he wasn't telling this story well.

"I went with her to Sean's place. I fired Sean and kissed Taran in his kitchen." His frown turned into a scowl.

Will could have gone in a lot of directions, but he just smirked. "And?"

Corey didn't have to ask what he meant. He dropped the beer he didn't want onto the coffee table and groaned as he let his head fall back against the back of the sofa. "I'd like to do it again."

His friend chuckled. "I knew you were screwed when you were rude to her."

"Huh?" Corey said, looking up.

"Come on, Cor, the only other girl you've ever hooked up with who you weren't sweet as peach pie to was Beth," Will said as he took another sip of his beer.

Corey and Beth had dated as teenagers, which had ended in a media disaster—much like everything else in his life. He'd say it started his hatred for the press, but that would be a lie. His hatred started as soon as he realized his parents' need for attention constantly drove them into the headlines. The implosion of his relationship with Beth had only added to his burning hate of the press. But regardless of how he and Beth had ended, one thing was true.

"I was always great to Beth." Corey frowned at him. "None of you Evanses would have let me live if I wasn't."

"If you'd meant it, you're right. We wouldn't have, but you always pissed and moaned and bickered with her like it was foreplay. You did the same thing with Taran. That's how I knew you were spewing a load of shit with the whole *I'm not hooking up with her* act," Will explained as he kicked his feet up on to his coffee table. Will must have just come home from the gym where he coached one of the area's most premier swim teams, because he was still in his red swim trunks and warm-up jacket.

Corey glared at him. "You're full of crap."

"Why do you think Danny jumped all over a chance to annoy you the second you got bitchy?" he asked.

Corey paused. That was true.

"Because he's Danny?" Corey mumbled, and Danny was too much like his brother Bob.

"No, because he knew you wanted to tap that." Will laughed.

"Yo." Corey frowned. They normally laughed about women, but Taran, well, she wasn't like that. Corey didn't know how he knew it, but he did.

"Sorry, I didn't mean any offense." Will put both hands in the air, smirking again. "But what are you going to do about it?"

"I think she's doing a story about Clay." Corey didn't like that idea. Most likely because Will was right; his desire for Taran grew every time he saw her. And now that her soft lips had pressed against his, he knew he needed more. He'd never had a woman respond to a kiss the way Taran had. It was almost like she was drinking him in like oxygen as she kissed him. Like he was something she needed more than wanted—and it was *hot*.

Corey could handle wanting Taran, but he was struggling with his ability to trust her. In so many ways, she was his enemy. The press had always been his enemy. And there had to be a saying about fucking the enemy, although he couldn't remember it.

Moreover, he never did casual hookups. The world's unending interest in his love life had ensured that he needed to trust a person to spend time with them. And he wasn't sure he could trust the woman who wrote "In Case You Didn't Know." But he struggled to believe the woman he kept seeing was that gossip reporter. Although knowing Taran was writing about Clay made it hard for Corey to ignore that aspect.

"She is featuring Clayton," Will agreed. "He called an hour ago. He's stoked about the story."

Corey frowned.

Will just raised his eyebrows.

"I don't know." Corey sighed.

"You better figure it out," Will suggested. "Because she'll be hanging around with the whole family, and they'll want to know what's going on with you two."

Corey shook his head, reminding himself that he loved the big, noisy, highly involved family he'd been brought into. He had always craved a supportive family, and although he'd been welcomed as a part of the Evanses, there was always that tingle of outsiderness. He was included, but they weren't his.

"Lucky for me, the team is going on the road where the family won't bug me."

"Want to bet?" Will asked.

9

TARAN GLANCED AROUND the dingy hallway of the apartment complex Clayton called home during the school year. She thought, considering who Clayton's family was, he would have had better digs. She double-checked the address Sean had texted to her and knocked on apartment 301. It was a third-floor walkup in a rundown building just off campus.

The door was opened by a man who could have been the dictionary picture of the word huge. His black eyes were just about even with the doorjamb, and he had to duck to look through the opening.

"Jermane?" Taran asked. Having done her research, she knew Clayton's roommate's name without having to check her notes. Although she would have recognized him anywhere with the way the TikTok video of him and Clayton dancing to "I'll Be Missing You" had taken off, encouraged by the fact that most of the Evans family had jumped on board to duet it, going all-in on the war for the most views.

"Sup." The single syllable seemed to say: *Who are you? What do you want?* And *How do you know me?* All at the same time.

She reached her hand out to the tank in front of her. "Taran Murphy, *Sports Illustrated*."

Jermane shook her hand and smiled. "Ga-erl, I thought you were a co-ed." He laughed, and his whole body shook.

Taran smiled. Jermane had one of those contagious laughs.

"Is that Taran?" Clayton called from behind the huge mass that was Jermane.

"Yeah, and dude, she could be Phi-Beta Kappa," he answered with a whistle Taran took as a compliment. He opened the door in a gesture that said *come in.*

The apartment was exactly what you would picture for two college guys. Empty beer bottles and dirty dishes cluttered the room filled with a mismatched mess of what had to be secondhand furniture. Again, Taran was surprised at the normalcy of the would-be first-round draft pick's apartment.

After her quick scan of the apartment, Taran met Clayton's gaze. "Taran Murphy," she said, holding her hand out to the young heartthrob.

He was six and a half feet of perfection. If she was a few years younger and not constantly thinking about another guy who kissed like fire, she'd be in trouble. The blond hair and baby blues were the stuff of fairy-tale princes, and she realized he looked like a better version of his older brother Danny.

She watched Clayton glare at his roommate. "Dude, I told you she's taken."

"Huh?" Taran asked.

Jermane smirked as he shrugged, sending her a wink.

Clayton's gaze turned sweet as he turned to her. "No worries," he assured her. "It's nice to finally meet you. I've been hearing about you all week." His smile could melt a teenage girl into a puddle.

"Have you?"

"I don't know if you heard but my family is chatty. It's fun when they aren't talking about me," Clayton assured her.

Ah. Although she hadn't seen or heard from Corey since Sunday, she guessed the Evans family hadn't forgotten her.

"I'm surprised they aren't talking about you. A few weeks until the draft, and you aren't the topic of every conversation?" Taran tried to steer this back where it belonged. She was there to learn about him, not be part of his story.

He shrugged. "They'll all be there on draft day. But in a family as big as mine, there's so much going on; it's hard to harp on any one person."

In no way was it a complaint. It almost seemed like he couldn't understand how his being drafted into the NFL—as the possible first pick—was anything close to a big deal.

"Plus, my brother's getting married this week, so all the attention is on the bride and groom." Clayton smirked. "If Corey hadn't brought you home last week, it would be wedding all day every day in the Evans news cycle."

"I think they might be making too big a deal about that," Taran replied.

Clayton laughed. "You don't understand a big family news cycle if you think they're making a big deal out of you."

Taran frowned. She was very familiar with a family's news cycle. Being the youngest of three, she had plenty of experience. She knew Corey was close with the Evanses and Demodas, but she'd had no idea he was one of them. But after spending one night with the family, it was clear. Corey wasn't a friend; he was an Evans. It was surprising that he could hide that from the press as well as he did. And it would be a great "In Case You Didn't Know" about Corey because no one had any idea.

Taran shook her head. This was supposed to be about Clayton, and she needed to focus. "I'm the youngest of three. I understand a nosy family better than you think."

Clayton's eyebrows rose. "Totally sucks to be the baby, huh?"

That she could agree with.

"I hear you on that," Jermaine agreed, and when Taran turned toward him, he added, "Youngest of six."

"We bonded over that," Clayton explained.

"Maybe we can too," she said and tried to refocus. The point of "In Case You Didn't Know" was finding something the press didn't know. Something that humanized the person. Something that made them relatable to the public. And her inability to choose an athlete this month gave her a very short deadline to get to know Clayton.

"Babies of the family always bond," he agreed. "But we have like nine hours for that."

She had flown out to California last night, only to have to fly back today. It might have seemed ridiculous, but she wanted the time with Clayton, and she knew she wouldn't get much one-on-one time when he was back in his hometown.

"Can I help you with any of your stuff?" she asked.

Clayton scoffed. "My sister and Will would kill me if I let you carry my bag." He rolled his eyes, grabbed a small duffel, told Jermaine not to enjoy his absence too much, and held the door for her.

She walked out thinking that so far, Clayton seemed like the most normal, down-to-earth, professional athlete she'd ever interviewed.

A few more hours with Clayton didn't change her mind in the least.

"How are we getting home?" she asked as they walked down the terminal at the Newark Airport. "Uber? Car service?"

He looked at her like she was nuts. "Were you ever allowed to Uber home from school?"

Taran didn't want to admit that Uber hadn't existed when she went to school. But then he continued.

"My sister will be here waiting. Along with a few others, I'm sure."

Although Clayton tried to make it sound like a nuisance that his family would be here, she saw how much he really loved it. And after security, there was a party waiting for them. Beth, Marc, and their four kids were all there, along with Danny, Will, and their other brother Joey. The welcome home hugs and high fives began at once.

It reminded her of her family. She remembered coming home from college and finding her two siblings, their spouses, their kids, and her parents waiting just past security. Jeremy, her high school sweetheart, always stood a little apart from them. The only child unable to really understand her big overly loving family. As a kid, she always thought her family was a bit too much. It was always a weird feeling remembering things from back then. To Taran, it felt like remembering a movie she'd watched rather than a life she was a part of.

"Taran." Danny was the first to notice her standing just out of the way.

"Yo, I told you she's not here; she's only my shadow. She wants you guys to ignore her and be normal." Clayton frowned at Danny. "And for the record, she and Corey aren't a thing."

Will looked surprised, but Danny asked, "So, why'd he have that *hurt you so good* look going on?"

"I don't know. She seems chill, but it sounds like he blew her off," Clayton said.

Taran shook her head. How had Clayton gotten *that* from their conversation?

Beth sighed. "It's amazing the amount of time I spend apologizing for my brothers' idiocy. How was your flight?"

"It was fine, but seriously, Clayton's right. I'm not really here. Pretend I'm one of them," Taran said, pointing to one of three men in dark suits—and earpieces—fanned out around the Demoda family.

"Wow, Clay, you're so pathetic you need a pint-sized bodyguard?" Danny teased, earning smirks from a few of the brothers.

"I'll send you the signed cover of *Sports Illustrated*, asshole," Clayton shot back.

"Language," Beth grumbled.

Clayton dipped his head in remorse. "Sorry." Then he turned to the eleven-year-old boy Taran knew was Marc and Beth's son. "Don't cuss. It makes your mom nuts."

The way the kid smiled said he'd heard this spiel a few too many times.

"Dude, it took you until you were twenty-two to get on a magazine cover. That's pathetic in this family. Marc, Corey, Beth, and Nick all beat you," Danny teased.

"What exactly did you do that was so special?" Clayton demanded.

Danny came toward Taran, pointed to the bag on her shoulder and gestured for her to hand it over—which she did.

"I live and breathe awesomeness, right, doll?" he asked her.

She couldn't tell if he was serious or not, but he got a lot of eye rolls and sighs from the group.

Danny just smiled, wrapped his arm around Taran's shoulder, and said, "You two are riding with me." He looked over his shoulder at Clayton and added, "And be a gentleman. She gets shot gun, douche."

"I'm going with Will, then," Clayton whined.

Joey crossed his arms over his chest. "I've got shotgun with Will."

Clayton's eyes shot to Beth and Marc, but their son added, "There are six of us. If you go in our car, it's the middle of the way back."

"Fine," Clayton huffed.

Taran just watched and appreciated the normalcy of this big loving family. She was starting to understand how Clayton stayed so down-to-earth. No matter what Clayton became in life, he'd always be the well-loved, well-teased baby of the Evans family. And that would forever keep him in his place.

The last few days had been all kinds of fun for Taran. She liked the Evans family more than she realized she would when she'd started the article on Clayton. She had finished last night and had dropped a copy off earlier in the evening at the Demodas' house, giving the entire crew a chance to read it.

What she learned wasn't anything she hadn't observed in the first few hours. Although he looked like a real-life Prince Charming, and threw like the next Tom Brady, he was the most normal person she'd met in a long time.

She had also sent Hot Shots a copy. Although she wrote color pieces, she always had the agent and the athlete's approval before she published. It was contradictory to what many journalists did, but the only way she got athletes to agree to work with her was because of the reputation she'd created for herself. She assumed she would know everyone's thoughts when she heard back from Sean the next day, and then it was time to pick her next subject.

She was already settled in for the night when her doorbell rang at eight thirty.

Clayton stood on the doorstep with a rolled-up bunch of papers, knocking them against his leg.

"Am I the first one here?" he asked, as he walked past her. The lack of an invitation didn't stop him from coming in and looking around. "This looks more like Morgan's place than what I'd pictured for you."

She ignored the comment everyone always made about how feminine her house was. "What do you mean 'first'?" she asked, eyeing the roll of papers he had tossed onto the glass table. "Is there a problem with the article?"

"No, it was great. Although I don't think my brothers will ever let me live down the Disney prince comparison." He frowned at the thought. "Will I break any of this if I sit down?"

A knock on her door interrupted her before she could assure him he wouldn't. Will and Danny stood on her front stoop, and as she let them in, she saw Marc and Joey both parking, so she waited at the door for them.

Once she got them all inside, she asked, "To what do I owe this pleasure?"

"Beth said when you dropped off the article, you told her to thank all of us and that you were done," Marc said, frowning.

"Yes." She had no idea where they were going with this.

"Well, doll," Danny drawled, wrapping his arm around her shoulder, "we don't let people into the inner sanctum very often. You were an exception to our no outsiders rule. We can't just let you go without a sendoff, so we're here for one more beer night."

Another knock filled the air. "Luke?" she asked, already knowing the answer.

Will nodded. "And he better have the beer. He's been freeloading all week."

"Got any more of that banging lasagna?" Clayton asked. "I've been telling the guys it's my new favorite food."

"Sean said I need to try your brisket. It's apparently heaven on earth," Marc said.

Taran did a mental inventory of her freezer before agreeing. "They're going to take about an hour though."

"We have all night," Danny informed her.

Taran rolled her eyes and got to cooking. Well, reheating. She was flattered they'd come to say goodbye, and she was sure she'd miss these guys. It took less than five minutes to get the food in the oven before heading back into her living room.

Three steps in, she froze, as Nick Evans turned his intense slate-blue eyes on her. He sucked in a hard breath as his eyes widened.

"Holy shit." The words left his mouth in an almost whisper.

She'd successfully avoided Nick until this point, and for good reason. He'd been busy with work and his wedding, and she'd planned her time with Clayton and the Evanses carefully. But now she had no choice but to face him. He shot to his feet, and she braced herself. God, she didn't want to do this.

10

"T-CUP," NICK SAID, staring at her. He almost moved toward her, but as his eyes scanned her face, he stopped.

"Hey, Hawk," she said flatly.

This was the problem with emotional numbness. Nick's appearance should cause a reaction. She should feel sad or scared or maybe some kind of bittersweet remembrance. She should feel *something*.

Although she didn't know Nick well anymore, she'd known him what felt like a lifetime ago. Before Jeremy died, Nick and her fiancé were on the same SEAL team. But through her time with the Evanses, she'd avoided this run-in with Nick because she knew her emptiness was hard for people to accept.

All the eyes in the room were on Taran, curious but smiling. That would all change in a few minutes when they learned about her connection to Nick.

Danny, tipped back in her winged chair, watched them. "Do you two know each other?"

Nick blinked and cleared his throat. "Hell, yeah."

"What?" Clayton asked. "You two didn't sleep together, right? Morgan's pretty chill, but that could get awkward."

There were a few uncomfortable chuckles.

"Somehow, I doubt you'll believe me, because now I'm known as the gossip reporter of sports, but I wanted to be a serious journalist at one point. I did an internship with the *Associated Press* a couple of years ago." Taran walked over and opened a drawer on the bottom of her bookshelf. The photo didn't seem heavy enough to hold the weight of her old life in it. But her life changed twenty-four hours after it was taken. The girl in the photo didn't look like Taran anymore. This girl stood in the middle of a team of male United States Navy SEALs and one male reporter. Her long ebony hair fell to her waist in waves. Big silver hoops hung from her ears, and bleached white teeth flashed around a perfectly made-up face, fake lashes included. She remembered the men laughing at her as she did her hair and makeup. Handing the frame to Nick, she said, "The guys called me T-Cup."

She looked over at Nick and saw it flash in his eyes—that which could only be understood by someone who'd been there. Everyone else seemed confused.

"I traveled with Nick's SEAL team for a few days," Taran said, but she still watched the horror in Nick's expression. In that split second as their eyes met, they relived it. Hours of hell.

She blinked.

"You're different," Nick said and continued before she could respond. "The girl these idiots keep telling me about isn't that too-sweet, ditzy southern girl I remember. Man, you were so innocent, so shallow, so focused on seeing the good everywhere. Sunshine and rainbows in a war zone," Nick said, describing the Taran in the picture. The girl she didn't know anymore.

He shook his head like he needed to release that time, but the words that came out of his mouth were the words Taran had written. She was shocked he had them memorized.

"Not one of us got up that day thinking it was the last time we'd wake; not one of us knew that last dirty joke we told at breakfast was the last laugh we'd have; not one of us had a death wish that day. Yet half of us died. Not because we had nothing to live for; most of us had families back home. Each of us had an 'If you're reading this' for that important person in our life, and half of those important people read tear-streaked letters later that week. We knew what we signed up for, and so that day, we did our jobs. When it was over, those who could walk carried the fallen home because we left too much of ourselves on that roadside to leave anyone behind."

Taran nodded at her words and swallowed as she remembered the weight of the men on her back as she'd dragged them from the SUV after the roadside blast. The smell of blood and blast powder. Very rarely did she give any of the subjects of her stories a piece of herself, but with Nick, she couldn't not. They were bonded by one thing.

"I don't think any of us left those twenty-four hours the same person. Living through something like that changes you."

Nick's haunted eyes pierced her again. "That piece—that story you wrote." Nick swallowed.

She'd written the story for the *Associated Press*, and it appeared in multiple places, but she'd refused a byline. Her name hadn't appeared anywhere the article was printed. No one who wasn't there that day would know she had written it.

"It was hands-down the best story ever written about what it's like; what we're like."

"In Case You Didn't Know," she said, quoting the name of the monthly column she wrote.

Nick's eyes widened. "Oh, fuck. I've read those, and I've never made the connection."

She shrugged. No one was supposed to.

"That was an 'In Case You Didn't Know,'" Nick said.

"Looking back, yes. I never intended it to be. I didn't want it to be." She paused and shook her head. That wasn't exactly what she meant. "I couldn't be known for *that* day. Or *that* story. Before that tour, I wrote freelance 'In Case You Didn't Know' articles for *Sports Illustrated* about athletes when I could get a big name to agree. I got offered a full-time feature position after I wrote that piece."

Nick looked her in the eyes. "Thank you."

She shook her head. "No. Thank you. I left. I wouldn't go back. I couldn't go back. You did it more than once."

"We've all reached out so many times," Nick said finally. "But you changed your phone number; emails started bouncing back. You changed your name—Murphy?"

Taran shook her head. She'd never admitted this, and she was in a room full of people, but she would have to trust them with this truth. "It's a pen name."

"What's your real name?" Clayton asked.

"Kuppton, Taran Kuppton. My fiancé…" She watched Nick carefully.

He was taking deep breaths through his nose, but his eyes stayed focused on her.

She raised her eyebrow in a silent question, and he gave a clipped nod without words. "Jeremy had called me T-cup since high school, and all the guys jumped in on it."

"I don't get it. What happened?" Clayton asked, holding the photo.

Taran explained. Syria. Normal supply run, roadside bomb, surprise attack.

"It's why I could write the story correctly. I lived as one of them for twenty-four hours," Taran said. "And it's why I insist that I spend time getting to know people when I write a story. You can't phone in the truth."

Every man in the room was looking at her differently. They passed the photo around, and she was sure they were comparing the her in the snapshot to the story and to the her they had known for a few days now. It was a long few minutes, the men silently trying to understand what she and Nick had been through. But she knew that would never happen. They couldn't understand.

"Listen, I'm gonna go," Nick said.

He walked to the door, and his brothers let him go without a word. It was like they had seen this before. This pull-away. Taran understood it, but she felt responsible for it. So, she followed him.

"Nick," she called as she pulled her front door shut behind her, the cool night air sending a chill down her spine.

"Don't be sorry," Nick said. "I'm going home to Morgan. I need to feel real right now. It's the only way I know to pull back from the edge."

Taran nodded. She couldn't say she truly understood, because she never felt on an edge.

"Are you okay?" Nick asked. "And I don't mean this minute."

Nick's intense eyes flicked over her face.

"Yeah."

"I've thought about you a lot since I met my fiancée, Morgan." Nick looked away from her. "I can't imagine what it would be like watching her die, pulling her body from a car, carrying it to safety—*living* with that." He swallowed. "You're allowed to not be okay."

"A lot of people have told me that, but I want to keep moving forward." She watched him fighting a battle. She could see emotions flicking over his face. She could tell this was hard for him. Times like this, it was easier to just feel empty.

Finally, he met her eyes again. "I've always wanted to thank you. My boys—without you, we wouldn't have made it. They always wanted to thank you. You should say yes, to Danny. Come, please. Because all six of us will be there."

Taran stared at Nick. Danny had invited Taran to be his date for Nick's wedding at least four times. Taran had repeatedly turned him down because she didn't want any of Nick's brothers in arms to see her. To remember her. And she knew they would. They all knew Jeremy. And then there was Corey.

"Things with Corey are weird. It's not a good idea." She didn't love the words, because things with them were almost nothing. But at the same time, it wasn't completely nothing.

Nick's face morphed, like suddenly this conversation became easy. A smile played on his lips.

"I will deny this outright if you ever quote me, but Marc's sister Glory is coming to my wedding. And Danny is weird about bringing a date around her. Marc would kill him, but I'm pretty sure there's something going on there. So, I think he's looking for something no pressure as much as you are." Nick pulled at the back of his neck.

"I'll talk to him."

"We're brothers in arms, Taran. You can't forget that; you have to work through it, not run away from it. Jeremy would expect us to be there for you. You never gave us that chance." Nick hugged her. Then he flashed a grin. "It's fine if you don't. We'll come get you. Remember, you're only a hundred pounds, T-cup."

11

THE CEREMONY HAD been long, but the pictures were worse. When he said he'd be in the wedding, he had no idea it would mean three freaking hours of pictures. Although Morgan looked absolutely stunning and Corey almost laughed at the whomped-upside-the-head expression on Nick's face when she appeared at the end of the aisle, her *no drinking until after the pictures were finished* rule was utter crap.

"On a scale of not too bad to I'm screwed, how mad is Genni?" Will asked.

Corey turned his head and saw a group of women standing on the deck that surrounded the country club overlooking the golf course. Will's longtime girlfriend, who Corey, out of respect for his friend, would never say aloud was a bitch, was glaring over at the bridal party.

"You're screwed." Corey nodded. There were three other women with Genni. "Who are the others?"

"Yeah, almost missing the start of the wedding means you skipped introductions," Will joked.

"I flew in this morning with the team. Nick knew I'd be here when he said 'I do,' but I had to skip everything else. Even Morgan was fine with it."

Will grinned. "I'm just messing with you. The brunette is the flight attendant from Luke's flight home yesterday." Will shook his head in utter disapproval. "I can't remember her name. Not that it matters."

Corey chuckled. That was true Luke Evans. He had a new girl in every city, and although he always claimed he left them on good terms, the family never saw a repeat.

"I don't know if you remember the ginger. She was a couple years behind Clayton in school."

He remembered she used to babysit Beth's kids. "How old is she now?"

Corey watched the pretty red-head laugh at something Genni said. It made sense that Genni would be talking to her. Never forget a face, smile, shake hands, kiss babies, all the crap that she lived by. Corey couldn't understand why his best friend dated such a fake woman. He suspected it was because Will knew he could never be serious about her, and he wasn't ready to settle down.

"Julie's twenty-one already, if you can believe it." Will shook his head. "I'm starting to feel old."

"Definitely could drink to that," Corey agreed. "Oh, but wait—we can't drink."

Will rolled his eyes. "You're such a dumbass."

"So, the blonde is with Danny?" Corey assumed. If one of the Evanses hadn't brought a date it would be Joey. He was a little less social than the other boys. Most of his time these days was spent in a lab working on a cure for diabetes or something.

"No, she's with Joey. One of his lab assistants. Her name is Penny or Polly. I'm sure I could ask Genni," Will said.

"Danny doesn't have a date?" That was hard to imagine. If there was an Evans who never spent a night alone, it was Danny. The man had more women flocking to him than most picnics had ants.

"Pfft, of course he does." Will laughed, but it seemed uncomfortable. "I'm surprised you didn't see her at the ceremony."

The church had been packed. Corey wasn't sure how Will thought he'd pick out some random woman and peg her as Danny's date.

"Maybe she went home between the ceremony and the reception since there's such a long gap."

Genni took that moment to turn another heated glare their way.

"Uh, Nick, are we wrapping this up?"

Corey tried not to laugh at the trepidation in his best friend's voice.

Nick nodded and waved them away while the photographer set up another shot of the couple.

The door to the country club opened, and Corey was pretty sure his eyes bugged out of his head. He knew the petite frame of the woman holding six bottles of Coors Light, but that and the beer were the only things that looked familiar.

Corey's eyes started on the strappy sky-high black heels and ran up the lean legs on display in the dress that stopped well above the knee. The black dress fit like cellophane, and the strips of material on the bodice wrapped around her body like bondage. Her hair was long, way too long to have grown in a week, and done in big curls that softened her entire look. Her face, although unconventionally pretty without makeup, was drop-his-jaw perfect made up, and those sea greens were flanked by long, thick curved lashes. The woman looked like a fantasy, especially with three beers in each of those hands ending in French manicured fingernails.

"Danny's date. Although, in fairness, date probably isn't the right word. It's more like they were both coming, so they came together—*platonically*," Will said, clearing his throat nervously.

Corey looked at Will incredulously.

"Cor, I don't meddle, you know that. So none of this is on me." Will raised both hands up.

Corey turned his eyes back to Taran in time to see Danny heading up the steps to her.

"I'm in love," Danny said as he reached her.

She frowned at Danny. "Cut the crap. I've known you just over two weeks, and I've heard you say that to at least three different women, so don't even start with me."

Danny replied with a lazy smile that Corey had never wanted to wipe off the kid's face so badly. "What can I say, doll? I wear my heart on my sleeve. And I'm not sure what's more beautiful: you or the beer."

Corey could have easily answered that, and it wasn't the beer.

She sighed like Danny was her cross to bear and tipped one beer toward him. "Nick and Morgan have special drinks inside. I got Beth, Marc, Grant, Luke, you, and Clayton. Trish wanted nothing, and Genni said she and Will want to get their own drinks."

Corey would have laughed at the sigh he heard from Will if he wasn't twitching to hit something.

"Did you forget about me?" Corey demanded as he made

his way up the stairs to Danny and Taran. He wasn't sure if he was talking about a drink or something else entirely.

Danny turned and winced at Corey. Guess his face mirrored his current mood. Something sparked in Taran's eyes, and Corey met her gaze head-on.

"How could anyone forget about Corey Matthews?" she asked dryly.

Corey turned from Taran to Danny. "I need a minute with your *date*." The venom dripped out of Corey's voice and he didn't bother trying to hide that, at the moment, it was directed at Danny.

"You know what?" Danny asked with a smile. "Let's just swap dates. You take mine. I'll take yours, and it'll be all good." Danny shrugged like he didn't care.

If Corey had brought a date, which Danny *knew* he hadn't, Danny wouldn't have minded just switching, even if he was "in love."

"Excuse me?" The octave of her voice cut into Corey's ears. He didn't need to look at Taran to know she was offended. As annoyed as he was with Danny, Corey didn't want Taran to think he'd treat women that way.

"Great plan. I didn't bring a date, so just take the beers and go," Corey snapped.

Danny complied taking the beers from Taran as Corey took a hold of her upper arm, moving a fighting little lady inside and away from the crowd.

"Let go!" she demanded for the third time before Corey did.

He ran his hands through his hair and took a deep breath. He really wanted to do something physical. Shake her, hit the wall—or Danny, kiss her. But the last time he did that, he ended up kissing her like it was the last kiss he'd ever have, and he needed it to survive. To top it off, she seemed to have moved on to a different man quickly. Still, she was throwing those hot sparks out of her eyes, and he felt an ache inside him.

"I don't know what makes you think you can just ignore me for weeks and then go all caveman."

Corey raised his eyebrows. So maybe she'd been waiting for his call. He'd thought about calling. In fact, he'd gotten her number from Clayton. But he'd gone a different way.

"Someone upset about sitting by the phone?" Corey asked as he smiled down. Even in her heels, she barely came up to his shoulder.

He received a glare in return. "I've been too busy to sit by the phone."

"Which was why I didn't call, pipsqueak." He watched her mouth open to reply, and then her brow pucker in confusion. She was cute when she was thrown off. "I knew you were doing your story on Clayton, and I figured I'd let you finish with business before the pleasure."

She blushed before she regained herself.

"That's a lot of assumptions, Matthews. I never said I was interested in pleasure," she said and then paused. "With you. Pleasure with you."

He put his hand against the wall just over her shoulder, boxing her in, and had every intention of reminding her exactly how interested she was when a couple entered the hall. Corey saw something like misery flash in her eyes, and he turned to the intruders.

They must have been Nick's friends, because the man was in full Navy dress whites. But he'd never met Nick's friends from the SEALs. Nick kept that part of his life very separate from his family. However, recognition flashed on the man's face as soon as he had a good view of Taran. Corey didn't understand, even as the woman came right up to them, and Corey stepped away from Taran.

"Thank you for protecting my heart, for sending him home to me," she said, her hand on Taran's arm. He watched Taran swallow and nod once as the woman released her arm and stepped back so the man could salute her before they both walked away.

As the couple disappeared, he turned back to Taran, who had wrapped her arms around herself like she was holding her body together. There was an emptiness reflected in the beautiful green eyes that Corey hadn't seen before.

"Taran?" he asked, and she finally turned her gaze from the now empty hallway back to Corey. "What was that about?"

"Ancient history," she replied and walked away from him.

He had the urge to follow, but something held him back. Instead, he spent the next hour watching one of Nick's SEAL friends after another salute the little woman who seemed to become smaller with each gesture. He couldn't give her shit about coming with Danny because, although he didn't understand what, something was going on, and she was fragile because of it. Will answered the question Corey couldn't bring himself to ask the girl herself.

"She was a reporter with Nick's team in Syria," Will said.

"Which time?" Corey asked.

"The last one."

TWO MORE, TARAN thought as she sat at the table alone because Danny had avoided her completely since Corey had basically done the human male version of peeing on her. All she had to do was make it through two more thank-yous, and then she could get out of here. She'd promised Nick she would do this, so she was, but she hated it. Between feeling Corey's constant stare, being dressed up and looking like Jeremy's fiancée—a woman she'd tried to leave behind, and having every single wife of DEVGRU SEAL team six give her the wife's version of a salute was too much. She didn't know how to feel or react to any of it. Telling herself to be sad, stoic, melancholy, proud—anything was exhausting. And the only feeling that came naturally was the butterflies in her stomach when she met Corey's gaze, which made her feel incredibly shitty. But she stayed at the reception. Because if it had been someone else who saved Jeremy, she would have wanted a chance to thank them.

A throat cleared behind her, and she turned. There stood another of the six men. Seb Aston, Jeremy's best friend. Seabass, as the dark-haired grumpy man was known to the rest of the team.

"You don't need to stand. I've already thanked you. You know that," his deep voice informed her. And that was true. The only one of the men from the horrific day to find her again was Seabass, although he had the unfair advantage of knowing where her parents' cattle ranch was to check in on her. "You canceled on me twice last month."

Taran gave him a clipped nod.

"Hard month?" he asked.

March had been weird. Exhausting was probably a better way to explain it. Avoiding having to answer the same questions over and over again.

"March eighth. His last day as a Navy SEAL," Seabass said.

He put his hand to his mouth and blew a hard breath into his fist. "Fucked with me a bit. Remembering all his big plans, his promises to keep in touch with me even though I wasn't leaving the teams."

It was the promise Jeremy'd made to her when they got engaged. He'd finish the last tour, and then their life would focus on her career. Whatever she needed to do to become the journalist every outlet wanted telling their stories.

"When you canceled, I thought you were doing well. But now Nick made us promise to just say our thank-you and let you be. He said your demons are too big."

"They aren't," she said and then automatically glanced down at the leg she knew was metal and plastic below the knee. Seabass had lost his leg, but he made it home.

"Jeremy would hate that."

She shook her head and swallowed hard at the knot that was trying to creep up her throat.

"Don't." She didn't need the reminder of all Jeremy would want for her. She knew. "Nick asked me to give you all a chance to get closure and give the wives a chance to say thank you. I understand both, so I'm here. I'm probably the most well-adjusted of all seven of us. I just don't want to constantly relive it."

"Just because you don't have flashbacks, constant mood swings, or nightmares doesn't mean you should ignore *your* PTSD, T-cup."

"*I'm fine.*"

"Are you? Or is that the excuse you're using to not have to deal with hard shit?"

His question was exactly why she hated rehashing everything that happened. Why was everyone convinced she hadn't dealt with the trauma?

Before she responded, a chair moved behind her, and she was swamped with the smell of the familiar cologne. She glanced over her shoulder at Corey. She didn't have it in her to spar with him at the moment. But he simply set a pink drink in a martini glass in front of her before he turned his attention to the man standing next to her.

"I hope I'm not interrupting," Corey said to the man in his full-dress whites.

Seabass grimaced.

She wasn't sure whether they knew each other. Seabass wasn't done talking to her, but she relaxed, knowing he wouldn't continue the conversation with Corey there.

Taran turned to the drink Corey had set in front of her and took a long sip. She waited for him to ask her why sailors were saluting her or what was going on, but he didn't.

"I figured since you look like a girl today, the pink fruity drink wouldn't mess with your image too much," he said instead.

She tried to glare at him, but she couldn't quite pull it off. She was too relieved for the playful banter. "Thanks." She finished the pink liquid, leaving only the white orchid in the empty glass.

"Want another?" he asked simply.

She shook her head. Adding too much alcohol to the stress of the night would help nothing.

"How about a walk? There's a huge empty golf course out there," Corey offered.

She glanced at him.

"Unless you're afraid you can't keep your hands to yourself if we're alone." He waggled an eyebrow at her.

"Yes, Matthews, I'm lyin' and dyin' to get my hands on you." She rolled her eyes and laughed.

"Lyin' and dyin' huh, Little Miss Texas?" Corey said but stood up.

She couldn't deny it. Everyone knew no one outside the lone star state said things like lying and dying.

"And they say all big things come from Texas. How did you slip through those cracks?"

"Haven't you ever heard the expression? The best things come in small packages."

"Must be why I come from Rhode Island, since it is the smallest of all the states," he replied with a smirk.

She was trying to decide whether she should question it or ignore the information she already knew. He spoke again before she had a chance.

"But you already knew that, know-it-all."

"Has anyone ever told you you're annoying?" she asked, but Corey just laughed as he led her outside and down onto the golf course. And annoyed was the last thing she was feeling toward him at the moment.

Taran figured once he had her alone, he'd start the twenty questions about the Navy SEALs. She wondered how she would dodge them. But he surprised her with a ridiculous question instead.

"Do you have magic hair-growing syrup at home?" He glanced at her hair piece.

She didn't use it much. She'd learned to love her short hair, but today, Taran assumed the guys would recognize her better with her old trademark beauty-queen locks. The only reason she had it was because everyone back home expected her to have long ebony hair. "Yes, I got it at Hogwarts, or maybe it was from my fairy godmother. It's hard to remember."

"Does that mean it'll go back at midnight? Because I like it better shorter," Corey said as they headed down the golf cart path.

She glanced at him to see if he was joking or not. "I thought you were into the girlie-girl-long-hair-drop-dead beauties who giggle and smile with stars in their eyes."

Corey looked at her sideways. "*Why*?" he asked like the question actually confused him.

"Let's see. You're rich, you're famous, you're a star athlete, and I'm pretty sure you told me I wasn't pretty enough to be your type." She listed the obvious reasons.

He seemed to ponder that for a minute. "I don't remember saying that. I'm pretty sure I didn't because, from the moment I saw you smile at Demoda, I wanted you."

"What?" Her heels sank into the lush grass beneath her feet. Corey offered his arm as she struggled to walk. She wrapped her hand over his tux jacket. Feeling the tight muscle of his forearm caused her stomach to flip.

He leaned down, and his breath danced off her ear, causing her to shiver.

"Yep, you stood there in Marc's kitchen in that tent-like sweater, and all I thought about was getting you naked." Corey pulled back and smiled.

She really couldn't tell if he was kidding or not.

"Seriously, you know you look gorgeous tonight, but I'm old-fashioned. I like the simple things, like how you looked the other morning when I pulled you out of bed." Corey waggled his eyebrows at her again.

Now she was sure he was kidding.

"I'm not sure it was the right look for a wedding though." She pulled away from him and crossed her arms over each other as the cool spring evening breeze blew through the path.

"The outfits have some similarity." He took off his tux coat and wrapped it over her shoulders.

"They're both black?"

"No, they both leave me wondering if you're wearing a bra." His smile did something funny to her stomach. That warm zing of heat shot through it quickly.

She wet her lips. "What is it with you and my underwear?"

"I'm a guy. You're hot. I like the idea that you're pretty much naked under that dress because it means I could get you out of your clothes that much faster." There was a husky heat to his voice as he spoke the words.

Taran stopped walking and turned to look at him. In the dark of the evening, she could only see the outline of his blond hair. She couldn't see the two-toned brown eyes, but she could feel their gaze. He cupped her cheek in his calloused palm. Her eyes fluttered shut as the warmth from his hand spread over her entire body. She didn't understand how a simple touch could be so hot. A glance from his brown eyes, a heated smile, a caress of a warm hand—that was all it took to flip her stomach and get her heart pounding.

"Hmm, hmm." A cough came from behind her.

She turned to see Danny standing on the path a few feet back. Taran was glad for the interruption, even if part of her wished he wasn't standing there. She wasn't ready for whatever Corey wanted.

"I know I'm really on your list right now. But they think it's funny so they made me come find you. It's time for the shot bag." Danny cringed at Corey's death glare.

Corey sighed, and he rubbed his thumb against her cheek before dropping his hand and stepping back. "Come on, I'll get you another one of those pink girly things."

Taran smiled at him. Corey took a few steps and whispered to Danny before he reached for her hand. It had been a long time since Taran felt the warmth of a big calloused hand wrap around hers protectively. Standing there being wrapped in an oversized tux coat that smelled like Obsession for Men and holding hands with a man felt a lot more intimate than any kiss could have. She wasn't sure she wanted intimacy.

"I think I deserve credit for bringing you two back together," Danny said from ahead of them.

"Danny." It was one word.

Just one.

But Taran got the idea that it said a lot of things. Danny must have gotten that impression too, because he shut up.

Corey stopped on the porch that wrapped around the enormous white country club. He turned and looked down at her.

"If this wasn't a family tradition, I'd probably blow it off, but I have to go with the guys," he explained.

Taran laughed. "Danny left me for pictures and never came back. I think I'll be fine without you," she assured him.

Corey frowned. "You're not dating Danny," he informed her. "Give me ten minutes."

She nodded and let him go. It was better this way. She didn't want him overpowering her with all his hot Captain America mojo. When he was around, she focused on him; she couldn't seem to stop herself. But what she needed to do was go in, let the last wife have her thank-you, and then leave. It had been a long day, and she wanted it to be over.

Instead of moving, though, she watched Corey walk up to the pack of Evanses, and she could tell instantly that this was a tradition all nine guys enjoyed. Taran turned toward Morgan. No one could miss the beautiful bride in a dress made for Cinderella. The lace wrapped her upper body tight before it gave way to a skirt meant for a princess. She looked every part the fairy tale tonight, and she should—it was her special day.

Morgan waved her over to where she was sitting at a table full of people Taran didn't know. She wasn't only Nick's wife, but she was the sister of one of the SEALs killed in Syria that day over two years ago.

"One minute," Morgan said to her family before turning to Taran. "I'm not sure you want to hear this, but thank you. My brother…we were able to bury him because you helped get him home." She reached out her hand and placed it on Taran's arm. "Thank you for protecting Nick. For helping get him unpinned from under the hummer. For keeping him alive for me."

Instead of releasing Taran's arm, Morgan held on tighter. Taran looked directly above her head, like she had with every other sailor's wife, unable to meet their eyes, and nodded.

"I know your forever died that day, but I can't express what it means that you saved mine," Morgan continued.

Taran nodded again. She should have said something, but her voice wouldn't hold the right emotions. Morgan would expect her to be sad. Jeremy had died that day. He had died in that second car, one car behind her. And then she'd carried his body out of the car and back to the base so she could bury him. She should have had the white dress, the rings, the party. Instead, she had a black one, a gravestone, and a cold emptiness.

Seabass came up again beside the women. Morgan smiled at him.

"Enjoy the rest of the party," Taran said before she walked away.

"You and Matthews a real thing?" Seabass asked, following her. There was a hopeful tone to his voice.

Everyone wanted her to move on. But she didn't want to give him that false hope.

She shook her head and took Corey's coat off her shoulders. She just needed to find his place card to leave the coat; her night was done. She had finished what Nick had asked of her. And if there was one person in the group she owed, it was Nick. Although Nick gave her credit for helping that day, she knew if not for him, they never would have gotten Jeremy out of the hummer. If Nick hadn't risked himself, if he hadn't gone into the unstable hummer to get Jeremy out, leaving himself pinned under the car, she never would have gotten his body back to the US. She owed him.

It wasn't hard to find Corey's place card. There were two tables of Evanses. She was at one; he at the other.

"T-cup," Seabass called out.

She sighed before she turned.

"You and Matthews?" he asked again.

She went with the only truth she could give him. "He's an Evans, and they're all my friends."

With that, it was time to go, because if there was something she was good at, it was running away.

12

THE STUPID SHOT bag had put Corey back on edge. He'd almost gotten over Danny bringing Taran as his date before the shot bag. It was an Evans tradition, and he didn't know how it started, but at every Evans wedding, the best man—this time being Grant—brought a bag filled with one-shot booze bottles. All the guys had to grab a bottle, and then together, they toasted the new life ahead of their brother.

Corey didn't hate the tradition. He hated none of the Evans family traditions. In fact, he always felt honored to simply be a part of them. But at the moment, he resented the hell out of the bag of booze. Especially since none of the guys were in any hurry about it. And he was in a hurry to get back to Taran.

Corey craned his neck to see where Taran was. Her appearance was still a bit jarring because he looked for the short-haired girl in cutoffs every time he scanned the room for her. He wasn't lying when he'd told her, although she looked jaw-droppingly beautiful today, he preferred less makeup and the shorter hair. The gorgeous version of Taran was talking to Morgan, but he couldn't decipher what they were saying. He'd guessed by the look on Taran's face it was the same thing all the wives of Nick's SEAL team had said to her.

95

"Cor, can we clear the air?" Danny asked while the other guys got their mini bottles out of the bag.

Corey sighed and turned back to Danny just as Grant passed him the brown paper bag. He didn't even look at what he pulled out before he tossed the bag to Luke and gave Danny his attention.

"I'm sorry I didn't talk to you about bringing Taran, but you didn't ask her. Did you really want her here with anyone else? Because Nick wanted her to come. At least this way I got her here. I get that your trust issues are a hot button, and you overreact to things, but *come on*. You know you can trust all of us."

He might overreact. Danny wasn't the first person to point it out to him. Corey's gaze flicked around the group. The Evans men had squeezed around the high-top cocktail table. Joey punched Clayton for flicking his ear for the third time, forcing Marc to grab Clayton by the arm to switch places with him. Will shook his head, watching them while Luke laughed about it. Nick was telling Grant that his black wedding ring was far superior to the titanium one Grant wore. Grant's face said without words that his brother was an asshole.

Danny's words were true; these guys were trustworthy. But a small voice in his head reminded him that he'd never truly been able to trust anyone.

"Cor, seriously, I like Taran. She's cool. We've all been having fun with her pretty much every day, but we're all on the same page."

Corey's eyebrows shot up, and he clenched his jaw. He had no idea Taran had spent that much time with the Evanses while he was away.

Danny flung his arms out. "Look, I get it. You're another asshole who's taken the plunge and can no longer take a joke." Corey was confused by the statement, even as Danny continued. "Although you're all falling like dominos."

Corey caught Will's headshake at Danny out of the corner of his eye. He turned to Will, shooting him a questioning look. Will grimaced.

"What are you talking about, Danny?" Corey asked.

"One," Danny pointed at Marc. "Two." His finger moved to Grant. "Three." Then Nick, "Four." He settled on Corey. "Mark my words, you'll all be dragging me to another jewelry store within six months."

Corey reared back. He had no idea what Danny meant, because although he was interested in Taran, he wasn't anywhere near marriage. He was hesitant to even say he was interested in a relationship. But he did want to get to know her better so he could decide.

"You're ten steps too far into a future I don't want," Corey informed him.

"Hmm," Danny said sarcastically. "Marc told Will the same thing, then Grant told Luke that, and Nick said that to me less than four months ago. Yet I'm almost certain we're at Nick's wedding."

The guys around them all shrugged.

"Pick your bottle," Corey snapped at Danny. "You and me—we're good. But I'd like everyone to butt out of anything going on with Taran and me."

"Um, dude, do you *know* us?" Luke asked. "Because although Danny does need to pick a bottle, none of us are ever going to butt out of anything."

Danny smiled but did as he was told before handing the bag off to Clayton.

"Grant, why in God's name would you put schnapps in the bag?" Clayton asked. Although it was a good question, because schnapps sucked, it meant that everyone had their bottles. Groom, then oldest to youngest. Always the same order, and if Clayton had his bottle, everyone did.

Corey had hardly glanced at his scotch, confirming it wasn't a schnapps too, before turning back to Taran. She was talking to the grouchy guy who worked with Nick, or he was trying to talk to her. Corey didn't know Seb well, but he didn't seem the type to harass a woman.

"I'm not one for long speeches," Grant said, gaining Corey's attention. That meant open the bottle, which he did. "But Nick, we wish you all the happiness that comes from family. From seeing the woman you love next to you every step of your forever. Even if some of us don't realize that's a good thing yet."

Corey almost rolled his eyes, but he didn't. It wasn't that he didn't believe being with the woman you loved was the best kind of forever. He could easily toast Nick's happiness, and he held up his bottle and clinked it with the other guys' before the burn of scotch slid down his throat.

"Cor," Nick said before he could escape. The rest of the Evanses started to disperse, but Corey stayed by the groom. "Danny might be a moron, but now that I finally figured out who Taran is, I've got to say this. Taran's my sister in arms, and I would protect her as fiercely as I would protect Beth or Bex or Trish. Be careful with my girl."

He didn't want the story from Nick. If she wanted him to know what happened, she'd be the one to tell him. Corey frowned and then turned back wondering what exactly Taran had been through, but he couldn't find her.

"It wouldn't surprise me if she was gone," Nick said. "She didn't want to come. I used our history to force her hand."

Corey nodded. That was probably for the best. Nick smirked and then headed for his bride.

"Want to dance?" The voice came from behind him. He turned to see Beth standing there, none of her usual energy surrounding her. He took her hand and led her to the dance floor.

"Long week?" he asked as he settled a hand on her waist. He still scanned the room in hopes that maybe he'd see Taran, but he was starting to believe Nick was right and she'd left. Without even a goodbye—that kind of sucked. Beth had been talking, and he wasn't really listening.

"But with the wedding over, the article done, and everyone going back home soon, it should be quiet," she finished.

"Taran's article is done?" he asked, and Beth rolled her eyes.

"Yip. She dropped it off two days ago. She isn't sending it in until after the draft, though, because it talks about Seattle."

He simply looked at her not asking aloud.

"I like it. Don't make fun though. He's starting to get annoyed with the guys."

Corey wondered what he could mock Clayton about. But he wasn't worried about the article. If Beth approved, then it was fine. She was fiercely protective of Clayton.

But the excitement sparked in his stomach at the knowledge that the article was finished. His plan could move to the next step.

13

"HOLD ON, SOMEONE'S here," Corey said and muted the mic attached to his ear so the other players wouldn't hear.

He opened his door, and there in the hallway outside his apartment stood his former agent, looking uncomfortable. Corey crossed his arms and glared down at him.

"Whatcha doing here?" he asked.

"Official business," Sean explained. "I tried to go through your agent, but apparently you don't have one."

Corey *had* to get around to dealing with that. It had been well over a month. He'd signed the Sideline agreement without representation, which was always a bad idea. He just didn't know who to sign with. He'd only ever been with Hot Shots, and he'd gotten bad vibes from the five agents he'd interviewed.

He stood there not knowing what to say to Sean but not really wanting to invite him in either. Finally, Sean sighed.

"First, there's an article coming out about one of my clients this week, and it needs your official okay before it can go to print," Sean explained.

Corey narrowed his eyes. What the hell was that about? The voice from the game he was ignoring got louder in his ear, and he glanced back at the television.

"Is this a bad time?" Sean no longer looked uncomfortable as he crossed his arms over his chest.

Corey shook his head. "Come in but make it quick."

He headed straight for the coffee table and grabbed the PS4 remote. He hit some buttons to keep him and his partner from getting killed while he dealt with whatever this was.

Sean dropped two sets of papers on the table, along with a pen, and sat on the couch.

"I'm surprised you have time for that shit during the season," Sean said, nodding at the television.

Normally he didn't, but he was making time. However, that was not Sean's business; it'd probably lead to another fight he didn't want to have.

"What's the article about, and why does it need my okay?" Corey wondered if this was some attempt to get him to re-sign with them.

"Clayton, and although a half-assed contract written on the back of a car registration doesn't seem likely to hold up in court, Ms. Murphy insisted I get a formal okay from you."

Corey chuckled and scratched his head. "Girl's got integrity. Don't see that too often with reporters."

Sean grunted a non-reply. "Can you just read it?"

"Don't need to. Beth said it was good to go." Corey picked up the pen and signed the papers.

Sean's long sigh had Corey turning his way. He was sitting with his eyes pinched shut, squeezing the bridge of his nose with two fingers and looking about as unhappy as he'd ever seen his former agent. "Did you *read* it before you *signed* it?"

"Why? Are you trying to pull something on me?"

Sean's huff was followed by a frustrated statement. "Matthews, I know you hate reading, but you *need* an agent."

Corey didn't disagree, but he just shrugged.

"Is every one of us against you dating the 'In Case You Didn't Know' queen?" Sean asked, frowning at him.

"Believe it or not, not everyone thinks I'm such a loser." Corey glared. *What the hell?* His reputation wasn't bad. He wasn't a heartbreaker, nor a playboy, by any means.

"What?" Sean demanded.

"Most people don't have issues with me. I'm not known as a douche bag."

"I never had an issue with you dating. I had an issue with my incredibly media shy client casually dating a gossip reporter, even if he thinks she has integrity," Sean replied, clearly a bit exasperated.

"Oh." Corey hadn't really considered that viewpoint. He might want to revisit the firing, although he wasn't craving crow at the moment, and he'd have to eat a bit of it to get Sean back.

"So, are you going to read this or not?" Sean asked. "Because I highly suggest you read what you signed."

"Nah," Corey said. He hated paperwork. Just dealing with texts was hard enough, he didn't need to read a multi-page contract that said the article about Clayton could go to print. He hadn't even read the Sideline contract. He'd given it to Marc and Beth to look at for him.

"Fine," Sean said and picked up the papers. "I'll let myself out."

Corey waited until the door shut and then unmuted his mic. "You almost killed us. It's a good thing I was near the television."

"You walked away in the middle of a battle!" The female voice growled in his ear, and he smiled. That voice was the entire reason he was making time to play. And hell, playing this game had made up the best moments of his last two weeks.

14

TARAN'S PHONE RANG beside her, and she glanced down at the name on the screen. She quickly muted her microphone and answered.

"Well?" she asked.

"T, he signed it," Sean said.

"As is?" she asked, shocked.

"Yup," he answered, but he didn't sound happy.

Taran fired off a couple more spells and listened to the guy in her ear asking her if she was asleep at the wheel again. She ignored him. She made sure they didn't die, but she wasn't focused on *Diablo* at that moment.

All she could think about was that Corey Matthews had just signed a contract giving her permission to write a color story about him for September without any input. She couldn't believe it. When she asked Sean to try to get him to sign it, she never imagined in a million years that he would. She had hoped that now that he knew her better, he would trust her enough to let her write an article on him, but she hadn't really believed it.

"You there?" Sean asked.

"Yeah, I'm here. Did he say anything about conditions or suggestions?"

"He didn't read it, so he has no idea he agreed to let you write an article about him."

"Oh." Just like that, her bubble burst. She didn't understand why she cared whether Corey Matthews trusted her, but knowing he didn't willingly sign it depressed her. "What did he think it was?"

"If I had to guess, I'd say something saying you could print the Clayton article. He didn't read that either."

"Why didn't you correct him?" Taran asked, mystified.

"He fired me," Sean said. "You didn't. You, as my client, asked me to get someone to sign a contract for you. He didn't even ask me what it was about. He just assumed. I suggested—*strongly*—he read it, but legally, I can't tell him what it says. That's not my job. I was representing you."

Taran always forgot that she was Sean's client, but he wrote up all her contracts with *Sports Illustrated* and with all the athletes she wrote about. And because of that, she got a nice fat monthly invoice from him.

"What do you want to do with it?" he asked miserably.

Wasn't that the million-dollar question? She had always wanted to write the Matthews story, but could she do it this way?

"Just hang on to it for now," Taran finally said. "I'm doing Tillerson for June, and that contract said he'd be the September story, so I have some time to think about it."

Tim Tillerson was another one of Hot Shots' clients who had the potential to be Major League Baseball's rookie of the year. Sean offered her the first real shot at him. She jumped on it knowing it would make Wayne do a happy dance to get a feature on the rookie catcher and get him off her back. Two good athletes in a row had her boss smiling. The only issue was that he was another Metro, and she knew that meant a run-in with Corey Matthews.

She hadn't seen or heard from him since she'd walked out of Nick and Morgan's wedding. Not that she had expected to. But a part of her hoped she would, so part of the temptation of this new story was that it would once again bring her into his circle, but that was also part of its downside.

"Nope. Not going to do *anything*? Great, thanks. Guess we're going to die—*definitely* going to die—yup, officially dead. Hear that? *Dead*." Her earpiece was now yelling at her so loudly she had to yank it out of her ear and toss it onto the table.

"Who's that?" Sean asked.

"It's just the TV," Taran replied, still ignoring the game. Dying wasn't the end of the world.

"Oh, for a second I thought—" Sean stopped. "Never mind."

Taran ignored the comment. "Let's put it on a shelf for now. We can think about it again in mid-July. Email me a copy with Tillerson's paperwork, but I won't do anything without your input."

"Fair enough," he answered and hung up.

Taran reached for the earpiece and put it back in. "You let us die?" A string of curse words greeted her.

She laughed. This guy really took this game seriously. "Sorry, I got distracted."

"This is why you need to eat meat. Carnivores don't space out," the man complained. She didn't know who sportnut85 was, but they'd been playing together for a few weeks now. He had messaged her out of the blue, saying he'd heard she was a pretty good wizard and asked if they could pair up for a bit. They did well together, and the guy seemed nice enough.

She never told people anything that would help them find her in real life. Not what city she lived in, her occupation, or what she looked like. Not even her first name, and this guy seemed to be on the same page. So, although they chatted while they played, she knew nothing of value about him.

"Sorry. I just can't. I grew up watching cows go to slaughter, and that forever made me a herbivore," she explained.

"What?" he asked.

"My family owned a cattle ranch, and it scarred me for life," Taran explained.

The guy laughed. "You're telling me that the daughter of a cattle rancher doesn't eat meat?"

"Oh yeah, you're the first one to find that funny." She rolled her eyes, and she heard what sounded like a dog in the background. "New pet?"

"Nah," he said. "Dog sitting for a friend."

"What kind of dog?" she asked.

"I don't know. One's black and fluffy and yappy and the other one is the kind women put in their purses."

"Ooh, girlfriend's dogs, huh?" Bummer. Although she didn't know this guy, there was an easiness about him. She didn't have to try so hard to interact with him. They had even been doing a little flirting, but if he had a girlfriend, that had to stop.

"Ex-girlfriend, actually," he corrected. "And her husband. They took their kids out west, and I get to watch the dogs."

"That's pretty big of you. Most people wouldn't do that for an ex who's married with kids," Taran said.

"Well, her husband's one of my best friends, so it's hard not to."

"Wow. Your best friend married your ex?" She thought there was a guy code about that.

"In reality, it played out differently than it sounds," he assured her.

"I hope so. Otherwise, you're a schmuck." Taran laughed.

"Sometimes I think I might be." He agreed, and she kind of felt bad for him. "But then I remember I'm me, and I could never be a schmuck."

Taran laughed, guessing he didn't need pity. "Just conceited."

"Bah, it's not conceited if it's true."

She grinned.

"But I don't currently have a girlfriend, so you don't need to feel bad if you're falling for me."

"Ha!" she replied. She liked laughing, flirting, and chatting with him while they played a game, but it would never be more than that.

Her family believed it was a choice. She was choosing not to find love or even a casual relationship because she was still mourning Jeremy. But that wasn't the case. She'd tried to force feelings for guys she dated but it didn't work. She didn't feel anything.

Until Corey Matthews and that kiss she couldn't stop thinking about.

He made her feel a lot of things. She'd like to say it was just lust for the Captain America look-alike, but that wasn't true. She smiled without meaning to with Corey. Around him, she easily got annoyed, frustrated. But she also felt relief—and maybe happy. But she definitely felt lust.

And before Corey, that was something she'd only ever felt for Jeremy. He was her first love, her high school sweetheart. It was going to be one of those sappy stories where she'd only kissed one man her entire life. It hadn't worked out that way. Because he was gone, and she was left here to try to figure out what she was supposed to do without him. Pivoting, adjusting, became part of life.

Taran had done a pretty good job of moving forward. She had sold the condo they bought in Pensacola and moved to New Jersey. She took a full-time job with *Sports Illustrated* and left the serious press behind her.

At first, she feared she couldn't write the news without reliving it, but that faded away to a different reality. She couldn't be cold and distant while reporting a tragedy. She'd need to feel in order to do the story justice, and since she couldn't, she'd had to find a new path. One that didn't require her to be passionate. But she liked writing, and she'd always liked sports, so this was the perfect way to write things that interested her while living with the emotional emptiness of her PTSD.

"Ha? What exactly does 'ha' mean?" He sounded disgruntled. "I'm lovable."

"It means that although I'm sure there's nothing wrong with you, that's not what I'm looking for," Taran explained.

"Every woman's looking for that—even when they claim they aren't."

"That's not true."

"Okay, I'll bite. What's the reason? Never interested, scarred by some horrible guy, or too wild and crazy?"

Taran paused. "It's complicated. I used to want the whole big love story. I had planned every detail of my wedding and even named my three kids. I wouldn't say I'm scarred, because that tends to make people think there's something wrong with me."

"So, you're not scarred, just had a bad experience?"

"Actually, the opposite. My fiancé was amazing. I could see our entire life. Our wedding, our first house, our first Christmas, our first child and grandchild. It was going to be one of those real-life fairy tales," she said, remembering what she used to believe.

"Experience has taught me there's no such thing."

"No, I guess not. Jeremy was killed by a roadside bomb in Syria, and since that day, I can't get back to a person who believes in the fairy tale." She expected the typical *I'm so sorry; that's so awful* reaction.

"I get it, totally different situation, but I lost my first love too. I used to crave a family of my own. My parents didn't exactly create a loving family or a stable home life. They were like a fairy tale with a dark, dark end. But with my high school girlfriend, I thought I'd found everything I wanted. Our relationship ended in disaster, so bad it took me a while to try again. Then the next one ended with me receiving an invite to her wedding to another guy, and somehow, I'm the asshole if I don't go."

"That's not fair."

"Only you're allowed to be jaded? Everyone else has to believe in love?" he grumbled, causing Taren to chuckle.

"I meant that it's not fair they expect you to go. But I'm not jaded enough to say there is no such thing as love. I see it all over."

"I hear you." He cleared his throat before adding, "One of my"—there was a long pause. Taran wondered if the connection dropped, but finally, the guy continued—"brothers just got married. He's got the whole package. A beautiful wife, great life, and I doubt it will be long before that turns into two point five kids since he already has the white picket fence." He chuckled softly as he said it.

"My siblings are married with kids, and as far as I can tell, they're both living their happily ever afters. Maybe it's just me. I just can't feel it anymore." Again, she braced herself for some kind of *I'm so sorry you're broken* reaction.

"Well, I'll apologize then. You really aren't looking for anything, even if you have two *x*'s."

She wanted to respond, but the only person she'd ever heard that expression from was Danny Evans—and it wasn't common. She closed her eyes and called his voice into her memory. She was terrible at recognizing voices. In the time before caller ID, she never would have survived, because she'd have had to ask "who is this" with every phone call. But she didn't *think* this guy sounded like Danny.

"Unless I'm wrong and you don't."

"I'm definitely female," she confirmed. But thoughts of the Evanses made her realize how personal this had become. *New topic*, Taran thought. "Are we going back in, or are we done?" Currently, they were sitting in the spawn city, not playing, and it'd been at least ten minutes.

"It's probably a good time to just cut out. I have to get to work," he said. He worked the oddest hours.

"Okay, see you around maybe," she replied, and then unlinked from him.

Her phone beeped, and she glanced down to see an unknown number had texted her.

> **UNKNOWN:** Hey Taran. You said to let you know when everything was done. Sean just called and gave his final okay to start. Do you want to meet me at the stadium around 5 to go over what you want from me? Thanks Tim

The Metros were home for one more day, so it would be a good time to start to get to know Tim, see what he does outside of baseball in his home city before they left for a few games on the road. She replied back that she would be there and then sat down at her computer to jot down what she knew and assumed about the up-and-coming star.

15

COREY STRETCHED HIS back and shoulders as he sauntered into the locker room. He'd thrown for over an hour, and
he was feeling it. A good ice down was in his future, not to
mention the magic hands of one of the many trainers of the
Metros staff.

It was four thirty, and most of the players were still out on
the field. Even on off days, in-season practices ran long. The
only people with short days were the pitchers.

He made a quick right into the trainers' room. "Who has me
today?" he asked and received a nod from the new guy. "Give
me five to strip," he informed him and headed to his locker.

An empty locker room was something he could appreciate
during the season because it was rare. Only the trainers were
about today, and they were easy to pick out: black pants, blue
polos. He narrowed his eyes. Tillerson must have some issue
because one was waiting for him, but Corey hadn't heard
anything. Hopefully it wasn't too bad; he was half the team's
bats in a game.

He pulled his shirt over his head, and the kid who had him
today appeared, ready to pack him in ice. Corey flopped into

his chair, shut his eyes, and let the kid to do his thing. The training staff was actually good this year. Not one of them annoyed him, and the work they did on his shoulder was helping. A Cy Young award was looking promising, and Corey would be damned if anything got in his way.

"I'm taking a hot shower, so I'll need a new pack when I get out. No ice bath today," he told the kid who tossed him a towel.

The twenty-minute shower gave him time to think. First, there was Hot Shots. He probably needed to rehire the guys. As mad as Corey was about it, he'd been wrong. Sean was doing his job by telling him not to date a reporter, which Corey really didn't want to do anyway. He never linked himself to any type of reporter or broadcaster.

That was a true statement, but he had to amend it, because he still was thinking about Taran. That was completely his fault too. His idea to get to know her on *Diablo* wasn't horrible. It had started innocently enough. He asked her to play, and they chatted. Teasing her was fun and the more he learned about her, the easier that became. That teasing had turned into flirting, which was better.

Today, they'd gotten a little serious. He hadn't meant to share his feelings, and he'd surprised himself when he did because there wasn't a soul in the world he'd ever admitted it to.

It wasn't until Taran had left the game that he realized what he had actually shared with her. But it had been easy because, as Taran was talking, he could relate to how she felt. He understood that pivot in life she'd described. He hadn't known she'd been engaged, and he'd had no idea she lost her fiancé in Syria—where she too had some kind of trauma.

Knowing she still carried a torch for that guy should have been off-putting, but when she talked about just not feeling it anymore, and how she still believed it existed for other people, it was like she'd taken the words out of his mouth. He was finding himself drawn to her in a way he'd never experienced before, but he also didn't know what to do about it.

Why wasn't he jumping on it? Because she was a reporter? As much as he told himself that could be an issue, she'd never once asked him anything personal.

Actually, she talked and questioned him more openly when she didn't know it was him, almost like who he was held her back. Plus, her interactions with the Evanses and how they reacted to her told him she wasn't a trashy gossip reporter. So he had no idea why he wasn't acting on what he was feeling.

He did have one big problem. In the hours they had spent playing and talking together, she had no idea it was him. And he knew if he told her, she'd shoot him one of those *I hate you* looks. On top of that, he'd admitted some really personal shit he didn't want the world to know. Although he thought he could maybe trust her, she *was* a reporter. That meant she couldn't find out he was the one she'd been talking to on *Diablo*.

Corey shut the water off but made no move to leave the stall now encased in a haze of steam. He cracked his neck left, then right before leaning back against the misty wall behind him. The shower had been hot, and he was still sweating in the steam, but he didn't mind. He did, however, have to stop wasting time. He had plans tonight.

He'd deal with Sean and Hot Shots as soon as he finished with his massage, and he'd have to back burner Taran for now. He'd still hook up with her on *Diablo* when he could. Although once he went back on the road, it might be tricky. He wasn't getting a solo room this time because Daily, his regular roommate, was making this road trip. Daily had bailed on the last two because they were short, and he didn't have to pitch either of them. If he brought the PS4, his teammate would never let it go. He was a closet video gamer, not a public one. Maybe he could somehow pull weight and get his own room for at least part of the eleven days. He'd done it in the past, especially when he was in a rut, but back then, his agent had done it for him. He had no idea how to do it himself. That thought circled him away from Taran and back to Hot Shots. He laughed at himself; he knew he'd circle back to Taran again, because his mind kept doing that to him.

Corey grabbed the thick white towel he'd hung over the stall, and rubbed his head dry, quickly moving down until he wrapped it around his waist and headed back to his locker.

The young guy was standing there with a new pack and Icy Hot, so Corey did nothing but flop into his chair and let him get to work. Ten years ago, in Houston, he hadn't needed so much work from a trainer to get him pitching. At this point, after more than half a lifetime of the repetitive motion, he needed all the help he could get with his shoulder to be ready to get on the mound. His shoulder wasn't so bad that he was done as a rotation pitcher, but he knew he was getting closer every day. He'd end up like his father, the great Orlando Matthews, as a closer for a while before he retired. Although, he wasn't quite old enough to worry about retirement yet, but watching Marc retire too young, had Corey thinking about it. He had the Evanses, but nothing else and sometimes he wondered what his life would look like when baseball wasn't center stage.

It was scary to think he might become a full-time video gamer. Because beside hanging out with the Evanses, he truly did nothing but play ball. He was a borderline loser.

"Matthews," Tim Tillerson called him, and he opened his eyes and turned to look three lockers to the right. Corey raised his eyebrows at the kid. He hated that all the veterans were assigned a rookie to show the ropes. It made him feel like he was in high school again. But it was the way the team worked, and unfortunately, Tim was assigned to Corey this year.

"What's the deal with bringing someone on a road trip with you?" the kid asked.

Corey wanted to sigh. The last thing a young player needed was someone wanting to go on the road with him. But it wasn't Corey's job to tell him that'd be a whopper of a fuck-up. That was something the rookie needed to figure out himself.

"Who's your agent?" he asked him instead.

"Same as you. Sean Taylor."

Corey frowned. No one knew he had fired them, even though it'd been a month.

"Call him. He'll take care of it," he told the kid and then added, "you hurting?"

"Nah, why?" Tillerson asked, his head cocked to the side. The dumbass looked like he couldn't imagine why Corey would ask.

"You had a blue shirt waiting for you. I just assumed." Corey tipped his chin to the woman standing next to Tim, her back to Corey.

Tillerson smiled. "Oh, yeah. I thought that too. I had brief flashes of failed drug tests."

Even if Tillerson was laughing, Corey didn't find it funny. "Is that seriously a possibility?" He'd have to get the kid off that fast, and that was the last thing Corey needed to add on to his life. Of course he couldn't get a normal rookie to look out for. He'd have to have the one hooked on something.

"What is it with old people and their inability to take a joke?" Tillerson asked, annoyed. There was a crack of an unmistakable laugh, followed quickly by a fake cough, and Corey whipped his head around to where it had come from.

Now that she'd turned to face him, Corey couldn't believe he hadn't recognized her sooner. Taran stood, black pants, blue shirt, hair clipped back, looking exactly like a trainer and blending in like she belonged. He frowned at her.

"Why are *you* here?" he demanded.

"Good to see you too," she assured him before turning back to Tillerson. "You don't have to worry about a thing, I'll take care of all of it on my end. You just sit back and enjoy the ride." Taran sent Tillerson one of those smiles that did something to Corey's gut.

"Just the kind of woman I like." The rookie wrapped his arm around Taran. He wanted to take Taran on the road?

"Fuck, you move through men faster than a two-bit hooker," Corey snapped at her.

Tillerson looked a bit put off by his comment, but Corey just found himself on the receiving end of one a Taran's withering looks.

"Every thirty days, but sometimes it's a woman," she assured him.

Did she really date women too?

She didn't explain the comment, just scooted out of Tillerson's grasp. "Wallpaper." She said it like it was a reminder, but even as Tillerson smiled in agreement, Corey was lost.

The locker room was filling up as practice was winding down, but Corey couldn't focus on anything but the petite, dark-haired woman who was hovering around Tillerson's locker, trying to blend in. He wanted to tell her she was doing a crappy job, because as the trainer finished up with his massage and retaped him, and as he was left to get dressed, all he noticed was her. The way she watched the rookie carefully, analyzing his every interaction. The way she noticed everyone in his vicinity, and the way her mint-green eyes assessed everything about the situation. It was pissing him off. This afternoon, she had told him she wasn't interested in anything serious, but she was seriously interested in watching the rookie from Alabama *good old boy* her. She didn't miss anything going on around Tillerson.

Anything, that is, but *him*. Corey, she systematically ignored.

He should be getting dressed. He should be gone already. Will couldn't make the trip out west with the rest of the Evanses for Clayton's big day because of an important swim meet, so Corey was supposed to meet him at six. They planned to eat before the first round, but at this rate, he was going to be late because he still had to stop at home and deal with the dogs. And yet he couldn't bring himself to leave.

"Tillerson, you up for Poison tonight?" Daily yelled.

Corey watched him almost agree before he looked behind him. Taran raised one slim eyebrow.

He sighed. "I can't. I have plans."

That galled Corey. First that Taran had plans with Tillerson, and second that the guy didn't realize what a lucky son of a bitch he was.

"We can push this back. You were the one who called me," she assured him, looking like she truly couldn't care either way.

"No." He sighed. "Everyone says it's important. I want to do it." The reluctance was ridiculous, even as he assured her he was interested.

Corey felt that burning desire to hit something building in his system. Any kind of physical outlet would work, even pinning

Little Miss Eyebrow against the wall. Yeah, that would work. Pin her up against the wall. Her body pressed hard against his. He'd lock her hands over her head and hold her tight against him. The swell of her breasts would press into the wall of his chest.

Grimacing, he stopped that train of thought. He was going to tent his towel if he wasn't careful. He dropped his elbows to his knees and ran his hand over his face. He had to get a grip.

"Hey, Matthews, you coming with us tonight?" Daily asked.

"Eh," Corey replied, looking toward Daily. He'd never been a huge fan of the bar or club scene in New York. Plus, his plans with Will, which he was now going to be late for.

"Come on. Aren't the Evans all in Cali for the draft?" another guy asked. Three years ago, not one person in the Metros knew he was close with the Evanses. Now, because of his friendship with Marc, everyone knew. Marc was a lot less private about things.

"Most of `em," Corey agreed.

"Oh, he has Demoda's so-called dogs then." Daily laughed. "You know, I don't think I'd do it. He might be your best bud lately, but they're still your ex-girlfriend's dogs."

Corey glanced over and saw Taran jerk upright. He shut his eyes. She'd just realized who she'd been talking to online. He couldn't think about it, though, because he had to answer the guys.

"Yeah, I have the mutts, so unless I want to live in Demoda's dogs' pee, I'm stuck home until after Clayton is signed."

He turned his eyes on Taran, and she mouthed one word: "asshat." His mood sank even lower. Until that moment, he hadn't realized he'd been hoping she thought they had become something—friends, maybe. But the look she shot him said that wasn't the case, and it bothered him even more because she had something going on with the idiot kid.

17

HE DIDN'T EVEN have the decency to look guilty as he chatted about watching his ex-girlfriend's dogs. She'd spent the last few weeks letting Corey Matthews get to know her. Flirting with him. Why? Why would he find her online and pretend to be some random person? She was pissed. She needed a minute to regroup and refocus on Tim, the reason she was in the room.

"Tim, I need to make a call really quick. You go ahead and get dressed, meet me in the tunnel and I can follow you home." She always did a first interview with her subjects at their place. She made them dinner and let them talk. It was surprising how much a person would say in a few hours over a couple of glasses of wine and good food.

"You're going home with him? Really?" Corey snapped.

Taran turned to look at him. She hadn't wanted to. She'd spent the last forty-five minutes trying not to look at him sitting there in just a towel.

She'd been in many locker rooms—probably a hundred over the last two years—and never had a half-naked or even fully undressed male bother her in the least. Yet she couldn't bring herself to look at Corey today. His bare chest and arms—all muscle from years of working out for hours a day—daring her not to stare. Not to follow the blond happy trail that led to the knot of the towel, making her wonder what was below.

If she wasn't a female reporter in a male dominated world, she might not have had the strength to make sure her stare was blank when she responded to the half-naked Captain America look-alike ten feet from her. But she was, and it was not her first locker room, so her eyes stayed up as she answered.

"I don't have time to deal with you today. I'll get there, trust me." She let her eyes tell him she was mad about the game he'd played with her. "But today, I'm going to have a nice dinner with Tim and get to know him." Basically, do her job.

"Just no meat—or are you making an exception for his?" he asked, but in a locker room where double entendres hung in the air, you didn't make that comment to a female reporter.

Taran's mouth fell open for a split second before she snapped it shut so hard her teeth rattled.

"Matthews, what the hell is wrong with you today?" Daily asked, coming to her aid.

She'd known Daily since she'd interviewed him two years earlier.

"Murphy, don't hold that against us. He's not usually such a douche bag."

She glanced back to Daily. "Actually, I'd have to disagree with that." Although he was known for being the boy's boy with the media, and never doing anything out of line—polite, humble, sweet—Taran hadn't met that man at all. "I'll meet you outside," she added to Tim.

As she walked out of the locker room, she heard Daily say, "She's a reporter asshole. You should thank her if that doesn't end up in her blog."

Taran wouldn't post anything about Corey. Whatever his problem was it seemed way too personal for her to speculate about.

She was a reporter who, in a few months, would be writing a story about Corey Matthews. Although it annoyed her that he'd sought her out on *Diablo*, he also gave her quite a bit of information. Some of it she'd known. His parents were always in the news, so that wasn't new. But he basically confirmed his relationship with actress Mel Holly, something there had been a lot of speculation about. He'd also implied he had a lot of unresolved feelings for both Beth Demoda and Mel. Taran wouldn't ever put that in her story, because it truly was no one's business, but it might give her insight into who he was.

Then again maybe it wasn't even true. He *definitely* knew who she was when they'd talked online. Corey Matthews didn't seem like the type to open up to a reporter, but he *did* seem like the type to punish her for her attempted blackmail with the Clayton story. That hurt, which was a weird feeling. A pain in her chest and an uncomfortable turn of her stomach. It had been a long time since she'd felt that. And instinctively, she pushed the feeling aside. Drawing away from the pain.

At Nick's wedding, Corey had been the one bright spot in an otherwise awful day. She had spent the last few weeks wishing he'd reach out, only to find out he'd been playing her. It pissed her off. And she felt that knot come back, but she had no intention of letting it continue to grow.

She took a deep breath and tried to get her professional mask back in the place. The one she needed to do her job. The one that normally took up every moment of her day. Taran breathed in another deep breath and blew out everything that had to do with Corey Matthews. She'd learned how to let things go a long time ago.

Feeling the knot disappear and the cool relaxation wash over her, she leaned against the wall and pulled out her phone. She had a text from her sister, one from her sister-in-law, and one from Erin. She answered all of them, smiling about the family updates from home and assuring Erin she would not be at this weekend's barbeque because she'd be on the road with Tim.

She then flipped to Erin's husband and made the quick call to get him to take care of her actual plans to travel with the team.

The air filled with Obsession, and she knew who was headed her way before she even raised her eyes from her phone.

"Don't find me again, *sportsnut*. And I expect a bit more professionalism from a team captain," she said, still not looking at him.

"Do you have a sixth sense?" he asked, and she finally raised her eyes from her phone.

"Huh?"

"How'd you know it was me, little bit? You didn't even look." He frowned at her.

"I have four other senses. I didn't need to see you." She rolled her eyes.

Her phone buzzed, and she looked down to see a text from Sean telling her everything was set to go. Corey rested his arm next to her shoulder, invading her space with all his Captain America Mojo. She licked her lips, steeling her resistance, before she met his eyes.

"Professionally speaking—"

Nothing about the way he invaded her personal space was professional. It created a serious lump in her throat.

"It's not my business what you do with him when he's not playing, but you shouldn't be traveling with him on road trips."

She was sure her confusion was written all over her face.

"Rookies don't need distractions, and I'm sure none of the management would want you becoming one."

What the hell? She knew how to do her job, and she had never been an issue for any of her subjects. In fact, she was known in the industry for being anything but a distraction because most of the time, no one noticed she was around. That was what she told every single athlete before working with them. As far as they were concerned, she was just the wallpaper. She made it a point to blend in.

"Look, Matthews, I don't know why you're suddenly so interested in what I do or don't do, but before I even thought about touching Tim, I got approval from everyone from the owner down to his batting coach. And Sean approves too, so maybe you could just step back and mind your own business." She glared at him—his face so close his breath was on her lips. His two-tone eyes sparking angry fire at her before they flashed with something else.

He swallowed and shook his head, but he didn't step back. "The *Diablo* thing."

She cut him off. "I get it; I crossed a line that I didn't understand at the time with the Clayton stunt. If I'd known how close you were with the Evanses, if I'd known they were *family*, I'd have never, *ever*, pretended I'd use you to get to Clayton. But I did. So you got back at me with all that stuff you said on *Diablo*—feed a reporter fake news."

She swallowed the hurt and anger the entire thing brought up again.

He blinked and then frowned, but remained silent.

She looked over his shoulder, avoiding eye contact so she could finish. "I don't like it. In fact, I hate it. But I know why you did it. And clearly you don't know me well enough to know I'd never write or blog about anything that wasn't approved by both you and your agent. *But. I. Wouldn't.* So it would be nice if you could just stop assuming the worst about me."

By the time she finished, her voice was hardly a whisper, and her throat was thick. She dropped her head and focused on their shoes.

He didn't move or answer, so she slipped under his arm and went back to her phone for the simple task of something to ignore him with. She was as tense as nails waiting for him to say or do whatever maddeningly unpredictable thing he'd come up with next, but nothing happened. She let her shoulders sag, wondering if he'd left, when he finally spoke.

"Taran." He said her name just above a whisper, and the deep tenor of his voice moved across her skin like a caress.

She shivered. Finally, she looked over her shoulder at him. He hadn't moved—he leaned against the wall on one arm and stared at his hand.

"Corey," she replied softly.

He sucked in a breath at that. His focus moved to her, and those multicolored eyes of his were liquid. The heat in that simple glance cracked through the hallway around her. She couldn't move. She was paralyzed by desire for the man who couldn't even be civil to her.

"Yo Taran," Tim called out, and Corey's eyes raised above her head.

It broke the spell she had been under. Taran cleared her throat before she turned to him.

"Did he apologize? Because he owes you one."

"Sure," she said, even though nothing about their conversation had been apologetic. But she had to shake it off and do her job. "You ready?" she asked and moved to Tillerson, leaving Corey standing in the hallway. A quick glance over her shoulder told her he was once again pissed off.

18

"SHE'S TRAVELING WITH the fucking team." Corey slammed in to Will's living room an hour late without so much as a hello.

The she in question was tying him in knots. Somehow, even though she was dating another guy, he was still an ass for the *Diablo* incident. The incident she twisted in her head to be a big joke *on her.* That was so far from the truth he didn't even know how to correct it. How did he tell her it was easier for him to use the anonymity of the game to let her see him? How did he tell her she was all he thought about while she was *dating* someone else?

"Hi Will, how was your swim meet?" Will mumbled. "Oh, it was crap." The one-person conversation continued. "That's too bad. So sorry I'm late. I should have called," he confirmed to himself. "I agree, but life just got away from me." Will sighed, not even looking at Corey.

"What the hell are you talking about?" Corey asked.

"Nothing," Will assured him. "I ordered pizza. Since the clock's about to start for Seattle, dinner was definitely off the table."

"I really hope you have beer in the fridge," Corey said and went for a cold one before coming back to the family room. "You know why she's traveling with the team?"

"I'm going to assume we're talking about Taran, because she's the only thing that exists in your world anymore." Will reached for the remote and smashed the mute button.

"Tillerson," Corey ranted.

"Your new catcher?"

Corey slammed his beer on the coffee table. The liquid bubbled up over the lip of the bottle and cascaded down and onto the table. Will jumped up, returning with paper towels.

As Will mopped up beer, Corey continued. "Tillerson. He's like twenty-two. And she's dating him."

"There is no state in which that's illegal." Will's voice seemed annoyed, which was out of character for him. Normally, Will was pretty chill. Obviously, Taran dating Tim bothered him as well.

Corey glared across the room. First Danny, now Tillerson. He didn't understand. If she wasn't looking for a relationship, why in God's name did she keep dating everyone and his brother?

"And according to her, the entire front office and the whole coaching staff approves of this relationship." It had taken everything in Corey not to go after them when they sauntered off down the tunnel to have their romantic dinner.

Taran felt the lust that spewed out between the two of them; he knew she did. And as much as he watched the interaction between Tillerson and Taran, there was no heat. Nothing.

"That's a weird thing for her to tell you. I mean, it's a weird thing for her to even ask any of them." Will's brown hair fell down into his eyes, and he brushed it back. "Who does that?"

Corey had no idea what Will was saying.

"She was standing in the locker room, watching his every move like he was the most interesting creature on the planet. Rambling in some code about wallpaper."

Will full-out laughed at that.

"What is so funny?" he spat out through gritted teeth.

"She's writing a story about Tillerson. She's not dating him." Will shook his head.

Corey's gaze snapped to Will's. "How do you know that?"

"Oh, suddenly you hear me." Will snorted.

"What do you mean? Of course I hear you. How do you know who her next story is about?" he asked his best friend again.

"I don't *know* it's her next story, but that is exactly what she told Clayton. She's the wallpaper, meaning she didn't want to be part of anything going on in Clayton's world while she shadowed him. And truthfully, it makes more sense that she'd get front office approval to write a story on him. No one asks the team owner to date a player," Will explained.

Corey's chest expanded with a breath for the first time in almost two hours. The blinding anger vanished. "Writing a story," he said, and he replayed everything that had happened in his mind. He laughed. Of course, she was writing a story about Tillerson. *Every thirty days*, she'd said. It was a monthly magazine. Corey glanced at the time. "Dude, sorry we don't have time to eat. I got stuck at the stadium."

Will nodded. "Pizza." He pointed the tip of his beer bottle to the table.

"Oh, great!" Corey said, reaching for a slice. His mood had done a complete one eighty. "Why is the television muted? Don't you want to hear Clayton get selected?"

Will looked annoyed, but he grabbed the remote and unmuted the TV. "So Taran's traveling with the team?" The tone he used made it seem like Corey should be concerned about this.

"I guess she has to if she's writing a story on Tillerson." He shrugged. "But she's probably going to be grouchy. She's pissed because she found out I've been stalking her on *Diablo* since before the wedding."

"What?" Will coughed, choking.

"You okay?" he asked, giving Will two swift pounds on the back.

Will nodded. "Why are you stalking *Taran*?"

"Not really stalking. I searched for her and played with her a few times a week. I just didn't tell her it was me, but today she found out. She's pissed." Corey laughed. He shouldn't think it was funny, but she wasn't dating Tillerson, and that just made him feel lighter.

"It's a good thing I was around when you and Beth started dating. Otherwise I would really question your sanity."

What did that have to do with anything? "Why?"

Will never got to answer because Seattle selected Clayton as the first pick of the draft.

The next night when Corey stormed into Will's, he had a different agenda in mind.

"Why are you dressed like that?" Will's eyes narrowed. Corey glanced down. He thought he looked perfect. "Did you get a *haircut* since the game?" Will asked incredulously. It was an afternoon game, so it had been a few hours. It wasn't *that* odd.

"I just cleaned it up when I got a shave," Corey explained.

"Shaved implies a smooth face," Will said, and Corey crossed his arms. "You got a haircut, a beard trim, and put on an outfit that should be on a runway for some damn designer, all to come over to my house?" Will clearly didn't believe this was the case. Which, of course, it wasn't.

"Want to go out?" he asked his best friend.

"Out? It's Sunday."

"Yes. We always sit around here. Let's go out." Corey smiled.

Will stood up and crossed his arms. "What the hell? You want to go out Sunday night at ten o'clock?"

Normally this would be a very out-of-character request for Corey, but after the game, the rest of the team had been all about a night out. They talked about it the entire time he did his interviews and as he iced down and when he got dressed. He wasn't letting them go out without him.

"What kind of out?"

"Beatrice Inn," Corey said.

"You want to go clubbing the night before a long road trip?" Will cocked his head to the side as his eyebrows pulled together.

"You know if we wait until I get back, Beth and Marc will be home, and then we'll never go because they won't. They're no fun anymore," Corey explained.

"They have four kids." Will shook his head. "Whatever. Fine, I'll get dressed, but I can't stay out until three a.m. I have swim practice in the morning."

Corey didn't want to stay out that late either. He hoped this would be a quick trip. It didn't take Will very long to pull himself together, and less than an hour later they walked into the VIP area of the club.

"Where we headed?" Will asked over the music.

"Over to the team," Corey responded, nodding his head to the back where he could just see of a few of the guys.

"The team." Will's lips pulled into a firm line, but he nodded. "Of course, I must have been a dumbass not to realize."

"What?" Corey asked.

"Tillerson's here," Will responded.

Corey nodded, and Will rolled his eyes as they headed over. Corey's gaze zeroed in on the little reason he had come. She stood almost in the corner, about three feet behind Tillerson. She looked taller than usual, and Corey couldn't help but scan her body—from her short black shorts down her toned legs to the black fuck-me heels on her tiny feet. His attention moved back up to the loose silver tank with a deep scoop neck, the made-up face, and the silver dangles that danced in her jet-black hair. She looked exactly like she belonged in a club surrounded by ball players. No one would be surprised to see her leaving with any one of the many Metros around her. But Corey would be damn sure that didn't happen. She didn't seem to notice his approach because those sea-mist eyes of hers were focused completely on Tillerson.

"Taran." Will got to her first, and she turned her attention to him.

"Will?" she asked, surprised, but her full smile said she wasn't unhappy to see him.

Will leaned down and gave her a quick peck on the cheek. "I'd say I'm surprise to see you here, but that'd be an outright lie."

"Why? I never come here." A cute line puckered between her brows.

"All the same." Will laughed.

"I never understand the Evans' sense of humor," Taran said to him, and then her eyes scanned over. "Corey." She frowned.

"Taran. You look exactly like a ball bunny should." In another situation, he might appreciate that fact.

Will sighed, and Taran shook her head. "I'm just going to say thanks and pretend that was your form of a compliment."

"It was," Will assured her. "Where can I get beer?"

"It's bottle service; hard liquor only," Corey told him. Will should know that, but the look on Will's face said he didn't. "You can put it on my tab."

"I can afford bottle service, you asshole. I just wanted a beer." He frowned and turned back to Taran. "Someday, ten years from now, when we're sitting around laughing about this, I want you to remind him of how much *he* owes *me*."

Taran looked mystified, but Will turned to find a waitress.

"Is he always this cranky when the swim team does badly? Or is it the breakup with Genni?" Taran asked.

Corey stared down shocked. "How do you know about any of that?"

Will had told him about the split on the drive over, but that wasn't shocking. It was just after a wedding, and Will and Genni always took a break after a wedding. Mostly because she wanted a wedding and Will didn't.

Her mint-green eyes turned up to meet his, hitting him with that familiar punch in the gut. "Clayton. He called to thank me again for the article since it came out today. And he gave me an update on the entire family."

"Why?" he asked her. Not that he minded.

"Unlike you, I think your family likes me," she explained.

It warmed Corey's heart that she called the Evanses his family because that was how he wanted it to be.

"They usually have good taste," he agreed.

Taran looked like she had been insulted again.

"But we need to talk."

The small line reappeared between her eyebrows, but she didn't protest when Corey moved her closer to the wall and away from the group. She rested her back against the painted cinder blocks, and Corey placed his hand on the wall and leaned over her shoulder, close enough for her to hear him in the loud club.

"Are you going to lecture me again about leaving Tim alone? He explained you're like his big brother showing him the ropes and what not, but I promise this article will be good for his career. You can have approval too if he wants that."

Corey smiled. He couldn't care less about the Tillerson thing now that he knew what it was. "No, honey."

Her brows shot up at the endearment. But he ignored the question in her eyes. He had practiced this explanation multiple times in his head but there was this angst about it in his gut.

"Being famous, everyone always has ideas about *who* I am, or what I'm supposed to be like." He saw her eyes flash with understanding. "I assumed even you did."

She glanced away, unable to meet his eyes for a moment before she refocused. Her hand came up and tucked a piece of hair behind her ear. But instead of giving anything she said, "It's why 'In Case You Didn't Know' works. I take those things everyone knows and show them something else."

He'd never read anything she'd written so he couldn't agree. Instead, he continued. "For me, that makes getting to know people hard. *Diablo* gives me a chance to talk to people without expectations of what I'm supposed to be. I just get to be myself and let someone get to know me."

Taran's lips parted in surprise before her brow furrowed. "Uh—wait." She shook her head in confusion. "What?"

He smiled and reached out, tucking a silky piece of her dark hair back behind her ear. He wasn't sure if she meant to lean into his hand, but when she did, he took full advantage. His palm grazed the skin of her neck and settled on her throbbing pulse. It was nice to see he wasn't the only one nervous.

"I didn't find you on the game to trick you or feed you false info. I simply wanted a chance to talk without being Corey Matthews." He moved his other hand from the wall beside her and slid it down her waist to the curve of her hip. When he did, the pulse in her neck kicked up a notch.

"Why?" she asked the million-dollar question.

"Hey Tar," a slightly drunk Tillerson called loudly over the music and noise.

They both turned to find him waving them down, and Taran moved away from Corey quickly. He was sitting on a sofa flanked by two women who were obviously baseball bunnies. He sat forward as Taran approached and leaned down to him. Corey watched Tillerson's hand come up and rest on the back of Taran's neck, and Corey moved without thinking. He knew the conversation; Tillerson was leaving with at least one of those trashy women, and Taran was not going with them.

"Dance with me," he said and grabbed her tiny hand with his to pull her away from his teammate and the two baseball bunnies with him.

"Wait, Matthews—" She tried to yank her hand back. "I didn't say yes. I'm working."

"No," he assured her. "You're *not*. Because that right there is not part of your article."

She glanced back over her shoulder at the two women and Tillerson.

"He's young, short stack. It's a strange thing when throngs of attractive women are suddenly throwing themselves at you, more so en masse. But that's the bad side of baseball. No one needs to read about that."

She licked her lips like she was going to ask him something but shook her head instead. "You're right. Kids look up to him. I'd never include anything about the ball bunnies."

"Great—you owe me a dance," Corey said again and reached for her hand.

It slid easily into his, even though it was so petite. Each finger delicate, the skin smooth. So different from his own. He yanked her toward the dance floor, knowing he wouldn't be stopped because everyone knew better than to stop an athlete when they had a woman with them. Alone, it would take him ten minutes to get to the dance floor. With Taran it would be twenty-five seconds.

"Christ on a crutch, Matthews."

He smiled without looking at her as the very Texan expression popped out of Taran's normally accent-less mouth. She must have had a drink because the only time Texas ever came out was when alcohol was involved. He'd learned that playing *Diablo* because three times in the last few weeks he'd noticed it. When the anonymous man he had been asked her, she confessed a few drinks brought out her roots.

"Why in the name of all things holy do you think I owe you a dance?"

He stopped yanking her along and glared down at her. "You left me without so much as a word at Nick's wedding. You don't leave your date like that. You owe me."

"Danny was my date, and I said goodbye to him." She looked exasperated with him.

"You're not dating Danny." He didn't understand why he needed to explain that to her again.

"Okay, I can't argue with crazy," she begrudgingly agreed. "One dance."

But Corey knew he'd get a few more than that out of her. Because there was something between them. He was sure.

Dancing wasn't Corey's best skill by far, but that didn't matter much because it was something Taran was good at. Her small frame moved to the beat in ways that caused a whole different kind of pounding in Corey before the first song was even close to over. His hand started out on her hip, resting on the satin of her shirt. But it wasn't long until his thumb was moving under to find the heat of the skin below. Two songs later, the palm of his hand rested against skin at the small of her back that was softer and smoother than the satin that rubbed the back of it. He pulled her closer, and she looked up with those tempting bedroom eyes of hers fringed with thick black lashes that matched her hair. Her breath skated across his neck, and she wrapped her arm over his shoulder and pulled up closer against him. It was like heaven and hell all at the same time. To move against the small soft creature who had been driving him mad for weeks was heaven, to do nothing more than just hold her was hell. In a crowded club, there was nothing he could do because he wouldn't so much as kiss a woman in public.

In his haze of lust, it took Corey a moment to realize she was trying to get him to lean down so she could say something. He complied, letting his cheek rest against hers. The scent of feminine hair products surrounded him as cool strands of her hair brushed against his forehead. Their hips aligned, and all the softness of the woman pressed against him. He heard her sharp intake of breath. Yes, he was definitely on the border between heaven and hell.

"Come home with me," he heard himself say. "It'll be the best night of your life."

She jerked back like he'd slapped her, not invited her to share nirvana with him. And then she took two steps away.

"I may look like a ball bunny tonight, but I can assure you I am not and *never* will be." Taran spun and stormed away from him.

He didn't understand. He never went for ball bunnies. Everyone knew that about him. Even the bunnies didn't bother to try anymore. What the hell did she mean? He tried to follow her, but he got stopped by close to a dozen people for photos or a "good game" or autographs so by the time he got back to the VIP lounge, she was long gone.

"What's going on with you and Murphy?" Daily asked.

"Nothing. I don't even know where she went," he assured him before heading to Will.

Will's look said *you suck as a human being.* Corey flopped onto the sofa next to him.

"What did you say to her?" Will asked.

"How do you know I said something?" Corey demanded.

"She ran out of here like her hair was on fire, but she had that look Beth gets," Will explained.

Corey knew exactly what he meant; the look right before shit hit the fan.

"Apparently the thought of sex with me makes her lose it." Corey sighed. That was a clear message if he'd ever received one.

"What do you mean?" Will asked, and Corey explained what happened. "Do you think maybe you made her feel like one of the baseball bunnies since you called her one when we got here and then offered her a one-night stand?"

Well, shit. That hadn't been what he said at all. "I've never in my life so much as looked twice at any one of those trashy women. And I don't do one-night stands."

"I know that, and you know that. But Cor—she doesn't really know you," Will explained.

Corey rubbed his face. "Okay, I'll apologize. Any of those many hours you spent with her while she did Clayton's thing over breakfast?"

Will's eyebrows shot up as his mouth dropped open.

"I got her message loud and clear; she isn't interested. I'm not going to show up at her house again. But we have a six-a.m. flight, and I figured breakfast would be as good an apology as any."

"She stole the last butter rum muffin from me," Will complained. "And she takes her coffee black."

"I'll bring her coffee and a muffin and then I'll leave her alone." Corey sighed. That sucked, but he'd get over it. She was a hard-to-peg reporter with eyes that caused his gut to clench, but she wasn't the only woman in the world.

"Yeah right." Will scoffed. "Can we go?"

"Yeah, and I'll get you and Genni owner's box tickets to the Nationals game in DC as a thank you," Corey said, knowing he'd dragged his friend here against his will and then left him for most of the time.

"Genni and I aren't together," Will said. "I told you this."

"The game's at the end of our road trip, in almost two weeks. You will be by then," Corey assured him.

Will laughed. "You are the only one who never says good riddance when we take a break."

Will should know better than that.

"Bro, I would never say that. She's *your girl* until the day you tell me she's not. And I don't mean the *she's being difficult so were taking a break thing you* two do monthly, I mean until the day you tell me *you're* officially done. So, I got your back. And you know she won't say no to the owner's box."

"Every time I really want to be done with your ass, you remind me exactly why you're my boy." Will smiled.

19

TARAN WALKED ON to the plane early. None of the big names were close to boarding, and only a few players were already settling in. Not wanting to stand out, she made sure to look like every other staff member in blue and black. Most of them were on the plane already, and a few waved her way. She smiled and greeted them before finding her seat. Seven A, the window seat. Tillerson would be in the aisle seat next to her. She knew he'd be one of the last on the plane; he was constantly late for everything.

She was facing the struggle of every not quite five-foot person, attempting to get her bag into the overhead bin, when *his* scent hit her nose like a tanker truck. Not again. He wasn't supposed to be here yet. She'd boarded early so she wouldn't have to deal with him.

The bag was no longer in her hand as the fingers of the million-dollar hand took over and easily put the bag into what had been the unreachable bin. She was swamped in Obsession.

She wasn't in the mood to deal with him today. She had let her guard down for twenty minutes, and he had managed to stomp on her. Agreeing to dance with him had been a mistake to begin with, but as she'd tried to tell him she needed a drink, he'd offered her a one-night stand. Maybe it wouldn't have offended some people, but as a female reporter in a business where men swore women only got ahead through one-night stands with the talent, she was more than affronted. And she was mad at herself too. She knew better than this.

Taran had never had to worry about sleeping with the talent before because she'd never had the inkling, and no one had ever shown serious interest.

That was until Corey Matthews.

Which was ridiculous. The man wasn't even known as a playboy, and she'd never heard stories of him sleeping with a reporter. So his sudden interest seemed not only weird but completely out of character for him. And on top of that, she wasn't anything most people couldn't ignore. In fact, it was rare that anyone but her subject and one or two people close to that person even noticed her when she did a story. But Corey seemed to always find her.

"What do you want, Matthews?" she said instead of thanking him, and she moved into her window seat.

He slumped into the seat next to her. No way in hell was she making the five-hour flight to Phoenix with him.

"You want some coffee?" he asked, and she met his gaze. Besides the locker room, Taran had never seen Corey look anything but perfect, and today was no exception.

The Metros required a suit to travel, and Corey's charcoal gray jacket with the white button-down was perfection. Cool gray accented the ring of light brown in the center of his eyes, causing the contrast to make them sparkle. He didn't have a tie, so the open collar rubbed against his tan skin. He held a beverage holder with two cups and a brown paper bag. She had no idea how he'd juggled that and her suitcase.

He'd asked the question, but when she didn't answer fast enough, he lowered her tray table and set a to-go cup on it before pulling a butter rum muffin out of the bag.

"How did you know those are my favorite?" she asked and opened the coffee. Sure enough, it was black, just the way she drank it.

"Can't give away trade secrets."

And finally, after over a month, she found herself on the receiving end of one of Corey Matthews's trademark media darling smiles. She should've been happy to get a smile and not a glare. But the fakeness of the gesture left her disappointed.

"Thanks," she replied and then looked out the window toward the tarmac. A few more cars arrived, dropping the many Metros men at the plane.

"Taran."

Something about her name coming out of his mouth gave her goosebumps every single time. What she needed to say was "Matthews, I'm a female sports reporter. I can't casually hook up with athletes on the team I'm traveling with and keep any of my respectability, so please leave me be." She turned to say just that, but he beat her to the punch.

"I'm sorry." In his two-tone brown eyes, she saw genuine remorse. "I get the impression that I made you feel like one of those trashy women who throw themselves at athletes. I've thought of you a lot of ways, but never like that. I *never* intended to make you feel like that. Plus, even as a young athlete, I never had any interest in that type of woman. I've avoided them my entire career. I don't go within a few feet of them, and they stay away from me."

Taran had noticed none of the women surrounding the team went anywhere near Corey last night. Like it was some unspoken understanding that he wouldn't welcome them. Still, when Corey talked about Tillerson leaving with them, it almost seemed like he'd been there. Taran had nearly asked him about it before she realized it was none of her business. However, it was clear Corey wasn't lying now.

"Apology accepted. But Matthews, I'm here to do my job, and I have to focus on that."

He nodded. "So that said, I'll take a hint and leave you alone, plus the damn kid should be here any minute. If I have to go get him again, I'll kill the little shit. He's like a ten-year-old sometimes." Corey grabbed his coffee and the empty brown bag and left.

Taran smiled at Corey's retreating back. Tillerson had told her the story about the flight he missed and how Corey had to come to drag him out of bed. The two had to take a commercial flight to St. Louis, and Corey had promised to kill Tillerson if he did it again.

She didn't know how long Corey Matthews would leave her alone, but she was grateful he seemed to understand that she needed to focus on her story.

20

EIGHT DAYS LATER, he'd kept his word and was still leaving her alone, but it was killing him. He'd pitched like old dog balls again because of it. He slammed the towel into the locker and flopped into his seat. He'd gotten pulled in the fourth and couldn't even stand to sit on the bench while the game finished.

"You ready for new ice?" the female voice of the trainer assigned to him asked.

Corey pulled out his phone as the ice burned against his skin. Seventeen damn messages. All from the Evanses. Six from Marc. He forced his brain to settle and focus on the words.

> **MARC:** What the hell was that inning?

> **MARC:** Where is your head at? Because I can tell you sure as shit its not thinking about what you're doing

> **MARC:** If they don't pull you now Monroe needs to be fired and Ashford too for that matter

> **MARC:** You missed every single mark for your left foot again. Are you on your period or some shit and that's why your head's a mess?

> **MARC:** How many times do we need to go over this? Figure out a way to get out of your own head. Maybe get laid

> **MARC:** I expect a call tonight

Fucking Marc. He was his personal pitching coach, and the guy knew his shit, but Marc texted him every time he sucked, all game long. Marc was a former pitcher; he knew that sometimes you just had a bad day.

He glanced around the locker room and watched as one person after another looked away before he could make eye contact. He knew what they were all thinking. *There goes Matthews's good season right down the shitter.* Falling apart wasn't a new thing for him.

Corey grabbed the towel back from his locker and hung it over his head so he didn't have to look at anyone. He needed to get out of his head. The team was in Lake Tahoe, and Bridget was here. Maybe a few hours with her would help him stop thinking about Taran.

He'd met Bridget a few years ago when he'd done something for the Helping Hands charity. She was a pediatric nurse, sweet as hell, and gorgeous to boot. They met up when he was in town and had time. He flicked through his phone, found her contact, and shot off a text.

"Bro," Daily called.

The last thing Corey wanted to do was pull the towel from his eyes, but Daily did it for him.

"Bro," Daily repeated.

"One crap game doesn't make a slump," Corey said before Daily could ask.

Daily rubbed his beard before he nodded. "We all have 'em."

"So, what do you want?" Corey asked and yanked his towel back. He hung it over his head again and stared at his feet.

Daily chuckled. "Demoda wants me to take you out tonight; get you loose."

"Fucking hell," Corey snapped. "He's now mothering me while I'm on the goddamn road!"

Daily laughed. "Well, when two men love each other."

"Suck it," Corey demanded, and he heard the cough that was meant to hide a giggle. It took every ounce of control he had not to turn in that direction.

He hadn't realized Taran was nearby. She hadn't been there when he came out of the shower. He knew that because he checked for her every time he walked into a room. It was pathetic, but he couldn't stop himself from doing it. So he could only assume she'd come in with Daily. It sucked that she'd not only watched him melt down on the mound but also got to see the razzing he was going to take from his teammates—who, in fairness, were trying to get him out of his head. He needed to be loose, relax and not overthink. But he didn't want her to see everyone trying to help him. Mainly because it made him feel like a loser.

"Seriously, bro, we're going to Silver Lining, my sister's bar. Either drinking to the bats that saved our asses or to mull over the loss you caused." Daily's feet settled on the floor next to his, and Corey assumed he sat down at the next locker.

The buzz of his phone caught Corey's attention, and he glanced at it. Bridget's response made him smile.

"Can't. Got plans," Corey said.

"Hmm," Daily pondered. "No Evanses in Tahoe. It's my stomping ground, not yours." He paused. "Tahoe." He snapped his finger. "My naughty nurse."

Corey's eyes now shot up to find Taran, and the towel fell to his feet. She wasn't around. He didn't see her in the locker room, and the glass to the trainer and team doctor didn't frame her pretty face either. He let out his breath. Thank fuck. Although he wasn't sure why he didn't want Taran to know about Bridget, but he didn't.

"Bro," Daily said, pulling his attention back to him.

Corey let his eyes find Daily.

"Bring her. We all like Bridget. She's hung out with us plenty. She's my sister's friend," Daily pointed out.

The Silver Lining was a great spot to chill. The bar sat right on the lake, and since Ryan's sister and her friends had bought it, it had become one of the more popular bars in Lake Tahoe. With the live music outside on the sand, it was the go-to bar this time of year. But Ryan always had his sister close off an upstairs area for the team when they were in town. With the bar, some sofas, and pool tables, it was perfect for the team to relax and let off steam. Daily might be all into the club scene in New York, but he didn't want the big nightclub when he came home. He wanted a quiet night.

Corey frowned. He and Bridget had hung out with the team the last two times they were here. She was one of the silent owners of the Silver Lining, so it wasn't weird. But now Taran was here with them. It was stupid to worry about her because she'd made it crystal clear that she didn't want anything to do with Corey, but it still felt wrong to bring another woman around.

"Worried this time Bridge is going to ditch you for me?" Daily suggested, and Corey rolled his eyes. "You know I'd be more than thrilled to take that little lady off your hands."

Corey just shook his head.

"Bro, I'm 100 percent serious."

Yeah, Corey knew that.

Corey's hand grazed the warm burgundy material of Bridget's dress.

"You sure you want a drink with them?" he asked her again as they walked into the bar he'd been in many times before. Since it was a day game, it was barely eight o'clock, even after their dinner.

"Corey, enough. I'm the one making you stop at the bar."

She rolled her dark brown eyes at him. Her dark skin was flawless besides the dusting of freckles across the bridge of her nose and cheeks. She shook her hair, the tight curls dancing around the skin of her shoulders that the burgundy dress didn't cover. Corey knew the woman a few years his senior was gorgeous. Men had been staring slack-jawed at her throughout dinner, but she never noticed.

She'd also have his teammates' attention in about one minute, especially since they would be overdressed. When Daily took over the top floor of his sister's bar, it meant sweatpants. The idea was low key; an invite-only type deal, no ball bunnies, no groupies, no press. It was just the team and friends.

They headed up the last two steps before rounding the corner, and Bridget nodded to security, who let them pass into the top floor without question.

The four women had designed the bar with the wood-on-wood feel of a lakeside cabin or a ski lodge. But the windows sucked the breath out of his body every time he took in the lake view. Damn, the crystal water with the stars reflecting onto the small waves was something out of a movie.

"Quiet tonight?" Bridget whispered as she glanced around, ignoring the view she'd probably seen too many times to look at his teammates.

The last two times she'd been here with the team had been celebrations. Not tonight. Ninety percent of the team lounged around with beers in their hands; nothing crazy, because although they pulled out the win, it wasn't one to celebrate.

"I sucked," Corey said flatly.

"Pity party, table of one," Bridget answered, poking his rib. Corey frowned.

He felt the heat of the stare before he turned. Taran's mint-green eyes met his from across the bar. He glanced away. Just because he only looked for a blink of an eye didn't mean he didn't take her all in. Converses, cutoffs, and a hoodie announcing that if you say gullible real slow, it sounds like orange. Corey smirked and wondered how many of his teammates had walked around muttering orange tonight. But the smile faded because he hadn't expected Taran to come. Corey had checked with Tillerson earlier, and he'd said he wasn't going to the bar. In Corey's mind, that meant that Taran wouldn't either, but there she stood with Daily.

"We getting a drink or are we going to stand here like morons?" Bridget prompted.

Corey shook his head. "Yeah, sorry, pino?" he asked.

After her confirmation, he headed toward the bar, surprised to see who stood behind it.

"Shawn?" Corey asked.

The former LA Dodgers starting pitcher crossed his arms over his chest. His dark hair matched the five o'clock shadow on his jaw, and the glare said he wasn't thrilled. Much like Marc Demoda, an injury had ended Shawn's career long before it should have been over. But Corey hadn't realized the former all-star pitcher was now here—*bartending* in Salt Lake.

"Saw the win." There was something in Shawn's voice Corey couldn't place. When he'd played, he and Corey didn't come into direct competition often, but they weren't friends either.

"Yeah, wish today hadn't happened," Corey said.

Shawn's jaw locked. "You might have thrown crap, but you got to be out there, playing ball. Don't take that for granted, man."

Shawn threw off the same hurt Marc had a few years ago. Corey didn't exactly understand losing it all suddenly, but he knew what Marc had gone through.

"I don't, but you know what playing like utter shit feels like too, right?" Corey asked, and he saw the small almost smile Shawn gave him. "If you ever want to talk to someone who's been there, I'm sure Marc would love it. You can't have forgotten how much that fucker loves the sound of his own voice."

Shawn fought the laugh but had to clear his throat with a fake cough. "You come here for a drink or just to bullshit?"

It took two minutes to have his beer and her wine in hand and head back to Bridget. "So, you want to say hi to Daily?"

Bridget nodded, but multiple guys came up to say hello

before they could head that way. It took twenty minutes and another round of drinks to get to Daily.

"Gorgeous," Daily greeted with arms wide open. Corey watched Bridget step into his embrace without comment.

"Hi, Ryan," Bridget said shyly.

"When will you leave this douche bag and trade up?" Daily asked.

Corey rolled his eyes before turning his attention to Taran.

He had spent the night looking at a woman who was made up to perfection, but Taran's clean-scrubbed face punched him in the gut. There was nothing showy about her. She wasn't dressing to impress, and she wasn't made up to attract anyone, yet he didn't want to look away. Her eyes met his, full of questions. And he wasn't sure why she cared.

"Bridge?" Corey prompted when he realized that it would be rude if he waited any longer. "Taran Murphy, Bridget Adams." He introduced the two women, not giving either a label. While the three people around him made small talk, Corey looked for any distraction. Any reason to get the hell away from Taran.

TARAN TRIED NOT to glare at the beautiful woman standing in front of her. It wasn't often—in fact never—that Taran cared about her appearance. Nor did she ever compare herself to women around her, but standing next to the bombshell who'd arrived with Corey made her want to hide. Especially since Bridget looked ready to walk a runway in Milan and Taran looked ready to walk the garbage to the curb.

"Bridge," Corey said, and Taran watched with a sinking stomach as he leaned down and said something softly in Bridget's ear. The woman's large brown eyes glanced around before she finally smiled at Corey.

"Excuse us." he nodded to Daily before walking away.

Taran tried not to care that Corey had ignored her completely the entire time he was at the table. It shouldn't matter. She'd asked him to leave her alone, and he was. As she watched Corey, who looked fantastic in his tan shirt and dress pants that enhanced every asset of his six-foot-three frame, she didn't feel happy.

But she didn't feel nothing either.

"Hot damn," Ryan said from beside her, and Taran turned, but his eyes were on the ass of the woman walking away with Corey. Ryan's knuckle came up to his mouth as he bit down on it. "Every time I see her, it's like my walking wet dream came to life."

"You see her a lot?" Taran asked, and she heard the bite in her tone.

Ryan turned his attention back to her with a look of confusion. "Uh. Damn. Sorry. Sometimes I forget you're female."

That was precisely Taran's goal when she worked on a story. She wanted people to forget she was female—forget she was a journalist. Heck, most of the time, Taran was happy if they forgot she was there. She acted and dressed to fit in around her. Not to stand out. And typically, when she heard those types of comments, she was thrilled about a job well done. Tonight, she glanced down at her ugly cutoffs and the sweatshirt that was three sizes too big and felt unattractive. But she couldn't be hurt at this moment. Nor could she keep acting like she cared about any of this.

"It's okay, Daily, I forget you're human and not an ape most of the time," she joked, making sure he knew she didn't care that he was blatantly checking out another woman.

Daily threw his head back and laughed. His black hair was slicked back as he usually wore it. About a month ago, he'd been voted hottest bad boy in baseball. She understood why. Full sleeves of tattoos covered both arms, and his deep-set eyes always had that spark of trouble. He had broad shoulders and just enough scruff to announce that he didn't give a shit about shaving this week. Though the team often demanded the guys wear suits, Daily lived in worn jeans and tight T-shirts.

A lot of women would love a chance to sit and talk with him. All she wanted to do was leave, but she couldn't go yet. Leaving now felt like Corey and his date were driving her away. Even if that was true, she didn't want anyone to know it.

"You don't have a plan for next month's article yet?" Daily asked again, and then his dark eyes cut across the room.

Taran followed his gaze to where Bridget was bending over the pool table to take a shot, and she looked away. Unwilling to watch Corey and his date anymore, she had to get over it. Corey Matthews was a gorgeous, famous athlete, and he was going to have women around him all the time.

"Ry—I never plan the next article before I finish the one I'm working on. One person at a time," Taran explained, which was accurate, apart from September. Her neck tingled as she thought about the signed contract from Corey Matthews. Before the trip was over, Taran would have to talk to him about it. After she finished this article with Tillerson, she wouldn't have a reason to see Corey again. And she couldn't leave that agreement for a story hanging.

He paused and took a sip of his drink. "So, what do you do if someone doesn't just jump out at you when it's time to write the article?"

"Sometimes my editor makes suggestions or agents reach out to me. But for the most part, I see who's hot in the sports world. Whether it's because they're playing really well, or poorly, or just had a big scandal. Whoever people are talking about, I go after them."

"And you get full say?" he asked.

"Not really. My editor might veto something or insist I write about a particular athlete," Taran said. "And then if I want to keep my job, I do it."

After fifteen minutes of Ryan quizzing her about her writing, Taran had her fill, and she was about to leave when she heard a throat clear next to her. She turned and saw a very flustered Bridget. She watched the beautiful woman shift from foot to foot, fiddling with her hands before finally looking up.

"I'm so sorry for what I'm about to do." Bridget sighed and then rolled her eyes. She took a deep breath. "I lost a bet."

"What?" Taran asked and then glanced at Ryan, who looked just as confused.

"Before I do this, I just have to ask." She paused, and a flush colored her high cheekbones. "Am I interrupting something?"

What the hell?

Ryan leaned his forearms on the table and looked from Taran to Bridget and back. It was clear on his face that he had no idea what this woman was rambling about either. There was only one thing Taran could take the question to mean.

"I'm a reporter, and I'm writing a story about Tim Tillerson. Tim had some personal things to take care of tonight. Ryan,"

Taran gestured to him, "was nice enough to keep me busy so I wouldn't be bored in my room, but I was just about to leave. I can get out of your way."

"No!" she said quickly and then flushed deeper. She huffed out a breath. "I hate Corey Matthews," she mumbled, looking at the table as she continued. "Part of the bet is that I have to talk to you both."

Ryan chuckled. "Matthews made a bet involving us?"

Bridget looked up, nodding slowly. As her gaze shifted around the room, Taran didn't see Corey.

"I can't believe I'm doing this, but this happens every time I'm with him or any of the Evanses." Bridget sighed.

Taran knew that feeling. "If it makes you feel better, the last time I was with the Evanses, they talked me into being Danny's platonic date for Nick's wedding. Danny left me for the entire party, and he went home with another girl."

Bridget smirked. "Danny is something else."

Ryan cleared his throat.

"Right," Bridget said. "Okay, so, Ryan." She paused again.

Taran saw how uncomfortable Bridget was. "You two figure this out. I'm leaving."

"You can't. Corey wanted you to hear this," Bridget said pathetically.

"Why?" she asked.

Bridget just rolled her eyes, but rushed. "Ryan, Corey and I have never hooked up. Brocode thing because Luke Evans and I dated for a brief time. Corey brings me out with you guys every time you're in town because I keep hoping I'll be brave, *or stupid*, enough to admit I've wished to have a drink with you for a while." When she finished, her face was the color of a lobster.

Taran watched Ryan's eyes shoot around the bar, looking for Corey.

"He went back to his hotel room," Bridget mumbled. "And no, this is not a joke, just humiliating."

Ryan moved quickly and bent down, whispering something in Bridget's ear.

"Pino," she said quietly, a soft smile on her face.

"Do *not* leave this table. I'll be back in two minutes," Ryan said, and when Bridget nodded, he practically ran to the bar.

"I'm going to leave. It was nice meeting you. Sorry Corey made you have an audience for that," Taran said.

Bridget shook her head. "It wasn't about an audience, Taran. He didn't expect you to be here, and once you were, he wanted you to know that he and I aren't and never have been dating."

Taran glanced away.

"Corey just pushed me out of my *too afraid to admit what I wanted* box, and he isn't here, so I can't return the favor, but I'll do this for him instead."

There was a pause, and Taran almost looked back at Bridget.

"He talked about you all through dinner."

Taran picked at the coaster below her drink. "Nothing is going on between us." She finally looked back up.

Bridget nodded and smiled sadly. "I know, but he wishes there was. He's a good guy, Taran. Maybe you could give him a chance."

21

TARAN WASN'T SURE exactly what she was doing, even as she lifted her hand to knock. She'd left the bar intending to go back to her room, but here she stood in front of Corey's. Although hooking up with him while traveling with the team was a *huge* no-no, she couldn't just ignore the chemistry between them. They at least needed to talk.

Bridget's words sent a buzz through her system. The idea that Corey wanted her made her stomach jump and her body pulse with electric energy. She felt more alive than she had in years. And she couldn't stop herself from chasing those feelings.

"I swear, if you're already back, you're an idiot." Corey's voice came through the door. "Seriously, man, if I had the chance you've got, I wouldn't be running back to my room."

Who would Corey be expecting? And what chance would he want?

"And why the hell can't you remember to bring your key—" The door yanked open. Corey cocked his head to the side as his eyes widened.

It clicked together. The guys all had roommates. Corey stayed with Daily. Did Corey mean he wanted a chance with Bridget?

"Taran?"

Was the reason nothing happened with Bridget because she didn't want Corey? Or was it because Corey wouldn't go after someone Luke had dated, even if he wanted her? Taran's stomach dropped. This was a bad idea.

"Taran?" Corey repeated, confusion still in his voice.

"Sorry," she said and shook her head. "Never mind."

She spun to walk away, but his warm hand locked in a fierce grip on her forearm, pulling her inside the room. The door clicked shut behind them, and she stepped back against it. Corey's bare arm came up, resting above her head, boxing her in. Her body flared at the heat radiating off him as he stood in the white tank top and dress pants.

"No way. You just heard me say I wouldn't walk away from a chance I wanted," he growled. "You don't get to show up at my door and then run away either, Smurfette."

She glanced down at her blue hoodie, but her eyes landed on his chest. The tank top was too tight to hide his muscular frame. She could see the defined muscles of his chest leading into six-pack abs. Just as her gaze hit his belt, he spoke again.

"Eyes up. I need some words, Taran. Your body language confuses the fuck out of me, and I'm dying here." The hoarse words whispered against her ear.

A shiver raced down her spine as he cupped her neck with one hand.

His gaze met her straight on. "I've told you repeatedly—I'm interested, but I'm not sure where you stand."

"You went out with Bridget tonight."

He nodded. His eyes tracked her face before they met hers again. At that moment, she realized that he was deciding whether he trusted her. "I'm playing like shit. I needed to get out of my head, and I needed someone to talk things out with. She's a friend. *Just* a friend, but one I trust. Management is pissed because every game is worse than the next. And I know what the problem is—you."

Her body jerked as her temper flared. What the hell? Was he going to blame her for his crappy pitching? Her shoulders pulled back as she slammed her finger into his chest.

"You don't get to put your problems on me. If you're playing like shit, that's on you."

He pulled on her neck and leaned down, bringing them to eye level. Their noses were almost touching, and Taran sucked in a hard breath. His heated gaze pinned her to the door. The inside ring of brown in his eyes turned to butterscotch, while the outside looked more like warm chocolate.

"You *are* the reason I threw crap again today. You're making me *crazy*." Every word pounded against her lips as they left his mouth. "Management knows pitchers are creatures of habit, and no one thinks it's odd that the head case of the team isn't handling it well because a reporter is traveling with us. I didn't even need to tell them I—want isn't a strong enough statement. I'm pretty sure I'm starting to *need* you like my next breath of air."

Ten seconds ago, she was pissed, and now she was once again turned inside out.

She watched him stare as she wet her lips.

"Shit—I give up," he mumbled.

He dropped his lips to meet hers. She shouldn't be doing this, but his mouth possessed hers in a way she wanted so badly.

Rational thought left as his lips demanded she open for him. When she did, he dove into her mouth like a man dying of thirst—for the substance only she could provide. He leaned into her, sending her back into the door behind her, locking her between it and his rock-hard chest. She desperately clung to his broad shoulders while he hitched one of her legs over his hip. The second one followed as they locked together, only a few layers of clothing stopping them from truly being one. Heat against heat, they rocked frantically into each other.

Taran moaned, arching against him, wanting more. The aching need settled deep inside her core. Corey pivoted quickly across the room to lower her down softly onto a bed. And then his glorious weight was on top of her. Her breasts brushed into his hard, defined chest, their stomachs pressed into each other, and the entire length of him settled into the apex of her legs. Both sucked in a breath and stared for a heartbeat, neither moving.

Corey slammed his mouth down and reclaimed hers as her hips bucked off the bed into him.

"Taran," Corey groaned around her mouth, and she whimpered.

Her heart was pounding so loudly she swore he must hear it. *Boom, boom, boom.* Her hips seemed to pick up the rhythm of the pounding in her head.

Corey yanked back and glanced around. "Jesus," he cursed.

The pounding wasn't her heart—it was the door. And she realized what she had almost done. How could she almost sleep with an athlete on the team she was traveling with? And whoever was on the other side of that door would know it. If people talked about this, she'd never be taken seriously again. Her heart dropped.

IT TOOK COREY too long to process the sound of someone pounding on his door. But he had been in heaven. Exactly what he'd been dreaming about, imagining for weeks. And now, when he was close to finally sliding into all that Taran was offering him, someone was at the damn door. He glanced back down at the beauty under him. Her thin bubblegum pink lips were swollen; her chin and neck were scraped from the scruff of his beard. Her hair was falling out of her usual bun, framing her face. The face that was sporting a look that told him no matter who was on the other side of the door, Corey wasn't getting his hands on her again tonight. Taran's expression was silently saying this was a mistake.

But fuck that. It *wasn't*.

He pushed himself off her and glanced down. Anyone would know exactly what they had been doing. His privacy was essential to him, and he hated that he might be about to lose some of it.

"Son of a bitch," he cursed before stomping over to the door. He glanced through the hole, and his eyes narrowed when he saw who was standing on the other side.

"Open the door, Corey. I'm not any happier about this than you are. My wife is pissed off right now," Marc yelled. "I have no problem letting the entire team know they called me in *again* if you leave me standing here any longer."

Corey had told the general manager he needed to get his head on straight. He *hadn't* asked for them to bring in his pitching coach. Yet they must have. Corey was probably closer to getting pulled from the rotation than he realized. But he needed to get rid of Marc.

Corey yanked the door open and glared, "Your timing sucks."

Marc's eyes ran from Corey's mangled hair down to what Corey knew was the mother of all bulges in his pants. Marc winced.

"Should I come back in an hour?"

"No."

The voice came from behind Corey, but he was not letting Marc in to see Taran. He didn't allow his relationships to become fodder for gossip. Marc would eventually find out about them, but not when the team was around. Corey turned to look at her. She'd taken five seconds to fix her hair so she looked slightly less about to be fucked—but *still*. She wouldn't meet Corey's eyes as she said. "I'd rather not have a scene. Let him in."

"Taran." Marc's voice went up two notches, and Corey whipped his head back in Marc's direction. The man needed to shut up, not yell Taran's name. "I didn't realize." He shook his head and then frowned at Corey. "I don't need to be here. *This* is the problem. I thought you knew better than to bring someone on the road with you."

"I didn't," Corey snapped as he yanked Marc inside, letting the door close. Marc moved into the room, pushing past Corey. He walked toward the bed before spinning back to face them, crossing his arms over his chest. Marc's gaze flicked from Corey to Taran and back before lifting his eyebrows in silent questions.

"She's traveling with the team as a reporter." As Corey said it, he watched Taran's face lose all its color.

"Is anyone in the hall?" Wide-eyed, she desperately glanced around like a magic door she could escape through might appear in the wall.

Corey reached out to hold her, calm her down, comfort her. But she jerked away from him. That hurt more than he thought it would. He cracked his neck left and then right. Her glance slid away from Corey to Marc, and she winced. Her eyes flitted shut before she took a deep breath. Corey just wanted to make her feel better. The way she was acting was giving him an ache in his chest.

"Is anyone in the hall?" she asked again, and her voice cracked.

Marc shook his head.

Taran almost looked up at Corey, but she forced her head away, looking at the door. She moved without a word.

What the hell?

The door slamming shut sent Corey into motion. But before he could get out of the room, a firm grasp pulled him back.

"Cor—if you care about her, let her go," Marc warned.

Corey turned to Marc, bewildered.

"She's a *reporter* traveling with the Metros. No one on the team can know what was happening here if she wants to keep any of her credibility."

Then it all clicked. It wasn't just about Corey and his privacy. No female reporter could sleep with the athletes they wrote about and still have respect. If she slept with the talent, the talent all assumed she was fair game, and she lost her status as a serious journalist. Maybe Taran wrote gossip stories, but everyone in the Metros locker room respected her. He'd witnessed that in the two weeks she had been around. It hadn't occurred to him to worry about her job. He was an asshole.

Corey flopped down onto the bed and stared at the ceiling. "Ever meet a girl who you can't seem to get off the wrong foot with, even though you feel like you're jumping through hoops to get on the right one?"

He rubbed his face with both hands before pushing them back through his hair. Marc chuckled.

"I guess that's a no, then." Corey sighed.

"*Actually*, I know exactly how you feel."

Corey leaned up onto his elbows to look at his friend.

Marc perched against the wall with his arms crossed. "That's exactly how I felt when I met Beth. If you remember, I floundered like a moron for the first few weeks of our relationship."

Corey flopped back on the bed. "Beth's easy. You should try dealing with Taran."

"Uh-huh." Marc didn't sound like he agreed, though. "Want advice?"

Corey stared at the ceiling. Marc was a good guy. A lot of people thought it was weird that one of his best friends was his ex's husband, but it had never felt strange to Corey.

"Sure."

"If you want it to work, don't let her walk away."

Corey flew up. "The fuck? You just told me—"

"Stop." Marc shook his head with a slight chuckle. "Not now—this second—but, in general. Corey, you let Mel walk. She walked away as soon as it got hard, and you let her. Even though it messed you up."

It wasn't that simple. Mel needed things Corey couldn't give her. He let her walk away, not because he didn't care or want Mel. But Mel needed Corey to let her go the same way

Beth had needed Corey to walk away. But he wasn't going to make it awkward by pointing that out to Marc.

"I messed with her head. All my need for privacy played on her insecurities. We sucked at communicating. We didn't work." Corey cracked his neck back and forth, not wanting to talk about Mel anymore. "You're right, though. You didn't need to come, and I didn't ask for you. You *can't* fix my head, and I know the problem. I'm working on it. So you can go."

Marc stared at him for two beats, not responding, and Corey wondered if he was going to push the Mel thing.

"I doubt I could get a flight out tonight. But even if I could, Beth wouldn't let me into the house. Like I said, she's pissed."

That was when Corey remembered. "Oh shit, you weren't supposed to travel until the twins were six months old."

"Yet here I am," Marc mumbled.

"Sorry, man. I don't think you're getting laid for a while."

Marc laughed. "That's okay. By the looks of it, neither are you. Let's get a drink. This is my big night out."

Corey shook his head, chuckling at how the former Metros pitcher's life had changed in the last few years. Marc used to be the guy who went out to the hot spot of the moment every night. Now his big night out was a drink in a random hotel bar. It left Corey just a bit jealous that although Marc was home every other night, today was probably the worst night of Marc's month. Why couldn't Corey find that with someone?

<h1 style="text-align:center">21</h1>

TARAN STARED OUT past the cement patio into the miles of green around her. She always forgot how flat Texas was when she hadn't been home for a while. It seemed like she could see forever here, the endless yellowy-green going on until it met the sky. It was blisteringly hot and humid, but the blue sky against the green fields made it worthwhile to sit out under the umbrella on her parents' patio with a glass of sweet tea.

"I still can't believe you cut off your hair," Teagan, her sister, said for the hundredth time. She flicked her long locks over her shoulder and shook her head at Taran.

When Taran had run out of her hotel room a week ago, she'd gotten on the first flight to Houston. Nothing like running home to hide. However, she hadn't brought her hairpiece, so it was the first time her family had seen how, as her mother said, she'd hacked off all her beautiful curls.

"Hair grows," she replied, not bothering to tell them that she'd done it two years ago. It was ridiculous that her hair that danced just above her shoulders was considered too short.

Usually, her family's nagging didn't bother her. Not much did. But the truth of it was that she had a lot of feelings for the first time in a very long time. And no idea what to do with any of them. She'd left Corey's room both shocked and pissed at herself. Taran wouldn't pretend she hadn't known what would happen when she went to Corey's room that night. She had. But she'd been high on feelings and not thinking through the consequences.

She'd grabbed her stuff and fled back to the one place that might make her numb again. She had hoped memories of Jeremy would make her forget her confusing feelings for Corey Matthews. But although she was back in Texas, where she and Jeremy grew up, Corey was still front and center in her brain.

Every time she closed her eyes, she could see him looking down at her. She could feel his hands moving on her skin, his breath dancing across her face. She dreamed of him pressing against her, moving inside her.

"So you ready to tell me what's going on yet?" Teagan asked, jarring her back to the moment. Her sister's brown eyes, surrounded by long lashes, sparkled with uncontained curiosity. "Mom and Dad are thrilled you're here; they can't care why. Dana's too busy to be nosy, and my husband and Tristan hate drama, but I'm none of those things. So, spill."

Teagan was almost nine when Taran was born. Tristan, their brother, was fifteen. By the time Taran was eight, Tristan was married to Dana. So unlike Tristan and Dana, who were more like her parents, Teagan was her best friend. Since the days when the two sisters were competing in beauty pageants all over Texas, Teagan had been her confidant. She taught her about makeup and boys. The first time she skipped class, Teagan forged her note. Teagan was who she'd run to when she kissed Jeremy for the first time. And she was the one who got her on birth control before she and Jeremy started having sex. Teagan was the first phone call when she got engaged. But her big sister was also the person who missed the old Taran the most.

Teagan leaned forward, resting her chin on her hand. Her engagement ring and wedding band sparkled on her finger as she tapped her manicured nails against her jaw.

"You told me you almost crossed one of those stupid lines you journalists have." She had no patience for things like journalistic integrity when it got in the way of a good love story. "So it must be about a man." She flashed her bleach-white teeth at Taran. "But looking at you, bless your heart, I can see why he didn't let you cross that line. You've let yourself go."

She wasn't trying to be insulting, and Taran knew that. Teagan just believed it was a woman's job to look like she was about to be crowned with some tiara, be it a homecoming queen crown or a Miss Texas crown or a you're-the-hottest-wife-in-the-world crown. She had her teeth bleached monthly, her lashes done bi-monthly, her nails done weekly, and she never left the house without her hair done and a full face of makeup. Teagan always looked perfect. Taran had given up that lifestyle two years ago.

"Don't bless me," Taran rolled her eyes. "And I told you, I stopped myself. He didn't stop a thing." She attempted not to blink while stating the complete and total lie. Marc knocking on the door was the only reason Taran hadn't had sex with Corey Matthews in a random hotel room while she was traveling with the Metros.

"So who is he?" she asked. Teagan's black strappy sandal tapped impatiently on the cement. "The last two stories you wrote were about Clayton Evans and Tim Tillerson. Although they're both beautiful men, they're both younger than you, and I can't see you falling for either of them."

This was not the first time Taran had assured her sister that neither of those young men was the reason for her sudden trip to Texas. Then her sister ran through a hundred other people, all too young, too old, too married, too ugly. She'd run the gamut of athletes and never even got close.

Taran sighed. "It's Corey Matthews."

The tapping foot stopped, and Taran heard her sister's arm fall to the table. "Lord love a duck," she whispered.

Taran rolled her eyes; no one but a Texan would ever say something so ridiculous. "What does that even mean, Teag?"

"Corey Matthews?" She blinked as she placed her palm on her chest. "Oh my goodness."

And this was why she hadn't told her. Ever since he'd helped the Astros win the World Series, Corey Matthews was like Superman in this family. A legend on a pedestal for all to see. Teagan brought her bright red fingernail up and tapped her lips twice as she looked past Taran into the fields. "Crying all night." She smiled.

Taran looked at her incredulously. "What?"

"I'm just trying to imagine Captain America in all his glory."

"For crap's sake." Taran sighed.

"You talk like such a New Yorker." Her sister's nose scrunched up as she pursed her lips. "So now you're here because you feel guilty?"

Taran slammed her hand down on the tabletop, causing the entire table to vibrate harshly. "I'm tired of telling you that me not dating has nothing to do with Jeremy. I don't feel guilty, and I don't think he would be upset with me. Just the opposite—he told me to move on if something ever happened to him. Everyone wants me to date. Holy shit, you all try to shove it down my throat so much I should feel guilty *not* dating, except normally I don't feel anything."

"Whoa," Teagan said, wide-eyed. "That's the first outburst I've seen from you in a long time."

Taran glanced away.

"You want to unpack this with me?" Teagan asked.

"He makes me feel things again," Taran admitted.

Teagan sucked in a hard breath with a single eyebrow raise that their mother used on them. It always made them look intimating as hell. "That's an excellent thing, so what's the problem?"

Because it made the knot in her chest come back, because it made her uncomfortable, because it made her mad. But she didn't say that. She just swallowed that thought down and pushed it away.

"I've told you—"

"Yes, I know. Some kind of sexism that makes it okay for men to sleep with whoever at work—even force themselves on their employees. Yet woman must keep even consensual sex away from the workplace." Teagan always had a way of twisting facts to make her point.

Taran shook her head.

"Regardless of your sexist viewpoint," Teagan continued not letting Taran correct her. "Your story with the Metros is finished."

It was true. When Taran left Tahoe, she had enough to write her article on Tillerson.

"Technically, it's going through review for edits," she corrected.

"So, what happens when it's finished? Are you going to call him?" Teagan asked as the eyebrow of doom popped up.

That was a good question, followed quickly by a second one. After the way she left, would Corey want her to call?

22

TARAN GLANCED AT the four shades of white with a slightly greenish blue tint.

"Erin," Sydney said as she took a sip of the wine. "I still don't understand why you need a haint-blue porch. Nor why white with the tiniest blue tint is called haint."

"Not the entire porch, just the ceiling, and it's to keep the spirits away," Erin explained again.

The half-full bottle of red sat on Taran's glass coffee table between the women. Although they each had a glass of wine, none of them were drunk as they talked about spirits.

"My grandmother always taught me that the spirits think the blue is the sky. According to the Gullah, this makes them pass through and not come into my house," Erin explained again. Her grandmother's Native American roots came out not only in Erin's stories but in her features.

Sydney scoffed.

"It's a thing people used to believe. A lot of people still do it," Taran assured Sydney, who rolled her eyes. "My mom, sister, and sister-in-law have haint-blue ceilings on their porches."

"I told you. Taran gets me." Erin put her fist out to meet Taran's.

"My porch ceiling is white," Taran said after she tapped Erin's hand with her knuckles. Erin huffed, but Sydney laughed.

"Fine, you two want to mock me, then we'll talk about Corey instead. Sean said Tim's article's done. Now you don't have any reason not to reach out." Erin sat back and crossed her arms smugly as Taran groaned.

"What are you thinking?" Sydney asked. "If you reach out, you have to tell him about the contract for the article."

Taran nodded. "I have to do that, no matter what happens with the rest of it. Unless maybe I just throw it away."

"It seems dumb not to at least ask him," Erin pointed out.

"I guess the worst he can say is no. It's not like I gave Wayne the contract, so if I explain what happened—how mad can Corey be?" Taran waited for either to answer, but no one responded. "No, that was a real question. How mad can Corey be?"

"Well, Corey is pretty umm—emotional?" Erin winced.

"Yeah, he'll probably freak out before he calms down." Sydney nodded. "But you're still giving him complete say if he wants to do it, so I think it'll be fine."

"And if Corey says no, I'll throw it away." Taran sighed. "As mad as Wayne will be that I never do a feature on Corey, he can't blame me if Corey won't agree."

Erin nodded. "Even if he's an ass. I wouldn't think his bosses would let him fire you over something an athlete won't agree to."

"Especially when you've been getting almost everyone else on Wayne's list." Sydney took another sip from her wineglass just as a knock sounded on the door.

Taran got up and was shocked to see who stood on the other side, hands deep in the pockets of his jeans. She hadn't heard from Corey since she fled his room, not even on *Diablo*. Every time she signed on to play with her niece and nephews, she looked for him. But here he stood on her porch, the dark night shadowing his two-toned eyes.

The second their gazes met, a tingle shot down Taran's spine. A strong pull had her wanting to step toward him. Let him wrap his arms around her, but she didn't move.

"Hi." The barest hint of a grin whispered against his lips.

"Hi," Taran repeated.

His hand twitched at his side like he wanted to reach out to her.

She leaned against the open door. Even though she hadn't talked to him, she'd seen him play, and his pitching was better. Tonight, he made it seven innings without letting up a run. "Good game."

His mouth tightened into a straight line.

"Yeah, my head's in a good spot, I guess." However, he didn't look pleased by that statement. "Can we talk?"

"Uh." She glanced over her shoulder to see Erin and Sydney craning their necks for a better view. Taran raised an eyebrow, and they stood up quickly.

"Am I interrupting?" he asked, and Taran turned back to him. His Adam's apple bobbed as he swallowed.

She studied the line of his neck, remembering how it felt to press her lips against his pounding pulse. The heat of his skin. She wanted the scrape of his beard against her jaw, on her neck, running down her body.

His gaze tracked down her like he knew what she was thinking. Her breath caught, and his eyes flared.

Erin cleared her throat, breaking the spell. "No, *you're* not interrupting. *We're* leaving." She and Sydney moved past Taran onto the porch. "Let me know which haint," she reminded Taran as they both waved.

"Come in," Taran said.

Corey walked into her living room and stood awkwardly in the center. His plain white T-shirt pulled tight across his broad shoulders, not hiding the tension in his stance. Every time Taran had seen Corey step into her house, it had been with the firm assurance of a man who thought he belonged. But at the moment, he looked like he was waiting to be kicked out.

"I didn't mean to ruin your girls' night." He tipped his head to the three half-full glasses of wine next to the table.

"They were leaving anyway. Only so much Gullah and ghost talk before Sydney decides she's out," Taran said, and Corey turned his focus to her.

"Ghosts?" he asked.

"Erin thinks blue porches will scare the ghosts away," she said.

He opened his mouth and shut it twice before she laughed.

"Are you messing with me?" He stepped closer. His cologne swamped her senses, and although they were at least a foot apart, she swore she could feel the heat radiating off his body.

"Always," she assured, but her voice came out in a breathy whisper.

He swallowed, his stare dropping to her mouth and then lower to the scoop of her fitted cropped shirt. He lifted his hand and brushed his thumb across the bare skin above her cutoffs. Goosebumps broke out across her hips and a shiver racked her body as an ache pounded low inside her.

"Tillerson told me your article is finished." His deep voice vibrated through her as his fingers finally settled on her waist, biting into her skin.

She nodded.

"Your next story won't be a Metro." His hot grip on her tightened.

Wait—what? Her eyes narrowed, and she reached up to push him away. But he didn't give an inch as she pushed her palms into him. Her body might be ready to melt into a puddle at his feet, but did he think he could tell her what to do?

"Who do you think you are—"

Before she could get more words out, his free hand covered her mouth, and he spun her, pressing her back firmly into the wall.

"I *know* I'm the man who's about to make you come so hard you won't be able to walk," he growled. His erection rested firmly against her hip.

She gasped as desire swamped her system. Her hands fisted his T-shirt, no longer pushing him away. This man could turn her inside out. He ran his hand along her jaw, cupping the back of her neck. Every cell in her body electrified as he lowered his forehead, resting it against hers. Hot breath danced around her face. Her body clenched.

"Only things that will stop me: if doing this puts your professional credibility in jeopardy or"—his fingers tangled in her hair as he yanked it tightly in his fist, forcing her gaze up to his eyes. Genuine concern showed in his expression, which only made her want him more—"you tell me to stop."

His words vibrated off her lips less than an inch from his. But as forceful as he was, the ball was in her court. He wasn't moving closer. His eyes begged her to close the distance. To give in to him. "Give me words, shortstop."

"Not a Metro," she whispered and wrapped her arms around his neck, closing the distance to press her mouth against his.

Immediately, he took control of the kiss. He groaned as his tongue invaded her mouth, and the raspy echo pounded through her, settling between her legs. Once again, the rough scrape of his beard grazed against her skin. His thick thigh forced her knees apart, demanding room for him. The arm around her back pulled hard, settling her against him, slowly dragging her up against his leg. The denim of his jeans rubbed torturously but didn't give her nearly enough friction. She arched harder against him. His mouth didn't leave hers, and every swipe of his tongue sent a new thrill through her. She rolled her hips against his thigh and whimpered at the delicious burst of lust the movement elicited.

"Fuck, shorty, you're killing me." His breathing was hard. He swept his hand down her neck, over her shoulder, to her breast. His firm pinch of her nipple caused her to buck harder against him. "Exactly why no bra is so hot." He pinched again, and the prick of pain rocketed through her.

Corey dropped his head again. This time, his mouth moved along the skin of her neck, kissing her throat, just behind her ear. Her head fell back, knocking into the wall.

"Corey," she moaned.

"I need to touch you." His eyes were liquid caramel and milk chocolate desire, causing the ache inside her to strengthen.

"Now," she begged.

He slipped his hand into the back of her shorts.

"You and these cutoffs, they torture me." His voice was hoarse as his fingers ran along the curve of her ass cheek. "I know this perfect crescent is here, but these shorts hide all but the idea. All day long, I see this peekaboo of heaven." He curved his hand under her, fingers sliding not where she needed him. Simply teasing her. "*Soaked* for me."

He grabbed her ass with his free hand, guiding her higher on his thigh as he sank his finger into her. She squirmed against his hand, against his thigh, the pressure inside her building.

"No, you don't," he demanded. "Your job is to hold on to my shoulders. My job is to learn exactly how to make you scream my name."

Half of her wanted to argue, but the pounding ache inside her won, and she didn't bother to fight, just did as he ordered. He added a second finger, almost like a reward, and she cried out. "Yeah, just like that, baby. Use my body to get off."

Scissoring his fingers, he guided her hips to rock against his denim-clad thigh. Her stomach flipped, and her heart pounded in her ears as he pulled her once again across his leg. She was so close. The pressure swirled deeper and deeper inside her.

"Give me what I want," he growled as he nipped at her earlobe.

"Corey," she moaned as her release exploded around her.

"Yes." His fingers didn't stop milking her until the last spasms stopped.

She slowly slid off his leg, letting her own feet get under her. Her body was still vibrating, and now they stood fully dressed in her living room. Corey smirked, delighted with himself.

"You good?" he asked, entirely too cocky. God, this man drove her insane.

Taran shook her head, and Corey's eyes widened.

"You promised I wouldn't be able to walk, but look at me. Still moving around."

He chuckled and shook his head. "It's going to be like that, huh, itty bit?"

"Like what?" She raised an eyebrow as he lifted his shirt and tossed it to the floor.

Holy shit. The man was cut. Her eyes raked down his tight pecs and every wave of his firm abs to the mouth-watering V between his hip bones. The bulge in his jeans implied the V pointed to something that wouldn't disappoint. She sucked in a hard breath.

"See something good?" He chuckled.

Oh, fine. Let's play.

She let her fingers drop to the button on her cutoffs. She teased her hand into the waistband, watching his eyes zero in before she popped the fly open. Her shorts and panties hit the ground at the same time.

"You don't play fair." He focused on the apex of her thighs, unable to look away for two beats. Then he reached into his back pocket and pulled out a condom. "Couch or wall?" he asked, holding out the foil packet. "Fair warning, with as hard as I plan on fucking you, I might break the couch."

She locked her knees as her body clenched at the possessive growl in his voice.

"Wall."

"Hell, yeah."

He smirked as she took the foil and watched him kick off both shoes and drop his pants. His erection jutted out, and it didn't disappoint. She opened the foil packet and stepped toward him.

She took him in her hand and gave him a slow tug, pulling a groan from him. Hot, heavy, and thick, she toyed with him.

"As good as that feels, it's been a year, so this will be over real quick if you keep it up."

Her gaze shot up to his face. Was he serious? He nodded once and pulled her hand away, taking the condom.

"I don't do this without a lot of trust, so feel special, shortcake."

Her heart twisted at his words, and the burn in his eyes seemed too intense. Not sure she was capable of intense, she had to remind him of what this was.

"You promised I'd come so hard I won't be able to walk—less talking."

He laughed but lifted her into his arms, backing her against the wall. He hooked his hands under her legs, guiding her to wrap them around his waist. "You know you want this. Why do you always have to be so difficult?"

"You like it," she reminded him.

"I like *you*," he replied.

And her heart stuttered. Even though his body had her pinned against the wall with her legs around his waist—his cock teasing her entrance—it was his eyes that pinned her in place. This was a silent demand for words.

"I like you too, Corey," she answered.

A smile broke across his face before he dropped his mouth to hers and slammed into her. The stretch was everything she needed—everything she'd missed for the last two years. It was pain and pleasure. It was a gift and a demand for more. But instead of moving, Corey froze.

"Damn it, Taran. I'm good with rough, but I don't want to hurt you. And you're like a vise gripping my dick." Corey sounded tortured.

"You're not hurting me," she assured. "I want you to move. I need you to move."

He met her eyes, checking before he pulled out and thrust again. Her back slammed into the wall with every drive. He was rough, hard. And it was making her crazy. Her breath came faster as he drove her higher, making her world focus on the pounding pleasure.

His teeth sank into the soft flesh of her shoulder. The pain meshed with the ache of need pounding her system, and she cried out. She thrust against him, changing the angle as he pounded the exact spot.

"Oh, don't stop," she said. "Harder, Corey, please."

He thrust again and again until finally, she shattered into pieces as euphoria swamped her.

"Taran." Her name left his lips like a prayer as his body tensed in its own release.

He pressed her harder into the wall, as if he needed the extra support. She felt his arms around her tremble as he buried his face in her neck. Neither moved, just stayed wrapped together, breathing hard. Something she hadn't felt in a long time fluttered in her chest, and she relished the unnamed emotion. She wanted to stay like this forever. But he finally pulled back.

"Are you okay if I set you down?" he asked.

Her legs were quivering—they both knew it. But she wouldn't admit it, so she just nodded into his shoulder. Although he let her down, he ensured she was balanced against the wall. His hand rested beside her head.

"I'll let you keep your pride. I'll admit that was amazing, and my legs are shaking. But I gotta get rid of the condom. Bathroom?"

"Just off the kitchen," she answered, and he dropped a kiss on her lips before leaving her.

As soon as he left the room, she slumped into the wall behind her, sliding slowly against the smooth surface to the ground. Corey Matthews knew precisely how to make a woman's body sing. And as much as she didn't want to admit it, she struggled to pull herself up and grab her shorts to head to her bedroom.

Five minutes later, he was fully dressed in her family room when she came down the stairs. The cocky assurance she'd come to expect from him was back in full force.

"I actually came to ask a question," he said, the ghost of a smile appearing again. "Want to come to beer night?"

23

COREY WALKED AROUND the front of his truck, attempting to get to Taran's door before she got out. Of course, she didn't wait for him, and she was shutting her door when he finally stood beside her. The ride had been almost silent. But every time he looked her way, he saw eyes full of the questions that had been there since she opened her front door to him.

Corey needed to say a few more things, but he wasn't sure exactly what they were. The look asked: *What are we doing here? Was this more than just a quick one-off? Are we going to try to make this work?* And he didn't know the answer to any of those questions.

Corey had given her space to finish her job with the team without any unprofessionalism on account of him. She had every right to be taken seriously as a journalist, and he wanted to be someone who helped her with that goal, not someone who took it away from her. But that didn't mean he hadn't been thinking about her.

Even on the mound, she drove his consistent pitching. In his head, pitching a good game became second to figuring out how he'd get her to spend time with him. So instead of stressing about his game, he relaxed about it. He was getting praise all over the place about how loose he was lately. However, if anyone knew that he cared less about pitching, they probably wouldn't be praising him.

Tonight, from the moment after the game when Tillerson said Taran's article was done, all Corey wanted was to find her. Hell, his shower and post-game interviews were almost painful; he just wanted to get to her house. He hadn't planned to take her against the wall, but damn, that might have been the best sex he'd ever had. Still, none of that meant he had a plan of where they were going.

Back to the bedroom would be high on his list, but he meant what he said about liking her. He didn't want this to be a sex only thing.

Beer night was an easy reason to hang out with her because the family loved Taran and she was comfortable with them. Maybe that would put them both at ease, and hopefully, it would give him some time to figure things out by letting her make some choices. Starting with the choice to join him tonight and including every move going forward.

He'd been pushing Taran without really asking her what she wanted.

So instead of just taking her hand, Corey held his out to her. Her eyes flicked from his face to his palm and back again before she linked her fingers with his. Holding her small hand shouldn't have made his gut clench, but it did.

Her soft floral scent filled his senses. He wanted to bury his nose into her hair, the crook of her neck, run his face over her collarbones, down the valley between her breasts, rest his ear against her heart, kiss her stomach. His pulse pounded.

He wanted the experiences that a quick fuck against the wall didn't give him.

"Corey?" she asked quietly.

They hadn't moved a step.

He swallowed thickly. "Right, we should go in."

They moved off the circular driveway and onto the front steps. He juggled the bag in his hand as he opened the front door.

"What's that?" Taran glanced at the brown paper bag.

"You don't like beer."

Her eyes flew to his face in sweet surprise.

"You told me that the day you stole my car," he said.

The sweet smile disappeared, and a glare came back. Now it was his turn to smile. She was cute when she got all mad. She yanked her hand from his to cross her arms.

"It's not theft if it's forced on you."

"Keep telling yourself that, munchkin." He chuckled.

"You don't need to hide tonight, Corey. You pitched well again," Marc called from the back of the house.

"I'm not fucking hiding," he yelled back.

"*Corey!*" Beth's voice chided.

"Shit," he mumbled, shocked he'd let that slip because he never forgot Beth's rule. Then he looked down at Taran. "You can't curse here. Did I tell you that last time?"

Taran shook her head. "Clayton did. Beth's strict about it."

Corey nodded and placed his hand on the small of her back, guiding her into the kitchen. Her spandex white Sideline tank top stopped about two inches shy of her cutoffs, so two of his fingers once again got to touch warm, soft skin. They moved along the silky flesh, and Taran shivered.

Yeah, me too. Me too.

"I brought company," Corey said as they passed through the archway from the foyer into the house's open concept kitchen and living room space. Marc and Beth were standing at the island, while Danny and Will sat at the table, drinking beer.

"Hey, Taran, we didn't know you were coming," Marc said, moving toward them.

Corey automatically pulled Taran closer, causing Marc to stop in his tracks and nod his head in welcome.

"You want some pinot noir?" Corey asked.

Taran's green eyes met his. "How do you always know my favorites?"

"He cheats," Danny called across the room. "We missed you, doll. Come sit those dirty eyes next to me."

Corey sent a glare to Danny as Taran moved to the table. Danny just smirked. Corey gritted his teeth but moved quickly around the kitchen he knew as well as his own.

"You pitched well," Beth said, and Corey looked at her for the first time. Pale skin, dark circles, red eyes.

"You okay?" he asked her.

Beth sighed, looking across the room to the baby girl in Will's arms. "Peyton's trying to kill me through sleep deprivation. Whoever said having kids was fun was a *liar*."

Corey laughed. "You love your kids."

She flopped her head onto her arms, resting on the stone countertop. "I know. I'm a masochist."

"And a drama queen." Corey chuckled and headed to the table with Taran's wine and his beer. "I think your wife needs to go to bed."

Marc's eyes cut to the wide-awake baby girl on Will's lap. "As soon as Peyton closes her eyes, you're all kicked out."

Danny leaned in closer to Taran, and Corey's whole body clenched. Danny flirted—with everyone—and he meant very little by it. Corey needed to work on trust, but that would be easier if Taran wasn't sitting next to Danny.

"Taran, let Beth have your seat. She's dead on her feet," Corey said.

Marc's eyes narrowed, and Will blew out a breath, shaking his head.

"I'm not going to have her stand," Beth said.

"Me either," Corey said and patted his leg. Once again, Taran's green eyes, full of questions, met his. "Unless you're going to steal my keys again."

She scoffed, and he reached out and pulled her onto his lap. Marc sent his wife a look that had her dropping into the chair Taran had just emptied.

Corey snaked his arm around Taran's tiny waist and tucked her against him. He let out his breath, feeling calmer now that she was in his arms.

The curve of her ass pressed against his thigh. She turned her head slightly, and the ends of her hair brushed against his jaw, causing his senses to whirl with bursts of lavender. He tucked his nose into her hair and pulled in a deep breath. She smelled like everything good in the world. And although a half hour ago he'd just come so hard he swore he saw stars, his pants were becoming uncomfortable. The skin of her lower stomach was warm, and he moved his hand slightly to feel the satiny softness against his rough fingertips. She was warm, soft, everything he'd want a woman to be, and he finally had her in his arms. Then that perfect ass shifted over, brushing against his erection, and he sucked a breath through his teeth.

"You okay?" she asked.

Perfect. Awful. He didn't know.

Peyton started to cry, saving him from an answer, and Will shifted the baby to his shoulder, but Danny stood up.

"Give me the demon child, and I'll work my special magic," he said.

"If you get her to sleep, I will give you anything you want," Marc called.

"Promises, promises." Danny chuckled as he left the room.

"It's still crazy that idiot's the baby whisperer," Will said.

"Huh?" Taran cocked her head slightly, causing her hair to dance across his cheek again.

Corey swallowed hard at the sensation. "Danny can calm any baby down. He settles the crying and gets them asleep," Corey said. "It's weird."

"It's not weird," Danny said, peeking his head back from the foyer. "Even babies know I'm full of awesomeness. I can't help that."

Beth chuckled, Will groaned, and Marc shook his head.

"Don't hate on me if you want me to work my magic," Danny warned as he walked back out of the room.

Taran shifted so suddenly that if Corey hadn't been holding her, she might have fallen off his lap.

"Taran?" he asked, but she had her phone out and had pushed off Corey's lap to stand.

"It's my boss." She licked her lips. "The only reason he'd call this late is because there's a problem with Tillerson's article. It's supposed to go to print tonight. Shit." Then her eyes shot up to Beth. "Shoot, sorry, *shoot*."

He watched her swallow and glance around at everyone at the table. She didn't appear to want to answer it with them around. Or maybe it was him. The article was about his teammate. The phone stopped vibrating.

"Just go out that door and call him back. The patio has privacy," Corey said and took a pull off his beer.

If she had to redo Tillerson's article, that meant tonight was a one-time thing.

Fuck.

24

TARAN STEPPED OUTSIDE on the pavers surrounding the Demodas' pool. The house was on the Jersey coastline, and just past the wrought-iron fence, she could see the dunes and the beach beyond. She could make out the crashing ocean waves with the light of the half moon. She turned back to the house. Through the large windows that covered the entire side, she could see them all at the table. Corey's eyes stayed on her while his jaw clenched.

When he'd asked her to come here tonight, she thought he would maybe say something about what this was. He hadn't. Instead, he'd been almost silent. His actions seemed to imply he wanted this to be something—keeping her close, holding her hand, and bringing her favorite wine.

She hadn't seriously dated anyone but Jeremy, and in high school, dates were dates, not this gray area of hanging out. She didn't wonder if Jeremy was just hoping to sleep with her, wanted a fuck buddy, or just wanted to be friends. That was fourteen years ago, and so much had changed. Maybe dating now was like this mind game she was going through with Corey.

He turned back to his family and laughed at something one of them had said. He tossed his head back, and that dirty-blond hair shook.

Her phone rang again.

"Hello?" she said absently, watching Corey's broad shoulders shake as the laugh rumbled through him. He turned to look at her again, his eyes narrowing slightly. She glanced away but felt the heat creep into her cheeks that she'd been caught staring.

"Sorry to bother you so late, but somehow I don't have the Tillerson contract. I've gone through my email four times—don't have it," Wayne said. "Legal wants it tonight before it goes to press."

"Oh," she replied. "That's weird. I usually send them straight over." She put it on speaker and flipped to her email. She searched for Sean's name.

"You got one, right?" Of course that was his reaction. To imply she hadn't done her job or was too stupid to do it right.

"Definitely. Sean emailed it to me," she said, and Wayne snorted. "I can always ask him to resend if I need to." But her eyes flitted up, and she saw Corey heading her way. She swallowed and scanned quickly, finding one this month with the subject contracts. "Found it." Weird, Sean made it plural. Why would he send two? She glanced up again, seeing Corey almost to the door, so she quickly forwarded it. "I sent it over, but I gotta go."

"Hot date?" her boss asked just as Corey pushed the door open, and his eyebrows shot up.

"Uh," she said, and Corey nodded. "Y-eah?"

Both her boss and Corey laughed at how unsure she sounded.

"I see your email, so we're good. Have fun, Taran."

Her boss hung up before Taran could even reply. She stood awkwardly, unsure of what to say.

"I didn't mean to interrupt, but you looked worried, and I wanted to offer to take you home if you needed to go," Corey said.

"It's okay."

He nodded before he continued.

"Taran, I want this to be a date."

"Oh." She felt the smile creep across her lips.

"Unless you don't want it to be," he continued.

"No." She shook her head. "I do."

"Good," Corey said. Then he shook his head, chuckling a bit. "Damn, this is awkward."

She laughed. "Yeah."

"I'm just going to spit this all out so it stops being weird." Corey frowned and shook his head again. "I like you, and I'd like to keep seeing you. But I'm very private about my personal life. I'd love to bring you here with me or have you hang out at my place or your place or any of our friends' houses." He swallowed, and then his words started to come faster. "But I'm not comfortable dating in public. And it's not because I'm embarrassed about you, or ashamed, or—"

"Corey." She cut him off, reaching for his forearm. "It's okay, and I get it."

He swallowed and pulled her closer to him, letting his hands rest on her hips. "Do you?"

"You and Beth had a very public relationship that ended with a massive invasion of your privacy and her getting crucified by the media." Taran knew the story well. Corey had won Olympic gold pitching, and Beth had won the gold medal in the gymnastic all around. They were the new *it* couple. But his college roommate had released a sex tape of Corey and Beth to the press, who ran wild with it. She couldn't imagine how he felt about it. But she understood he wouldn't want to throw himself into that fire again. He pulled her into his chest and dropped his head so his lips pressed into her hair.

"I can't let that happen to you," he whispered.

Her breath caught at how fiercely protective those words sounded.

"Going out is overrated. I'd rather stay in, play *Diablo,* and order a pizza."

"My kind of girl." He chuckled.

And for some inexplicable reason, that statement made her heart stutter.

The door opened behind them.

"Sorry," Marc said. "But Peyton's out cold on Danny on the sofa, so Beth and I are going to bed. Will just left."

"We'll get out of your hair, man," Corey said and stepped out of her arms.

COREY PRESSED THE ignition button to start his car, and the truck roared to life. Taran had been quiet since Marc had walked out onto the patio, so he left the radio off, hoping they could talk.

There was something he should ask her about, but he'd been leery of hearing the answer. If her fiancé had died recently, he needed to back off, and *shit,* he didn't want to. Maybe it was better if he just ripped the Band-Aid off again. It had worked with the dating topic.

"How long ago did Jeremy die?" he asked and winced at how badly that came out.

Taran turned and raised a single eyebrow.

"Sorry, I probably should have eased into that more." Nerves had him cracking his neck.

"I'm just shocked you know his name."

"Why? You told me."

"Oh." Her eyes widened. "That's right, playing *Diablo*. I can't believe you remember that." She turned to face him and tucked her hair behind her ear.

He didn't understand why she'd think he could forget anything she told him. All the little details, be it her allergy to roses, how she loved the smell of cut grass, or that she would only sleep in satin sheets because she loved the feel against her skin. That one had kept him up at night.

"He died two years ago," Taran said, finally answering her question. "In Syria."

He paused. Will had told him she was with Nick two years ago.

"You were there?" he asked, and he heard her sigh out a breath the size of Texas. When she didn't answer, he turned his head to glance at her. Her eyes were closed, and her jaw was clenched. He had no idea how deep the rabbit hole they might be heading down was. "We don't have to talk about it."

"Yeah." She sighed again. "We do. I was there covering a story about Jeremy's SEAL team. It was supposed to be for the *AP*, but the story ran all over. I can't mention names because DEVGRU is classified."

"Hmm." Corey filed away the fact that Taran was with the team Nick led, meaning Nick was the former leader of the highest trained special ops that existed.

"I probably shouldn't have said that since you know Nick." She shook her head.

"I'm a vault," Corey assured her.

"I went out with the convoy because it was a supply run, supposed to be stupid easy." Taran took a breath. "We were dropping water and canned food off in town. I was going to get some good pictures of the men handing out supplies to the women and children. Feel-good story."

She swallowed, and Corey reached over to take her hand in his.

"We were barely out of the city when the convoy hit a massive roadside bomb. Jeremy was one of the four men who died on impact. Another two didn't make it through the hours it took us to get out of the cars, get cover, and call for help."

"Nick almost lost his leg that day. Were you hurt?" Corey asked.

"No, I'm one of those stories where everyone in my car died, or almost died, and I walked away." She swallowed. "I think that helped a bit."

"What do you mean?"

"Jeremy was so mad when I told him I was coming to stay with his team for two weeks."

Corey thought she might pull her hand away from him, so he squeezed it, encouraging her to continue.

"He was thrilled to see me; his deployment had been long, but he was pissed and worried I would get hurt. I told him reporters traveled with soldiers all the time; it wasn't unsafe. But he said he'd never forgive me if I got myself hurt."

She cleared the rasp in her voice and shut her eyes.

Corey understood. He remembered how Marc acted when Beth was in an accident a couple of years back. Grant was a man on a mission when his wife Trish was threatened two years ago. Then a few months back, he'd seen Nick lose his mind about Morgan being in danger. So the idea of a man wanting his girl safe didn't confuse him.

What was currently screwing with his head a bit was that he wasn't at all jealous of the love in Taran's voice when she talked about the man she had planned to marry. Weirdly enough, he understood how she felt. To have her life mapped out and then suddenly, in a moment, everything changed. For her to have to move on and figure it out without the person she always thought would be her partner. Yeah, he understood that. Nothing about it made him jealous, but it did make him want to pull her close and wrap her up in his arms. Attempt to keep that hurt away.

"Since I didn't get hurt, I felt like he wasn't mad at me. Silly, I know," she said, bringing him out of his head.

"None of that sounds silly," Corey assured her as he parked in front of her townhouse. He turned to her and reached out to cup her soft, warm cheek in his hand. "It sounds like you're an amazing person to make it through all that, and your ability to keep yourself together is impressive as hell. I'd like nothing more than to get to know everything about the woman who is constantly blowing me away."

He looked straight into her sea-green eyes, and his stomach dropped. His eyes ran over her delicate nose and peachy skin. God, she was gorgeous. When her tongue snuck out to lightly gloss over her lips, he forgot to breathe.

"There's something I need to tell you," Taran said and glanced away.

Ten thousand thoughts flipped through his head in one second. She wasn't over Jeremy. She couldn't continue this. She'd never feel about Corey like she did about her former fiancé. He was trying to be open, to communicate better than he had in his last two relationships, but if he'd pushed her into not wanting to give them a shot, he'd kick himself.

"What—" His voice cracked, and he cleared his throat. "Whatever it is, I'm sure it's fine."

She sighed. "My boss wants me to do a story on you."

It took a second for that abrupt change of topic to sink in. Corey pulled back slightly and focused on the windshield in front of him. What was she saying?

"Him and every other sports outlet in the world." His tone was careful, but he white knuckled the steering wheel.

"Probably, but he's been pushing more these last couple months."

Corey gritted his teeth but couldn't look at her. "If you think letting me fuck you was the way to get me to agree—"

"Is that really what you think of *me*?" The sharpness in her tone had him finally looking at her.

Real pain reflected in her eyes. And it cut the breath out of him. He hadn't even let her talk, just jumped to conclusions.

"No, not at all." He reached out for her hand, and when she tried to pull away, he held on tighter. "*I'm* being an ass, and I'm sorry."

She relaxed and let him pull her small hand into his.

"My entire life, people have used me to get information about my parents, girlfriends, and me." Corey swallowed. "I'm not great at trust, but I'm working on it. So I'm sorry I lashed out. I know your boss wants my story. I knew it from the second you told me who you were. The second you said Taran Murphy, cold fear shot through my bones."

She brought her hand up and whacked him on the arm. "Oh, shut up."

He chuckled. "Seriously, I'm aware your magazine wants my story. You don't have to tell me that."

Taran flicked her bangs out of her eyes. "The thing is…" She paused.

Corey didn't breathe because he didn't know what she might say. And he knew her next words could break whatever was happening between them.

"My boss will keep pushing, and I'm sure you'll hear about it. I just didn't want you to think I was hiding it from you. That this was some secret or an end game."

He let out his breath. This he could handle.

"I'm choosing to trust you. I won't hold what your boss wants against you, because I want nothing more than to keep seeing where this thing between us is headed. But it's *never* going to be heading toward you writing an article about me." He focused on her reaction as he said the words, but she didn't seem upset or even disappointed. "You okay with that?"

She smiled. "I'm great with that, Cor. But I do have one more question."

"What's that?" he asked.

"You want to come inside?"

Hell yeah, he did. He liked this woman a lot, and it was turning out to be very easy to trust her too.

25

A MUSCULAR ARM wrapped around her stomach as his warm lips pressed against her shoulder.

"We've got to get up soon." His words vibrated against her skin, and she groaned.

"Don't tell me you're a morning person. I'll have to add that to the list of things I dislike about you."

"After last night, you can't claim to dislike me. You spent way too much time moaning my name for me to buy it." Corey laughed, and as she smacked his chest, he shifted so she fell back against the pillow. Rough fingers brushed against her temple as he tucked a lock of bangs behind her ear. "It's almost eight thirty. This is not me being a morning person, babydoll."

Until this point, she had been ignoring his many nicknames. But he needed to learn her lines. *"Babydoll?"*

He winced. "Yeah, not my favorite either, but nothing sticks, no matter what I try."

"What's your normal go-to pet name?"

The sheet rested low on Corey's hip as he leaned on his elbow. She reached out, letting her finger trace the smooth skin of his chest. Her nail scraped against the ridges of his abs as she waited.

"Corey?" she finally asked as he watched her finger.

"Huh?" He shook his head, but his hand snaked out and grabbed hers before she could let it run any lower down his body. "Cut me some slack here. I know you asked me something. But you're naked and touching me. I only have so much blood, and none of it's currently in my brain."

Taran laughed. "Pet names. You don't normally use one?"

"Holly, I just always called Holls," Corey said.

But Taran wasn't sure who he was talking about. As far as she knew, he dated Beth and Mel. His gaze ran over her face, and he met her eyes. It was another one of those moments where she could tell he was choosing whether to trust her. The odd part was, this time, her heart jumped. It was shocking to realize how much she wanted his trust. "Her real name is Holly Vanderbeek, but Mel Holly is a lot catchier."

It clicked in her brain.

"I use a fake name too," Taran agreed, but Corey's eyes narrowed. "Kuppton. Taran Kuppton."

"That's where T-cup comes from."

"Jeremy started that in high school," Taran explained.

Corey gave a clipped nod. "Makes sense."

He didn't say it, but Taran knew he'd never use it. Like he understood that piece of her former self couldn't be replaced. Corey made it easy to talk about Jeremy because although he was curious—open to hearing about him—he did it in a way that implied he respected Jeremy's part in her life.

"So, Holly was Holls, and Beth I always called baby." He smirked. "I did it a few times to get under Marc's skin when he and Beth were first dating."

"It's surprising you and Marc are so close," she said.

"Why? Marc's awesome. She's a lot with her dramatics and mood swings. It can make a person nuts, but he doesn't even seem to notice."

Taran scoffed. "When you put it that way, I can see exactly why you and Marc are friends."

"Are you implying I'm dramatic?"

"No." Taran shook her head. "I was outright saying out of you and Beth—*you*—are way more dramatic and emotional."

Corey laughed. "Just had to get your pot shot in, bite-size?"

"And we're back to the crappy nicknames." She waited for him to add more, but he didn't. "So what else you got besides Holls and baby?"

He shrugged. "No one else. Trust me, you would have heard a rumor if there was." Although his tone was casual, he couldn't mask the bitterness. "Until my parents died, I couldn't piss without the world hearing about it."

Corey shut his eyes and tilted his head, cracking his neck left and then right. Something Taran knew meant he was uncomfortable.

"My parents both thrived on the constant attention." The mattress shook as he fell back against his pillow, staring at the ceiling. "I'm sure you've read all about them. Their goal was to be on the front page of every magazine. I can't imagine what my life would have been like if social media had existed when I was ten."

The laugh was so bitter she almost didn't recognize it as Corey's.

There was a fairy-tale aspect to his parents' story—the star athlete and singer-actress dubbed America's Sweetheart. Of course people wanted a glimpse into their lives.

"Two people who are used to being the center of attention, too big to contain, should never get together. My life was a constant power struggle of which parent was more beloved by the world. And I played perfectly into that. As many media outlets have pointed out, I got a lot from both of them. Looks, talent, personality."

His dirty-blond hair, the exact shade of his mom's, rested against his forehead, and she reached out to brush it back, but he flinched away.

"Sorry." He pulled her arm, settling her against his chest. The gesture didn't seem comforting to him, though. Like he'd done it so she couldn't look at him as he talked. But he didn't give her the chance to say anything before he went on. "Dad said I got my roller-coaster mood swings from my mom. Anytime I was upset or sad, he mocked me. Mom said I got my temper from my dad. Anytime I was mad, she judged me. I couldn't live up to either of their ideas of perfect. So, I worried anytime I had feelings that I was doing something wrong."

He played with the ends of her hair.

"It got worse when I started school. They blamed each other because I was stupid."

Her body jerked, but he tightened his arms around her. "I'm sorry, *what*?" she asked as soon as she realized he didn't want her to look at him.

"It took a few years for the teachers to realize I was dyslexic. Mostly because my parents didn't want me tested. They didn't want anything to be wrong with me. It didn't fit their image."

Now she forced him to release her. His eyes were wary and guarded, but she wouldn't have that, especially when he started to look away. She moved his face back so he was looking at her. "Do not be embarrassed. My nephew, Noah, is dyslexic."

Corey's eyes softened at her words, so she continued.

"He's sharp as a tack, brilliant kid. He struggles with reading and works twice as hard as most kids, but he is *not stupid,* and neither are *you.*"

He swallowed. "For a long time, I thought I was, and—to sum it up, I still don't read well."

Oh wow.

The contracts he signed suddenly made a lot more sense. But anger rose in her stomach, and she wanted to chew Sean out for letting it happen. Corey might have fired him, but knowing how hard reading a contract for Corey would be, he should have jumped in. She'd never known Sean to be the kind of cut-throat who was out to screw someone over, which was why she used him, and she couldn't believe he would do that to Corey.

"I can see your brain working. It would be a huge story because this is *not* something anyone knows. My parents were so embarrassed that they didn't let it get out. So outside of my teachers, six people know this. And their last names are all Evans." He cleared his throat. His gaze swung down to her, and the vulnerability in his eyes was shocking. Because she expected the Corey Matthews who walked into the room as if he owned it, not the one who looked like he didn't know where he belonged. "Well, two are Demoda, but Marc and Beth might as well be Evanses."

"You can trust me, Corey," she promised. Although she couldn't be mad at Sean for something he didn't know, she needed to make sure he got rid of his copy of the contract. She had already decided to delete it, but this only confirmed she'd made the right call.

"I'm putting a lot of faith in you." The corner of his mouth lifted just slightly. "But since school was so bad, my activities became their focus—depending on the day, I should be an actor, a baseball player, a musician, a model." He yanked his hand away from hers as he ran his fingers through his hair. "They both had plans before I was *eight,* and they always wanted to know which I liked better—Mom's plans or Dad's. On the days they fought, they used me as a pawn in their competition against each other. On the good days when they were madly in love, I wasn't good enough for either of them."

That statement caused an unfamiliar crack in her chest.

"Corey—"

"You get that's wrong. Most people know that's not the way to treat a child, but few *understand* how it *feels.*"

Holy hell.

She'd been numb for months—years. But hearing the pain in his voice *hurt.* The satin sheet yanked against her skin, and she looked down to see it fisted in his fingers. She covered his hand with hers and went with encouragement.

"It's impressive that you didn't fall into the same patterns as your parents."

"I would have been a complete shit if it wasn't for the Evans family. Lynn Evans, the guys' mother, realized pretty quickly I needed some positive adult attention." His entire demeanor lightened at the mention of the Evanses, and he even chuckled.

She settled her palms against his chest and rested her chin on them, watching him.

"Will and I played on the same U-eleven little league club team. Mom and I were in New Jersey for the two years she was in *Rent*."

Debra Matthews had rotated between Broadway and Hollywood. But Taran hadn't realized that left Corey moving back and forth across the US every couple of years.

"Will started offering me rides to the practice and then invited me over to his house. Beth had moved in with them that year. The last thing Lynn and Rob probably needed was *another* preteen boy, but that didn't stop them from treating me like I was one of their kids. Without their dad, Rob"—Corey shook his head—"there is no way I'd read as well as I do."

Taran's eyes narrowed. She knew the eldest of the Evans brothers was Beth's late husband. Lynn Evans had been Beth's gymnastic coach for the Olympics, so Beth had known the family for a long time. From everything Taran heard, Corey had been very close with the family since he was a teenager. She always assumed Corey had become close with the Evanses when he and Beth started dating, but it sounded like he knew them first, which didn't make sense.

"How was it—" She cut herself off.

"What?" Corey asked.

She shook her head. "I was curious about what happened. You might as well share a last name with the Evanses. For as close as you are with them now, they're family. How was it ever okay for Bob to marry your ex-girlfriend? Were you and Beth not as serious as the press made it?"

He swallowed and sucked in a breath.

"At the time, I thought Beth was it for me. We had plans to become a family just like the Evanses. From the second we met, we understood each other. Her dad was as shitty as my parents. We were unwanted barnacles who were sometimes the grip our parents needed on the slippery rock of fame, and other times we were the things that cut them to shreds—it all depended on the moment."

Every instinct in Taran said to hug him. Offer him some form of comfort, but it was like invisible spikes were shooting out of his body, protecting him from the world.

Corey shook his head.

"But you know what happened. My college roommate, a guy I thought was my friend, used my name, my fame, and the fact that the world wanted every detail of my life to make money. He got paid hundreds of thousands of dollars for the tape of Beth and me having sex. I took a page out of my dad's book and lashed out—made stupid comments, and I almost lost the only family I ever had." He swallowed again. "Luckily, Beth forgives, and our promise of family forever meant something to her."

His eyes were closed, but he continued. "Every single time a media outlet asked questions, I reacted. The reporter twisted my comments, implying Beth was an out of control teenager." Corey sighed. "If I'd corrected that sooner, it might have been different, but I was dumb. So, I'm not blameless. But by the time I got my head out of my ass, it was too late, because she needed the only thing I couldn't give her."

"What?" Taran asked.

"Anonymity. A new name, a new life away from the media that trashed her. Even if I gave up baseball, I was famous. My mother won her fourth Tony award that year for her performance in Mama Mia and my father was arguably the best pitcher ever. Not to mention their crazy toxic relationship and need to drag me into it at every turn, which only got worse when Houston drafted me and he announced my games."

Taran remembered watching some of those games. The Astros were her father's and brother's obsession. They could do no wrong as far as either was concerned. But even they took issue with some of the harsh criticism Orlando Matthews spewed on his son.

"Beth needed an escape. So, I gave it to her. I told her to move on, and said I was over her. And I told Bob it was fine. She deserved to be happy, and she became a part of the family we had always dreamed of belonging to."

She didn't have to ask him to know he'd lied. He'd sacrificed to keep her happy.

"What about you?" she asked. "Didn't you deserve to be happy?"

He shrugged. "Houston was good for me. Besides the national games that my dad called, I had space from stuff. And now that Mom and Dad are gone. I get to set the boundaries that I can enforce with the press."

Taran respected that. She'd always felt like his stance with the media was harsh, but she understood it now. And there was no way in hell she'd ever disrespect his view on it.

"I'm going to add this because I'd rather get all of this out of the way now and we can move on." Corey cleared his throat. "All the rumors about Holls's eating disorders are true. My need for privacy fed on her insecurities. She thought if she was thinner, prettier, I'd be more willing to go public with our relationship. I didn't realize how much I was screwing with her head. I wasn't good for her." His hand brushed up and down her back. "But that worked out too because she's doing better. And Hunter and Holls work together. He's even become a friend, and I'm happy for them."

That didn't sound like a line.

"But you don't want to go to the wedding?"

Corey sighed. "I don't want to *be* the story at the wedding, Taran. It's their day, and I worry that if I'm there, the press will start talking about her and me again. That's not fair to them."

How perfectly Corey that sounded. And yet, two months ago, she would have assumed, like everyone else, he was either bitter about the end of his relationship with Mel Holly or the whole thing had been made up.

But the truth was, Corey just wanted some things that were his alone. Being in the spotlight meant he shared a lot with the world. But she got how he didn't want to share everything. Corey should be allowed the small amount of private life he created for himself.

"Does any of that make sense to you?" he asked.

"All of it," she said and lifted her head off his chest. She leaned forward, letting her lips brush against his.

He groaned. "Damn, I wish I didn't need to be at the stadium for pregame because I could spend another two hours in these satin sheets without complaint." He pulled his hand back and swatted her on the ass cheek. "I gotta shower. Want to join me?"

Taran ran her hands over his shoulders, imagining him wet.

"Nope, never mind." Corey shook his head. "If you shower with me, I'm never getting there on time."

Taran laughed. "Rain check?"

"Abso-fucking-lutely."

Taran got him a towel before heading down to make some much-needed coffee. She grabbed her phone off the table where she'd dropped it last night—three missed calls and two messages from Wayne. That was weird.

> **WAYNE:** Oh my god, you did it!

She cocked her head to the side, unsure of what he was excited about. He'd read her article about Tim a while ago. He hadn't been disappointed with it, but he was nowhere near this excited.

> **WAYNE:** I never gave you enough credit. Locked in another one. I am blown away. Call me.

What was he talking about? Although she was working on getting in touch with Edgar DeLeon's agent to lock him in for some time this summer, she'd yet to get anything tied down. At least, as far as she knew. It would be odd to have them reach out to Wayne and not to her. But anything was possible. She hit his name and let the phone ring.

"All hail the princess!" Wayne sang as he picked up. Man, he was in an unusually good mood. "I can't believe you did it. How did you get him to agree? I know I said it was the must-have article for the year, but I never thought you'd pull it off."

The only must-have he'd demanded this year was Corey.

"What are you talking about?" she asked.

"Corey Matthews. The contract you got for September."

Taran's eyes widened. How did he know about that? Her stomach bottomed out. There was no way.

"The way you snuck that in last night. I didn't even see it because I just forwarded it to legal. But they called this morning. And damn, Taran, I'm impressed," Wayne continued like Taran wasn't having a full-blown panic attack.

How did she send him that? She flicked to her email from last night, and her heart stopped as the names of the attachments came into view.

Tillerson June. Matthews September.

The reason she hadn't forwarded Tillerson's contract right away. Sean had sent it with Corey's.

This could not be happening.

26

THE TOWEL SMELLED just like Taran, or maybe it was her soap he'd used. Either way, that light lavender floated around him as he ran it roughly over his hair, feeling strangely relaxed.

He'd like to say it was the sex giving him this Zen. Because it was hot. But he knew it was the openness that was relaxing him. It was weird to have told her so much about his life. He had never said some of those things aloud before. But it was also like letting go of the breath he'd been holding for way too long, like it relaxed his whole being to have finally spoken the words.

He hadn't wanted things to be weird. So, when Taran had asked questions, Corey decided to put his cards on the table instead of keeping everything close to the vest. If they were doing this, he didn't want to have any off-limit topics hanging between them. He'd be an open book with her, and he'd make sure she could be too.

Once he threw on yesterday's clothes, he headed downstairs.

"Hey, half-pint—" he said but stopped as she glanced up from her phone. Something about the pinch in her forehead didn't sit well. He was on cloud nine, but she looked like someone had gotten her banned from *Diablo*. Had the ten minutes alone made her realize she had regrets about being with him? "You good?"

"Yeah." She shook her head. "*No*, not really."

Open the lines of communication, he reminded himself as he swallowed down the lump in his throat. Some things were hard to hear, but not saying them didn't make them disappear. He'd learned that the hard way—*twice*.

"Is this an us thing or something else?" He glanced down at her phone, but it sat, lifeless, on the counter.

"I just need to go into the office and get my boss on the right page about stuff."

Work—that settled the twinge between his shoulder blades. He relaxed, leaning onto the counter.

"Go in and drop that badass attitude all over him." He fought the smirk as her eyebrow rose.

"Attitude? I don't have an attitude." She crossed her arms, tipping her chin up.

He moved around the counter to her. "Sure you don't, little miss eyebrow." He grabbed the back of her neck, loving that he could kiss that sass right out of her system. She sank into him the second his lips pressed against hers. His body flared with a fire. The way she responded every time their mouths met called to his soul. But he didn't have time. He groaned, pulling back. "I should be done with the game by eight. Come over tonight before I leave for the road again."

"I'll bring dinner?" she asked. Her breath caught as his finger skimmed down her neck, dipping into the cleavage of her tank top.

"No. I got dinner. You're in charge of dessert."

Even sacrificing kitchen counter sex—which they'd revisit as soon as possible if he had anything to say about it—he was going to be late. He glanced at the clock twenty minutes later as he sat on the George Washington Bridge, headed into New York City. How late would depend on the god-awful traffic. It could take him anywhere from five minutes to forty-five minutes to get to the Bronx.

"Incoming call from Will." Siri's voice blasted through his car, overshadowing the music. "Should I answer?"

"Yes." Corey gave the phone the two seconds to connect. "Hey, man."

"Not a texting day or willfully ignoring the question?" Will asked.

Corey snorted. "Not a texting day, but now I'm worried about what the hell the question is?"

For most people, texting was like showering or brushing your teeth, just something people did. But for Corey, it took focus. If his mind wasn't on the words, he couldn't get them to make sense. And forget about group chats, because he read so slowly, he never could keep up.

"How'd things work out with Taran? You take my advice?" Will asked. "I was hoping I'd catch you in a good mood."

"I'm in a good mood," Corey assured.

Will laughed. "*Hell* yeah, you are."

"And for the record, I did take your advice. You were right—"

"Wait, I'm sorry. I think I misheard you," Will interrupted.

"Shut it. I said you were right." Corey rolled his eyes. He could imagine the cocky ass smirk on his best friend's face. "I went into this with the *I trust her; she's worth it* mentality, and we talked. It was good."

"Talked. Huh?"

"Among other things." Corey chuckled. "But I'm not buying that your question was about Taran, so what's up?"

"Genni's asking me—well, you know, if we're going to the wedding—or not."

Poor Will sounded like he was walking in a mine field. Genni had become friends with Corey's ex-girlfriend over the last three years. But Will, in solidarity with Corey, said he was only going to the wedding if Corey was. And no matter how much Corey said he didn't care if Will went or not, Will wasn't budging. Probably because Will had no interest in going, and he was using Corey as an excuse.

"I said—"

Will cut him off. "Last week, when we had dinner with them, both Hunter and Mel sounded like they wanted you to come."

Corey groaned.

"Don't stay friends with your ex-girlfriends if you don't want to keep getting invited to weddings." Will laughed. "But they did seem hurt that you were hedging about it, so this is actually me saying call her and tell her why you aren't coming, man."

"It's going to come back and bite you in the ass if Holls talks me into going. You know that, right?" Corey asked.

"You and Taran should come. I love hanging out with her. And it would save me the fight with Genni."

"I couldn't bring Taran," Corey scoffed.

"Why?" Will sounded lost, but to Corey, it was obvious.

"They made it clear that it's a small private thing. No press." Corey cracked his neck.

"Huh." Will huffed.

Corey waited for Will to add more, but he was met with silence. "Did I lose you?"

"Nope, I'm here." Will's voice was laced with disapproval.

"What bug crawled up your ass?"

"No bug. Just thought when you said you were trusting her, you meant opening up and trusting her. Not the same shit as always—"

"That's not fair." Corey cut him off. His hands gripped tightly on the wheel.

"I agree. It's not fair at all. You need to get your head out of your ass because you'll hurt that girl."

"Me?" Corey had opened up to her like he'd never done before. "You don't know what you're talking about."

"Yes, I *do*. Do you not realize that Taran is completely capable of dating you and being a reporter at the same time without confusing the line?"

Corey swallowed.

"She's written about Clayton and even done two blogs about things with the family—with everyone's approval. And I've yet to see your name mentioned. I've also noticed there have been no stories about Beth and Marc's demon child who they can't get to sleep. No gossip about the fact that you definitely dated Mel Holly. No stories about your crappy mood swings. Not once has this girl overstepped in any way. And yet she's not good enough to take to your friend's wedding. Just good enough to wet your dick—"

"Shut. The. Fuck. Up." Corey barely got the words out through his clenched teeth.

"Fine, but don't come crying to me when this explodes again. Because trust isn't pretending you believe she has your back while you're waiting for her to prove she doesn't—"

Corey slammed his finger against the red button, ending the call. He was trying so hard with Taran. How could it not be enough? After stewing for the last of the drive, he parked his truck and headed into the locker room on autopilot.

"Someone had a good night." Daily's cheery voice pulled Corey out of his dark thoughts.

"What?" he asked, dropping his phone and wallet into his locker.

"Ten minutes late and in yesterday's clothes." The teasing smirk made Corey roll his eyes. A few teammates turned their way, but Corey shook his head, causing them to lose interest.

"It's jeans and a white T-shirt—I own more than one."

Daily walked over and traced a line over his shoulder blade with his finger.

"What the hell?" Corey asked as he brushed him off.

"Watermarks from yesterday's ice. Don't bullshit a bullshitter."

Daily laughed, but Corey just yanked the T-shirt over his head and tossed it into the bin in his locker.

"Hey, bro, it's cool. I've been hoping you'd get your head out of your ass about it."

Corey glanced over his shoulder at Daily, braced for another lecture. The words hit too close to Will's statement to not put Corey on edge. Daily's dark gaze was teasing, not accusing. Still, Corey didn't respond.

"Gonna tell me you weren't with our favorite little reporter?" The corner of Daily's mouth rose as he finished the sentence. He crossed his arms and rocked back onto his heels.

Corey opened his mouth to deny it, but that didn't sit right. Daily wasn't just a teammate, he was a friend. And was it fair to Taran to outright lie about the fact that they were together? He cracked his neck.

"Why do you look like you're about to punch your fist through the wall?" Tim smiled as he dropped his bag on the floor in front of his locker. No one commented that Tim was late, but it was most likely because it was only ten minutes, which, for Tim, was like being on time.

"I'm not punching anything," Corey assured him. "Why are you so happy? You're normally a moody bitch for morning call time."

"Yeah." Daily's focus shifted. "Your walking-on-sunshine makes Corey's I-got-laid smirk look like the walk of doom. You got a girl?"

Corey shook his head at Daily. The man needed to stop. Otherwise, Corey might need to point out that Daily hadn't been going out with the team at night for the last couple of weeks. The only reason Corey could imagine that would happen was if *he* had a girl.

"Better. I got Taran Murphy."

Corey's body jerked at the words. What the hell was he talking about? There was nothing between Taran and Tim—right? Daily took two steps toward him.

"Settle down. I'm sure it's not what you think," Daily mumbled before adding at a normal volume, "Staff was buzzing about the article when I got here. So much so, I had to scan it myself."

Oh shit, that's right. He'd forgotten that came out today. He glanced over at Tim and his giant smile.

"She did a good job," Daily added.

"Hell yeah. That woman somehow made immature and irresponsible sound good. Two different kids' equipment companies already reached out to Sean this morning. It's awesome. She even turned the story of you coming to get me when I missed the flight into something cool."

Tim chuckled, but Corey's body went rigid. Taran didn't mention including him in the article. She never even *asked*. His hands fisted as he stood up turning to Tim.

"She wrote about me?" Corey worked to keep his tone neutral, but inside, anger burned. He knew this would happen. This was exactly why he had to keep her away from things like the wedding.

"Man, you're all over the place today." Tim shook his head, but his smile didn't fade as he bent into his bag and tossed the *Sports Illustrated* Magazine over to Corey. Reflexes had Corey catching it before it smacked into his chest. "Read it—but chill out. She just calls you the annoyed teammate."

Corey's shoulders slumped with the realization that he'd overreacted. Once again, he'd assumed the worst.

"Yeah, bro, relax. You're not mentioned at all, and no one who isn't part of the team would know it was you. I'm surprised you didn't already tell her she can't write about you."

"I did." It came out so low he was surprised Daily heard him.

"So what's the problem?"

Corey shook his head and turned back to his locker. But he knew the exact problem—Will was right. Corey claimed he trusted Taran, but both last night when she mentioned her boss wanting his story and right now, his brain had automatically decided she was out to get him. She'd done nothing to deserve that. His gut churned; he wasn't being fair to her. Could he really trust her? Or was this a sign they should have never started this?

27

TARAN PUSHED HARD on the number thirty-eight button and stepped back. Her light-blue shirt dress wasn't uncomfortable exactly, but business dress wasn't her go-to these days. The toe of her black heel tapped against the dark tile as the elevator moved up. She rarely came to the New York office. But today required a face-to-face conversation with Wayne.

He couldn't see her until one, so she had paced around uselessly at home. She should have used the time to come up with something to say, but she was still debating the best course of action. Mostly, she needed more time to dig herself out of this hole. She didn't have a grand plan. It was more of an iffy idea.

The elevator door finally opened on her floor. She stepped out nodding at the receptionist before she turned down the long gray hallway heading toward Wayne's assistant. Although Taran's heels didn't tap on the carpet, Nancy glanced up from her computer, almost as if she heard Taran walking.

"Oh, hey. He told me to let you know he's not ready."

"What?" Taran had spent the last hour psyching herself up for this conversation and Wayne wasn't available?

"Yeah, he said probably three thirty. Sorry, he got called into a meeting. But he figured since you were coming in anyway, you could just work here." She pointed off to the conference room Taran used when she was in the building. "He'd love to know July's feature by the end of the day." Nancy shrugged because it was typical Wayne behavior. He'd probably known he couldn't see her at one, even as he said it.

"I guess it's pointless to say he does this stuff to me on purpose," Taran mumbled.

Nancy's eyes softened. She'd worked for Wayne for probably twenty-five years, and the older woman wasn't blind to how he treated Taran. "I do think he's harder on you than some of the guys. But today, he wanted to chat with you about how you got the elusive baseball legend to agree, so it was a last-minute meeting."

Taran sighed and adjusted the strap of her computer case on her shoulder. "Okay, have him come get me."

After heading into the room, she closed the door behind her. She should have been focusing on work, but she glanced at her phone on the table. Corey'd texted his address with a message.

COREY: Dont no if you have this

COREY: I wanted to make sure you did

COREY: phones in the locker during game

COREY: but trust me my mind is with you

No punctuation, and it wasn't the easiest string of texts to read, but he cared enough to send them. She'd read it over and over, smiling each time. Corey was turning out to be so much more than the incredibly hot man with a hundred-mile-an-hour fastball.

But she had to figure out her next article, not pine over a text. The agent for her soccer guy wasn't getting back to her. She'd have to push back another month. No one else was standing out to her. Last month, she'd written about a baseball player, and in July, the other big four sports were offseason. She flicked through headlines and photos looking for somebody she might want to write about, but none of the athletes jumped out at her. This year, there were no Olympics, and golf had become quiet again recently. She should choose a woman because her articles had been male-heavy lately. After two hours, she finally stumbled on exactly what she was looking for.

The US tennis player currently ranked number two in the world had a baby three months ago and was training hard to get back into top form. It might not be what the typical *Sports Illustrated* readers were interested in, but it might pull in a wider audience.

She walked over to the door, calling out to Nancy. "Hey. Do you know who Jessica Walters' agent is?"

"I'll email you the contact info," Nancy said without looking away from her computer screen.

Three conversations later: one with Sean, one with the agent, and one with Jessica, Taran had her article set. At this point, it was almost four thirty, and she hadn't been summoned by Wayne. She packed up her stuff and headed back to his office.

"Is he in there?" Taran asked.

"He's waiting on you." Nancy nodded.

"Jessica's an interesting choice." Wayne sat behind his large desk. Behind him was what Taran liked to call the wall of brags. The entire wall consisted of him photographed with random famous athletes, showing off the fact that he'd met everyone who was anyone in sports for the last three decades.

Taran didn't want to fight with him over next month's article; she had a more significant battle to fight. She wiped her palms off on her dress and swallowed. "Want me to pick someone else?"

He shook his head, leaning back in the leather office chair. "No, just do a couple of moms in sports blogs leading up to it. That will help pique interest. Why do we need to talk about Matthews?" He narrowed his eyes as he clenched his jaw. Before she even spoke, he was unhappy with her. "By your tone this morning, I feel like you're going to pull out of this. So I'm hoping you're not about to give me some lame reason that you can't do the article."

"You said this morning you wanted to reach out to him right away," Taran explained.

"Why wouldn't we? If he's doing this, we need to make it the cover." Wayne shifted in his chair, leaning forward to rest his arms on the desk.

"Did you know he fired Hot Shots?" she asked. At this point, this was the only thing she could come up with, and she wanted a chance to talk to Sean about it. Although she talked to him about Jessica's contract, she didn't want to talk about Corey at work. But she wasn't even 100 percent sure this could get Corey out of the contract.

"Shit," Wayne snapped. "I'm assuming Sean told you that, and it's not a rumor?"

"It's confirmed." Taran nodded.

"Last time this fucking happened, we dumped time and money into the spread, only to have it ripped out from under us. These prima donna athletes claiming they were tricked and suing to invalidate the contract are killing us. Their new agents want to pad the billing and cause drama." Wayne's fist slammed onto the desk. "Who's the new agent?"

Taran shrugged. As far as she knew, Corey still hadn't hired one. "I can reach out to Matthews directly if you want. The Metros are on the road for a stretch after today's game, but I can get together with him and talk after I finish July's article."

Wayne ran his hand over his balding head. "Yeah, fine. But make it a meeting to lock in dates and details; don't hint that we believe he can back out."

"Of course," Taran agreed.

"It's times like these that I wish *SI* hadn't decided to go so heavily into the features' approval. *The New York Times* writes a piece, and they don't ask permission. They might ask for a comment, but the story runs anyway."

Taran forced herself not to roll her eyes. "It's hard to get an in-depth look into a person's life without cooperation."

"Yeah, I know," he grumbled but then looked at her. "Thanks for looking out for us. I was worried this would be an 'I can't write about Cory Matthews because I'm sleeping with him' conversation. I should have known better. You're one of the most professional reporters we have."

Taran chuckled uncomfortably.

"Plus, if that was the case, it's an easy fix. I'd pass it off to someone else to write it."

Taran's heart skipped a beat. "Wait, what?"

Wayne shrugged. "It doesn't matter now, but I was worried, so I checked with the legal. Nothing in the contract says you have to be the reporter who writes the article on Matthews. But it turns out I didn't need to spend the afternoon making sure it could be reassigned if necessary."

Her stomach bottomed out. It never occurred to her that anyone else could write the article. She assumed that if she didn't do it, the worst that could happen would be she'd get fired.

"Don't give me that look, princess. You know I won't take the story away. It'll be your baby." He waved a hand. "Check back in when you turn in the Jessica piece."

Taran nodded.

"Was there anything else?" he asked, and she shook her head. "Okay, we'll talk later."

With that, he dismissed her, but she barely remembered leaving the office and getting back to the car. The second she was in the car, she was dialing. Hopefully, Sean could help her work her way out of this contract. But she got his voicemail and left a vague call me message.

She sat in the car and banged her head twice on the steering wheel. There had to be a solution to this. Maybe she'd figure it out if she could talk it out with someone. She called her sister.

"Do not tell me that you're canceling on the kids." Her sister's voice echoed around the car.

"Canceling?"

"Yeah, *Diablo*, the castle hunt," Teagan prompted.

"Shit," Taran cursed. She had completely forgotten. It was unlike her to be such a mess. She glanced at the clock. She had over an hour, so she could still make it. "I'm not canceling. No issues. Just making sure it's all good on your end."

"Sure you are. What's going on, Taran?"

"It's just—" Taran swallowed. Although she had automatically reached out to her sister, she couldn't betray Corey and tell her sister anything she knew about him. And that made the contract issue so confusing. How could she explain and have it make sense?

"Taran?"

She couldn't tell her. "I'm good. Just tired. I picked Jessica Walters for the next article." Taran went on to chat about that and promised again she'd be on *Diablo* before hanging up. She called Sean next but got his voicemail again. The only good news about the *Diablo* game was it put off having to talk to Corey about the article; she wanted a solution before she told him.

She sent off a text.

> **TARAN:** I'm really sorry, but I forgot that I had plans with my niece and nephews tonight to do Diablo. I have to reschedule dinner for when you get back.

Once she hit send, she finally pulled out of the underground lot. But she was barely on the street before her phone rang. She looked down. Wasn't he at the game?

"Hey?"

"Hey." He sounded unhappy.

"Aren't you supposed to be playing?"

"I pitched last night. Daily was up today, but the game ended ten minutes ago." Definitely grumpy.

"You okay?" she asked.

He sighed. "Just thinking a lot. But, um, I'm hoping to change your mind about canceling tonight." He cleared his throat. "I actually like that thing you have to do."

"*Diablo?*"

"Yeah. Could we do it together?" He was hesitant. Although she wasn't sure if he was afraid she'd say no or if the locker room and everyone in it made him reluctant to say much.

"You want to play with my niece and nephews?"

"I want to see you." The hoarse declaration sent a shiver down her spine. "And there's some stuff we need to talk about."

Her stomach flipped—there was stuff they needed to talk about. She swallowed.

"I have to sign on with them at six-thirty. Will you be home?"

"I'm about to walk out of the stadium now," he confirmed.

She smirked as she put her blinker on, changing lanes on the busy city street. "Let me guess, you skipped all the post-game media?"

He chuckled. "Always got to give me a hard time, huh, half-pint?"

"Well, I'm still in midtown traffic, but I should make it by six thirty."

"I'll be waiting." Once again, the deep rumble of promise in his voice sent a shiver down her spine. And the idea that if he found out about the story, that would all go away knotted her stomach.

It took her almost forty minutes to get over the bridge, and she had just merged onto route four when her phone rang. Thank God it was Sean.

"Hey."

"Hey, Taran, what's up? I told you I'd get everything done with the contracts for Jessica tomorrow. This stupid ghost blue ceiling paint is taking all day." A slight huff to his tone implied Erin might be making him crazy with her back porch.

"I'm calling about something else," Taran said and nervously tapped her fingers on the steering wheel. The stupid emotions creeping up on her the last couple of weeks were messing with her. Her head wasn't in the game, and she was doing dumb things like sending over the wrong contract and forgetting about plans. But she had it under control. She was fine.

"What's going on?" Sean's voice grew serious.

Taran started from the beginning. The accidental email, the conversation with Wayne. Her plan to get Corey out of the contract. Sean was silent through all of it.

"Well, shit, Taran," Sean finally said. "I'm honestly not sure. That excuse works when a client signed while the agent represented them, and now they don't think that agent was working in their best interest. *This* is not that situation. He fired us a couple of weeks before he signed that contract. He knew when he signed it that I wasn't looking out for any of his interests. *SI* will jump all over that."

"So there's nothing I can do?" Taran's voice cracked. "Because if I tell Wayne I won't do it, he'll find someone else to write that story, and Corey will never forgive that. And Sean, I *like* him."

Sean sighed. "Let me look at the contract again. Talk to Mike and Austin. Maybe we can come up with something. But Taran, you've got to tell him."

"I know. I was just hoping for a solution first."

Sean grunted. "Erin should thank you, because I'm suddenly less annoyed about her porch painting. Why are you always such a pain in the ass?"

Taran forced a chuckle. "That's just what I'm good at. I'll call you tomorrow."

Sean hung up just as she pulled into Corey's building's parking garage. The security guard was expecting her, so he let her through and gave her a numbered space.

It was only 6:10, so she sat a moment in the car. It wasn't fair not to tell Corey, but he was leaving tomorrow. And this would mess with his head right when his pitching was doing better. It would be less stressful for him if she had a solution first. Maybe Sean would get back to her with an answer. A way that *nobody* could write the story. That seemed like a better idea than freaking Corey out. She wished there was an easy answer.

28

WHEN THE KNOCK finally echoed through his house, he practically ran to the door before forcing himself to slow down. *Don't be desperate*, he told himself, although he might be. Desperate, confused, and needy, because when Taran had tried to cancel tonight, he was hit with a tidal wave of disappointment.

He made himself stand at the door and count to ten before he opened it. Even though he'd slowed himself down, he wasn't prepared for the sight in front of him. He'd expected cutoffs and hoodie Taran, but that wasn't who stood at his door. She was his chameleon, and he should have known that she would be dressed to fit in at her office.

His eyes tracked the collar of what looked like a man's button-down shirt. But on Taran, it was a dress that pulled in tight at her waist and stopped mid-thigh. Her legs, the legs that had spent most of last night wrapped around his hips, were on full display. His body heated instantly. The plan to play with the kids, eat dinner, and talk sounded dull. His body demanded something different. Something hot and sweaty. And a hell of a lot more fun than *Diablo*.

"Inviting me to come in or just going to stand here undressing me with your eyes?" Taran asked.

His lips pull up. He loved this woman's sass, but she had to remember who she was dealing with.

"Oh, I want you inside, and I definitely want you to *come*, but I prefer you moan my name when you do it." Smug satisfaction erupted as her eyes widened and she swallowed hard. "You like that idea too, mini muffin?"

That caused her jaw to lock. She was easy to rev up in so many ways, and he enjoyed the hell out of all of them.

"Come in."

She took four steps before she froze.

He quickly glanced around the room, but it was clean. He'd called the service to come in and do a quick run-through when he'd invited her over.

"What's wrong?" he asked.

She shook her head and sent him a smile over her shoulder before her focus moved back to his apartment. "Every time I turn around, you're not what I'm expecting." She shook her head as she walked over to his large sectional and focused on the wall behind it. "Finger paintings?"

He eyed the pictures of the four seasons. "Beth's and Grant's kids made me one for Christmas last year. It's how they see spring, summer, winter, and fall. I had my decorator matte and frame them."

"I love this one." Taran pointed to a colorful explosion of what was meant to be flowers.

"Mandy's. I'm not sure if she was painting spring or herself in that chaos." Corey loved each painting because of how much of the kids' personalities came through in what they created.

"This one seems so serious." She studied the white and gray scene that depicted winter.

"It would make sense if you knew Nate," Corey assured.

She spun slowly, moving around the room, pausing at photographs to study them. Finally, his collection caught her attention. The five-foot glass vase sat next to the gas fireplace. It had started as a joke between him, Luke, and Will. But it turned into something that took on a life of its own.

"I've got nothing—are these *beer caps*?" She laughed, even as she squatted down to look closer.

"Yeah." He moved next to her. "From beer night. Will, Luke, and I keep them. You can see we went through beer phases over the years. It was Coors Light for a long time." His finger traced up about a foot of the vase that was all Coors caps. "But Marc blew in with his prissy tastes, so we all had to adapt."

Taran chuckled but didn't say anything for a minute, and he wondered if she thought it was dumb. But when she turned to him, her eyes danced.

"You guys are such a fun, unique family." She pushed back up to her feet and glanced around again. "Your *home* is perfect. Thanks for letting me come over."

His chest pinged at the term home because that was exactly what he'd told the woman who designed his space. He didn't need fancy, didn't care about the price, but he wanted a place he loved to hang out in.

He stood up. "We should probably set up. I figured we could eat when we're done." He gestured to the TV, which currently had his demon hunter spinning in a circle. "I have mine pulled up. You just need to sign in."

She sank into the sofa and groaned. "Oh man, this is the best couch ever!"

"Yes, it is." That was one of his demands, a sofa he could kick back on and be comfortable but would be durable enough for the Evans kids to jump or spill on without an issue.

He moved to sit next to her.

"Huge sofa, and you need to sit on top of me?" she asked, but it didn't really sound like a complaint.

"I'm happy to have you sit on a few different parts of *me* if you'd rather."

Her blush was the cutest thing he'd seen all day.

"You need to be a lot less R-rated because my sister and sister-in-law will kill me if this isn't a PG game." That eyebrow of hers shot up.

"Cross my heart."

"You talk like an angel but then shoot me a smile that's all devil."

He leaned in and finally placed his lips against hers. She moaned into his mouth. all liquid desire and he wanted nothing more than to say forget the game. But they couldn't.

"I better stop because this is going way past PG."

She groaned. "You're impossible."

Corey smirked. "Log in, chipmunk."

"That's another hard no. I may be little, but I'm not a rodent." She reached for the remote.

"So I should stay away from mouse, Minnie Mouse, and squeakers too?"

Her eyebrow shot up again, and he chuckled as she logged into the game and created a group for them.

"Noah's fifteen. He's my brother's oldest. Bryce is his thirteen-year-old brother. And my sister's daughter, Crystal, is twelve."

The commotion started as soon as the kids logged on. Even though he had an expensive sound system, he was having trouble hearing the kids over each other—their excitement of talking to Aunt Taran all at the same time made it impossible to catch much.

"Wait a minute, who's the demon hunter?" one of the boys asked.

"I was going to introduce you, but y'all are out of control, Noah." Taran laughed as she said it. "At this rate, we'll never take down the castle."

"Who is sportsnut?" A girl's voice, must be Crystal, asked.

"This is my friend, Corey. He wants to play with us tonight, and we could probably use his help."

Corey wondered what they would say. The kids were clearly excited to play with their aunt, and for the first time since she said she was canceling, he realized he might be intruding. He held his breath when the kids were silent.

"What kind of friend?" Bryce asked. "Like your *boyfriend*?"

"She hasn't had a boyfriend since Uncle Jeremy died. Everyone knows that," Crystal said with a matter-of-factness that only a kid could use about death.

Taran winced.

Corey couldn't force her to answer the question, nor could he claim to be her boyfriend to her family. "I'm hoping to someday be lucky enough to get to that title. Maybe you guys can help get her to like me?"

Taran shook her head, but the slight turn up in the corner of her mouth gave him hope she didn't hate the idea.

"Are you good at this game?" Bryce asked, cutting to the chase.

"Better than Aunt Taran," Corey assured because he spoke the language of winning. "I don't forget I'm playing and let my team die."

"Thank God," Noah praised even as Taran scoffed next to Corey.

"If you all gang up on me, I'll leave. Then this raid will fall apart." Her tone was too light to be a real threat.

"Corey, you have an adult account and can create a raid for us, right?" Bryce asked.

"Hey!" Taran's mouth fell open. It was apparent she was used to being the favorite.

"I'm grateful for the support, guys, but remember, we want Aunt Taran to *like* me," Corey reminded.

Taran whacked him in the stomach, and he laughed again.

That morning, when he'd asked Taran to come over, he hadn't expected this kind of night, but an hour and a half later, he wouldn't have changed a thing.

"I realize I shouldn't be surprised, but I had no idea you'd be that good with kids," Taran said once they had signed off.

Corey shrugged. "I'm the idol of a quarter of the kids in the world; I have to be good with them."

Taran frowned as she shook her head. "Don't do that."

"What?"

She crossed her arms. "You didn't *handle* having them ask you for an autograph like a trained pro. That's *not* what I meant. You connected with all three of them. Even if you never play with them again, they'll talk about you for the next year. And it's not because any of them realized you're Corey Matthews."

He shrugged. "I'm a kid person. Are you surprised? I'm like a ten-year-old. I literally play baseball and video games twenty-four seven."

She fell back into the couch, laughing. "You're such an idiot."

But he didn't feel like an idiot because that sparkle in her eyes and the smile were worth whatever it took to get there. A strange pull in his gut made him want to see that smile from now until forever.

He leaned close and let her soft scent encompass him. He ran the tip of his nose along the smooth skin of her jaw, and her breath caught. Corey pressed his lips into the hollow of her neck until she tilted her head back and moaned.

"Sex or food?" Corey asked as his lips danced down to her collarbone.

"Do I have to pick?" she asked.

"Only the order because I'm perfectly willing to have dessert first, but both are on the menu."

Her rumbling stomach made the decision easy. He wanted her, but he wanted to take care of her too.

"Dinner it is."

"Where did you learn to cook?" she asked, sitting on the island as he worked on the risotto.

"I like to eat, and I have a lot of time." He shrugged, but he watched her legs in the stainless-steel reflection. She'd taken off her heels, and her bare feet dangled. He'd never been a foot guy, but he wanted to run his lips from her feet up both legs. The risotto was on low, and the rest had about twenty minutes—enough time to focus on something else.

"Yeah, but this is like *real* cooking. I can do comfort food, but roasted asparagus with grated Asiago over a garlic risotto sounds like something I'd order at a five-star restaurant."

"Would you prefer something simpler?" he asked and held a spoon for her to taste. Her moan shot to his dick, which was already straining against his jeans.

"No, God no. This is amazing, Corey." She uncrossed her legs and let him step between them.

He tossed the spoon into the sink to rest his hands alongside her thighs and lean into her. Man, he wanted her to moan his name for a different reason. Right here on the island. He could push her back and taste something better than anything he could cook. Her scent tempted him as the silky strands of her hair tickled his jaw.

"But I want to know where you learned." Her words brought him back from the fantasy, but he didn't pull away. Just back far enough to look her in the eye.

"It's not a great mystery, Taran." He let his fingers run over the smooth skin of her lower thigh, slowly creeping them up under the cotton of her dress. "I had multiple personal chefs growing up. One on the east coast, one on the west coast, and one in the Florida Keys. A lonely only child to parents who didn't have time for me, so the staff became my friends. I also know how to wax a car and a boat, take care of horses, and power wash pavers."

"I'm sorry," Taran said, but her breath hitched as his hands circled under her ass, pulling her tight against his crotch.

"No one has a perfect life, but I have an idea if you want to make me feel better."

"Are you going to burn my risotto?" she asked, but she rocked her hips into him even as she said it.

"It would be worth it," he assured her, knowing he wouldn't.

"Hmm, I don't know about that."

"Challenge accepted, my little pain in the ass." He didn't let go of her ass as he lowered his mouth to claim hers.

Their lips met, and instantly, his entire body burned. Like the first time, their kiss was more than desire—it was need.

His tongue slipped into her mouth, owning it, touching every corner and marking it as his. The exact way he wanted to slide his dick deep into her body, driving them both to find that place that only existed with her. But first, he needed to taste her because she was a woman who deserved all the world's pleasures. And he was the man who wanted to give them to her.

Her hands snaked up under his T-shirt. Every brush of her delicate fingers was like an electric spark. He needed to feel all her sweet skin pressing against him. He reluctantly let go of her ass to pull his shirt over his head and toss it aside. The touch of her palms moving up his chest felt like a branding.

"So completely perfect," she mumbled, wrapping her arms around his neck and resting her forehead against his.

"So completely *yours*," he answered.

Her eye roll said she didn't believe his words, so he set out to prove it.

He pressed a kiss just under her jaw, smiling against her skin at the hum of pleasure rolling through her. Moving lower, he kissed her neck, shoulder, and collarbone. Slowly, he popped two buttons of her dress, his lips chasing his fast-working fingers. He paused to release the clasp of her bra and free her tits, letting them surround his face like soft pillows. The curve of her small breast kissed his cheek, and he couldn't resist running his tongue over it. As he teased the peak of a tight pink nipple, he glanced up to watch her.

Her head fell back, and a moan slipped past her lips. "Please." The almost silent plea ripped through him like wildfire, and he pressed his hips hard against her. He needed to make her feel good like he needed his next breath.

"Lie back," he commanded.

After the last of the buttons was undone, the dress spilled onto the counter, leaving her covered in only white lace. He groaned, appreciating the perfect buffet laid out for him.

Her breath caught in the best way as he blazed a trail up her inner thigh, teasing the soft skin.

"Damn, you're already wet," he said as his thumb traced the white lace.

"Don't sound surprised. You know what you're doing." She lifted her hips, forcing his thumb to press tighter against her slit. She whimpered when he gave it a slow, firm circle.

He couldn't help but smirk as he dropped his mouth to kiss her stomach, his tongue sinking into her belly button. He kissed both sides of her pelvis as her hips rocked up off the counter, begging him to show some attention to the place she wanted him most. He hooked the panties on his fingers, removing them so his tongue could lap over her.

The reward was a deep groan that would forever live in his fantasies. Between the sweet, breathy moans and the taste of her on his tongue, his control was hanging by a thread. But he needed to take care of her first. His tongue slowly lapped against her, but she wasn't having that.

"Please, Corey," she begged and grabbed his hair. He zeroed in on the bud of sensation that made her arch off the counter.

Damn, the way she rocked and moaned had him slamming hard against the counter just to keep himself in check.

"*Corey*." His name slowly dragged out of her lips, and he sucked as she convulsed on his face. He worked every drop of pleasure from her before grabbing the condom from his pocket and dropping his pants.

Taran still lay on the counter in front of him, and he

separated her legs, pulling her closer. Her hair was a mess from her head thrashing as she came. Her cheeks had a hint of red from the scrape of his beard. Her dress lay half on and half off her arms, and her pussy glistened, waiting for him.

"You're beautiful," he said, watching her spread out in front of him.

"You're horny," she replied and lifted to her elbows.

"No, you don't. Lie back; I like this view." He moved slowly into her tight wet heat. The groan ripped from deep in his chest as he sank in, watching her eyes roll back with every inch. She gripped him like she was his home. Like she was made for him. She arched up and closed the last distance so he bottomed out inside her.

Fuck. She felt incredible, and he worried this would be over too soon, but he needed to move. He swiveled his hips.

"Yeah," she moaned, urging him to do it again.

Once, twice, he pulled back to thrust deep into her heat.

"Harder, Corey."

Her wish was his command, and he pumped in and out. Instinct took over, leaving him rutting into her, hard and demanding. He was too close, so he dropped her leg to rub a tight circle on the bundle of her nerves, and she detonated. His heart raced as his control snapped while she milked his dick, gripping him like a tight wet fist. His stomach bottomed out, and he had to lock his legs so they didn't give out as he came in a burst of white-hot pleasure. He dropped her other leg and crashed onto his forearms above her.

"Holy shit, Taran," he huffed.

"Yeah, tell me about it," she answered. She was looking at him with those sparkling mist-green eyes, and without warning, something inside him cracked.

The decision seemed like a no-brainer at the moment, and the words spilled out of his mouth. "I have to go to a wedding in three weeks, and I'd really like you to be my date."

She tensed for a millisecond but relaxed quickly. "You want me to come to Mel Holly's wedding with you?"

"Yeah," he said. But the truth was he was starting to believe he wanted her everywhere. On his lap at beer night, on the sofa playing *Diablo*, on his counter while he cooked, and in his arms to sleep. Everything was better when this little spitfire was beside him. It was going to be a long nine days on the road without her, and who knows what their schedules would look like when he got back.

29

"GOD, I'VE MISSED you," Corey said in her ear as they swayed to the slow melody of the music. He'd been on the road for eight days, and when he got back, she was in Massachusetts with Jessica Walters. By the time Taran returned to Jersey, Corey was on the road again with the Metros.

They'd both flown into Miami that afternoon. But they hadn't even seen each other before the start of the ceremony because they'd gotten ready in separate hotel rooms. Although Taran thought it was a bit much, Corey assured her it wasn't. Everyone was on high alert for this wedding, and he was being followed when he wasn't with the team because the paparazzi assumed since he and Mel always claimed to be friends, he'd be invited. He said he was going to have to jump through hoops to get to the ceremony and he didn't want her to have to deal with it.

So far, she'd escaped the chaos because she'd been busy finishing Jessica's piece and setting up the following month's. She'd hardly seen Corey. The soccer star, Edgar DeLeon, had finally gotten back to her, and after her nephew Noah's rodeo this week, she was heading down to Guatemala to start work on him for her August column.

"I've missed you too. I feel like we haven't seen each other in forever," Taran agreed.

"Because we haven't. Our schedules *suck*," he pouted.

It was funny how much pouting the grown man had been doing in the last three weeks.

His hand ran along her hip, brushing over her ass. "I want to ditch this party and go back to my room."

His two-tone brown eyes turned liquid with his declaration.

"Basic wedding etiquette says we can't leave before the bride and groom cut the cake," Taran reminded him.

"Forget the rules—I need my girl." Corey's growl made her shiver. "I want to be wrapped up in all this soft skin." His thumb brushed along the open back of her dress. "And because I'm the best boyfriend in the world, I even pulled the *I'm famous and need special satin sheets* card."

She smiled as she rested her cheek against his white dress shirt. He was more than she would have ever expected. While she was busy with work, he'd made time to play *Diablo* with her family. He had all the Evanses call and check in on her when he was out of town. And during every interview, he managed to drop in the word chipmunk with a wink so that she'd know he was thinking of her. It was all swoony until she thought about her September article.

In the last three weeks, neither she nor Sean had gotten anywhere with getting Corey out of the article, and it was looking like she'd have to write it. Telling Corey was becoming more and more important, and she was feeling more like a dick every day she didn't. But it wasn't a conversation they could have on the phone. Nor did she think she could tell him in the middle of his very famous ex-girlfriend's wedding.

Mel and Hunter had done a fabulous job keeping the press away. The elegant mansion the couple had rented on the beach had been turned into a lush garden of green vines and white lilies. It belonged in a movie. Or a wedding for the movie stars. It was unbelievable to her that she was in a tent at the moment.

"No comment about the best boyfriend?" Corey asked. "Not even willing to let me own the title yet?"

"I agreed to the label last week, Cor."

"And I told you it doesn't count until you say the words." For one brief second, she heard the unusual vulnerability in his voice, and it cut at her. It wasn't that she didn't want to be together. It just didn't feel fair to label them until they had the conversation about the article. But she couldn't leave him feeling unworthy, because he was more than deserving.

She turned her head and let her lips press lightly against his neck. "My *boyfriend* looks hot in his navy-blue suit. Best looking guy in the room." Her breath bounced off his skin and brushed back against her lips.

He growled and pulled her tight, letting her feel his erection against her hip. "My *girlfriend* better be careful with that hot mouth of hers, or I might embarrass us both."

"I swear—why do you have to wreck every single wedding we go to?" the annoyingly high-pitched voice snapped from behind her.

The start of a growl rumbled in Corey's chest. Taran glanced up, but his face seemed impassive as he watched the couple over the top of her head.

"Come on, Genni." Will's voice was lower than his girlfriend's, but they were close enough for Taran to hear him.

"I'm not wrecking anything. I'm just not any more ready to propose now than I was in April. It's only been three months, for shit's sake."

"Well, maybe I should find someone who is," Genni snapped before Taran heard the tap of her heels walking off the dance floor.

"Maybe it's *me* who needs to find someone else." Taran barely heard Will before he brushed past them, heading straight to the bar.

"He does," Corey said.

"What?" Taran asked.

"That girl is a placeholder, and I think everyone but Will knows it." Corey pulled them off to the side of the dance floor, away from the crowd. He stood so he could watch his friend at the bar. "She's no one he's ever going to settle down with, and for whatever reason, Will has never felt like he wanted the dream."

"The dream?" Taran asked as she turned her head to watch Will talking to the bartender.

"You know, wife, kids, house." The statement was made without thinking, Taran could tell, but it shocked her.

"You dream about *that*?" she asked. Her attention jumped back to Corey.

His eyes widened comically. "Oh—uh—we used to talk about it. Nick, Luke, Grant, Will, and me. It wasn't that any of us thought it was a right-now thing, but, um, yeah. I never thought about what I'd do after I retired from pitching because—" He looked away. "Well." He swallowed. "I used to think I'd do the dad thing when I retired."

That flipped Taran's stomach. She could see it. She'd seen him with Beth's twins and with her older kids at Nick's wedding. She thought of the finger paintings and photos that covered his walls. The way he played with her niece and nephews. It wasn't hard to imagine him with kids of his own.

"You'd be a good dad, Corey," she said quietly.

He looked down, and just the corner of his mouth turned up. "I always wanted to have a family." He paused, but before she could jump in, he added. "Back then, I wanted kids because I wanted someone who would love me."

Every time he made those statements, he guttered her. Her heart ached for the kid he used to be. She wrapped her arms around his waist, and he leaned into her.

"That's not a reason to have kids, and I know that now. They're a lot of work. Look at Beth and Marc—they haven't slept in months."

"They seem to handle it together," she said.

"I always wanted that too."

Her breath caught at his last statement because she used to want that too. Before. Before she was broken. But the strange thing was, she'd never felt broken with Corey. He made her feel alive. He made her feel whole. He made her *feel.*

"Damn it," Corey said, and she looked up to see Will throw back another shot. "Give me a second, chipmunk."

She pinched his side hard, and he flinched. "I *hate* that."

But he laughed. "I know. That's why I picked it."

"You're so annoying."

He smirked. "But you like it."

Her gaze hung on his tight ass in the navy-blue suit pants as he walked away.

"The ass on that man," said a voice beside her.

Taran turned to agree, but her eyes widened at who stood beside her. "Oh wow, you're you. I mean. You're here." Taran winced as Mel Holly laughed at her. "Congratulations? Or—" Taran shook her head and swallowed. "I'm fangirling a little even though I promised myself I wouldn't, so just tell me to shut up, okay?"

She laughed again. "I came over to say hi and thank you, but if you really want me to tell you to shut up, I can."

"Thank you?" Taran asked, finally pulling herself together.

"He would never have come without you, so I appreciate you being here."

"She also planned to lecture you about not hurting our boy, but we can see that's not an issue," Hunter said.

And Taran's fangirling started again.

She opened her mouth and then shut it twice. "Hunter Cannon, I've literally seen all of your movies, and now I'm talking to you, and it's kinda blowing my mind. Thank God Corey is at the bar and not watching me act ridiculous."

Hunter shrugged. "If it makes you feel better, when Holly introduced me to your boyfriend, I called him my idol and asked him to sign my shirt."

"He did," Corey said, coming up behind Taran. "Stop overwhelming my girl or I will happily tell that story every time we're together."

"That was before I knew you were a dick." Hunter laughed.

His new wife whacked him in the stomach. "Corey's just an acquired taste."

"That's why you begged me to come today?" Corey rolled his eyes. But Taran couldn't stop the smile that pushed at her lips at the genuine affection between these three. Her mind flicked back to the conversation about just wanting to be loved. Corey had the kind of heart that made him so easy to love. It was crazy that anyone could not adore this man.

She swallowed hard at where her thoughts were heading; she couldn't fall for him. Not when it could all come crashing down around her as soon as he found out about the article. They had to talk about it tonight. It couldn't wait any longer.

"I hate to be that guy, but I'm leaving," Corey announced.

"Hey, I get you," Hunter said and put his fist up to Corey.

Corey's eyes cut to Taran and then back to Will at the bar. Taran got the silent message. Will needed him.

"Nice meeting you both," Taran said.

"I hope we see a lot more of you," Mel said.

Corey's hand on her back guided her away.

"Is he okay?" Taran asked.

"Yeah, she just makes him miserable, and yet he keeps coming back for more. Women make men stupid." He shook his head.

"I make you stupid?" Taran chuckled as she grabbed her purse from the table.

Corey threw on his navy suit jacket and cracked a teasing smile. "Probably." With his palm on her neck, he tipped her chin up with his thumb. His eyes softened, and the smile faded from his lips. "But you also make me better."

Her heart stuttered at the open truth in his eyes.

"I have a big ask."

"What?" Taran sounded breathless.

"You know how I said we'd have to leave separately?" Corey asked.

She understood—he didn't want them photographed walking into the hotel together. It made sense to her. She didn't want it either. If Wayne saw those photos, he'd question everything about the article. She'd convinced him to let her deal with Corey after she got back from Guatemala. Getting Edgar DeLeon had been a big win, especially since he was giving her a detailed look at the school he'd set up in his hometown. It was the first look into the place he'd spent the last two years working on. So Wayne was A-okay with her focusing on that and turning to Corey in August, giving her the time she needed to figure out how to tell him.

"I get it, Cor, it's really not a big ask to take our own car service." Her breath caught when he shook his head. Did he want her to leave with him? She couldn't do that. She swallowed hard.

His gaze shot back to Will. "He just downed his fourth shot in twenty minutes. It's going to hit him hard. I can't drag him into a hotel drunk in front of the cameras. He coaches kids." Corey's jaw locked. "When I walked into a bar with Marc after Mel and I broke up last year, social media blew up, claiming Marc and I were dating. Will doesn't need the attention."

She remembered that desperate plea for clicks that a few outlets used last year. It had been ridiculous. But at the same time, there was a reason it worked.

"I don't know if anyone has ever said this, but your stance on giving outlets nothing does cause some of the drastic attention you get." Taran tried to be careful with her words, but Corey went rigid. His eyes hardened, and he flexed his jaw. "Corey, I wasn't saying—"

He held up his hand, and his body relaxed. "I know you mean well. I've heard it before. I'm not testing the theory by dragging my drunk best friend into a hotel." He cracked his neck left and then right. "But maybe you could give me some pointers or ideas this week when we're back home."

Her entire being jumped. Did she hear that right? Might he be more open to the idea of a story than she thought? But he thought she was coming back to Jersey?

"Wait—you remember I'm going to my parents' in Katy and then down to work on Edgar's article, right?"

"Shit." Corey pushed his hand through hair. "So, another three weeks apart. Why don't you seem bothered by this?"

Taran shrugged. "I am, but I'm used to it. Jeremy and I spent months at a time apart. Between being at two different colleges, his BUD/s training, then his active duty deployments, we were apart a lot."

Corey wrapped his arms around her and pulled her into him. "Well, I hate it. Are you still in Houston next Friday?"

"Katy, but yes." Her voice was mumbled because of his jacket.

"We're playing the Astros. I could get you tickets."

"As long as you don't care that I'll be wearing my Astros hat and cheering against you." She glanced up to watch him roll his eyes.

"Of course you will, chipmunk." Corey's chuckle cut off when Taran pinched his waist. "Ouch, that hurt." He pulled back.

"Then stop with the rodent nonsense." Taran raised an eyebrow at him.

"Unlikely, but back to my big ask, which seems even bigger now that I remembered you're leaving again." His tone held so much complaint it was hard not to smile. "Can you get Will to our hotel room? He needs a place to stay. Knowing him, he'll let Genni lock him out of their room even if it means he sleeps at the airport. And if he stays here, she's just going to keep causing a scene."

Taran's eyes cut to the gorgeous woman in question currently chatting up an older man.

"He's a producer, but she's just trying to get Will to give her a reaction."

She nodded. "Go ahead. We'll see you in a bit."

He kissed her before heading out. She watched him go, wondering if he'd really implied that he'd be open to some media attention. Although Will staying with them meant she couldn't talk to Corey about the article tonight, maybe if they chatted about her other articles while she was gone, it wouldn't be the blow she was expecting. Perhaps he'd even be okay with her writing his story.

Just before he walked out the door, he turned back and sent her a heart-stopping smile and a two-finger wave. For the first time, she wondered how she would write his feature piece, because that man had become so much more to her than a story.

30

HIS LITTLE PAIN in the ass was probably going to kill him. He wasn't sure if Taran liked surprises. According to the GPS in his rental car, he'd arrive at his destination in less than five minutes. Guess he was going to find out.

She'd been great with Will the night of the wedding. Taran got him out of the reception and back to Corey's suite in what must have been record time. While he and Will talked, she ordered room service and took care of getting Will's bag delivered to the hotel. And as soon as Will called it a night, Corey took her to their room and properly thanked her. She'd just called it teamwork, which settled firmly in his chest in the best possible way.

It was strange to him to be the needy one in the relationship. In the past, he'd stay busy and coast through the time until he and his girlfriend were back together. It was different with Taran; he wanted to *make* time to see her, even if it wasn't easy. Which led to getting permission to skip the game in Atlanta, completing his workout early, and jumping on a flight to Houston. It was already two o'clock, and he had to leave before six to make it back to the hotel and check in with the team. As unpractical as it was, he couldn't be this close and not see her.

Especially since the craziness of Mel and Hunter's wedding had died down, and they had released a statement and some photos to the press. It completely stopped the frenzy of when would it be, what would it look like, and who would be invited. Corey had been thinking a lot this week about what Taran said. She might be right that releasing small bits of information could keep the press off his back. But if he was interested in that, he'd have to hire a publicist. And an agent. It was ridiculous that he still hadn't done it.

Next week, he had the all-star break, but he was playing this year, so he wouldn't get time off. There was a two-week home stretch in August, though. Taran would be back from her trip to Guatemala by that point, and maybe if he asked, she'd help him find the right agent.

The large metalwork arch announced his arrival at her parents' ranch, and he drove under the burnt red and black sign with the Texas star. Taran had sent him pictures of the land, the cows, and her nephew's rodeo all week, but the view still had him whistling. The flat land made the green pastures seem endless. What a place to grow up. He shook his head as he parked in front of the sprawling one-story home. The front porch stretched the length of the house. It was peppered with white rocking chairs and ceiling fans. Large unpolished stone overlapped to make a path from the gravel driveway to the front steps.

He pushed open his door and was hit with the familiar blast of Texas summer inferno. A quick internal debate had him pulling out his phone to call her while he leaned against his car to wait.

"Aren't you supposed to be at the game?"

"I'm pitching tomorrow, so I took a mental health day," Corey answered.

"Are you okay?" Her genuine concern had him almost backing out of his plan.

"I'm not sure I'm in a good spot." Corey bit his cheek.

"Give me a second to go out on the porch where we can talk. I've got too many eyes on me at the moment."

The front door opened, and Taran's small frame moved outside. She was in his favorite cutoffs with a black tank top that probably said something ridiculous, but he couldn't see it. He ended the call.

She glanced down at her phone. "Did he just hang up on me?" Taran said the words aloud, but Corey had no idea who she thought she was talking to.

"I figured it would be easier without the phones," Corey called out, and Taran jerked, bobbling her phone as she spun toward him.

"Corey?" Her smile made the short trip worth it.

She hop-skipped down the large, flat rocks and straight into his arms. He lifted her right off her feet, pressing her tight into him. The floral scent that was all Taran hit his nose at the same time the satiny strands of her hair danced around his jaw.

"How are you here?" Her lips brushed his ear, and he had to swallow a groan.

"Got a few hours off, and I missed you, chipmunk."

As it always did, the mention of the tiny rat-like creature got Taran heated up.

She pulled away, and he set her down.

"You know"—her eyebrow shot up—"I've heard chipmunks bite."

The grin split his lips so fast he couldn't stop it. "I like it. Sounds kinky." He waggled his eyebrows, and she whacked him in the stomach.

"You're impossible." Taran spun back toward the house. As always, she stretched the beat of playing mad for about five counts before she glanced back over her shoulder. "Brace yourself. You have no idea what you're walking into."

"What?" he trotted up the steps to catch her. "What do you mean?"

He'd never heard her say anything bad about her parents.

She paused with her hand resting on the wrought-iron handle of the enormous wooden door. "In this house, we live and breathe the Astros. It's like: God, family, the Astros—in that order—and you left daddy's team to play for the biggest rival we have."

Corey froze. "Wait. Taran."

She didn't stop, and he trailed behind as she headed into the big open foyer.

"I was traded. He knows that, right?" It probably said something about his ego that it had never occurred to Corey that her family wouldn't like him. But the idea that he'd start off having them all hate him *wasn't cool*.

She shrugged. "There was talk about prissy boys demanding trades."

Shit. He heard the noise coming from the back of the house, and it sounded almost as chaotic as Beth and Marc's on beer night. So it seemed likely it wasn't just her parents here.

"Who's here?" Corey asked.

"Everyone; it's Sunday dinner. We were just sitting down to eat when you called. So you're walking into an entire slew of 'Stros fans."

Corey cracked his neck. How hard could it be to win over her family? She'd hated him at first, and he'd changed her opinion. Plus, he'd won a world series for the Astros. He might have been traded to Metros a year later, but he was still the pitcher who won game seven and brought home the title.

"I'll win them over, don't worry. You're worth the work."

Her mouth dropped open, and her eyes softened. "Darn it, Corey." She crossed her arms. "Why are you being sweet? I was messing with you to get back for the rodent nickname." Her arms fell to her sides, and she stretched up on her toes to kiss him.

Not that he'd ever complain when her soft lips pressed against his, but he was confused as hell. So as soon as she pulled back, he asked.

"Huh?"

"They love Corey Matthews, so you'll be fine. Come on." She grabbed his hand and dragged him through a swinging door into the back of the house.

The door opened into a large dining room with a full table. All eyes swung to them the second they were through the door.

"My boyfriend stopped by," Taran said flippantly, like it wasn't a big deal, but her family stared, wide-eyed, at him.

Shocked fans were a regular part of his life, but Corey wasn't sure what type of shock he was dealing with.

He scanned the group. It was easy to pick out her parents. Her father had the build of a man who'd worked hard in the fields for years. The black hair filled in with gray, causing the salt and pepper look. Her mother was just as petite as Taran and had the same eyebrows, which were currently cocked in surprise. Her sister and brother had to be the other two dark-haired adults at the table because they had the delicate facial features that matched Taran's. He could even see the resemblance in the two teenagers and the two younger girls.

"I play *Diablo* with *you*?"

Corey recognized Bryce's voice and glanced over to see him sitting with a fork half way to his mouth.

"Yeah, did you check out the new patch?" he asked.

Bryce blinked, and the shock disappeared as the fork clattered to his plate. "Man, my new Barb melee looks tight, but I swear it's totally marshmallow."

"Marshmallow?"

Corey turned to the blonde at the table that must be Bryce's mother. "Soft. He loses lots of hit points when he wears it."

"I keep telling you it wouldn't be an issue if you cast more. I'm the monk. I should be tanking it; learn how to play," Noah said.

A flush spread across Bryce's cheeks as his glare tore through his older brother. Corey knew the look, and Noah would pay for the comment at some point.

"He's right; if we want to try the new category, everyone needs to stay in their lane," Corey agreed, walking closer to the boys at the far end of the table.

"It would help if we weren't stuck with a witch doctor and wizard," Bryce complained.

"Don't pick on the girls," Corey said. "Remember my life goals."

A throat cleared, and Corey turned to the rest of the table.

"What life goals?" Taran's brother asked.

"Get Aunt Taran to like him. Duh, Uncle Tristan." Crystal giggled.

A few others chuckled.

Her father stood up and walked over with his hand out. "Jake Kuppton."

"Corey Matthews." He shook his hand.

"I know who you are. I'm familiar with you on the field." Jake's eyes cut to his daughter. "Seems Taran forgot to mention who you were to her."

Taran moved next to him, crossing her arms over the words on her tank top. "I told you I was dating someone."

Jake scoffed, then nodded to the table. "You seem to know my grandkids, but this is my wife, Michelle." He pointed to the woman who had Taran's green eyes. "This is my son, Tristan, his wife, Dana." He moved down the table. "My son-in-law, Ben, and my daughter, Teagan, whose smirk is telling me she was well aware of who her sister's been dating."

"Lord love a duck. You're better looking in person." Teagan's comment had her husband rolling his eyes, but Corey glanced at his girl.

"Did she just pray to a bird?"

"Yeah." Taran shook her head. "I don't get it either."

Jake covered his laugh with a cough. "Join us. There's plenty of food. Taran, grab the man a plate."

"Thank you, Mr. Kuppton," Corey said as he sat in the empty chair next to Bryce.

"Jake would be just fine, especially since I intend to call you jackass tomorrow if you beat my 'Stros."

Everyone laughed at that, and even Corey had to smile.

"Pops!" Dana chided. "Not in front of the kids."

"Not his worst," Michelle announced as she passed a plate of steak to Corey.

Taran sat in the chair next to him, setting a plate down. Corey ate and discussed *Diablo,* baseball, and cows. Although he'd had a minute of panic walking in, Taran's family welcomed him without any issue, even though he played for the Metros.

"The steak's incredible. You raise cow well," Corey said after he swallowed his last bite.

"Uck." Taran gagged. "Don't remind me that used to be Bessie." She moved her broccoli around on her plate. Corey glanced down at Taran's shirt and snorted as the words finally came into focus. He tried but failed to stifle a laugh.

"It's true," Taran said, looking at her shirt.

"What does it say?" Noah asked.

"Read it," Crystal replied.

"He can't read," Bryce said, and Noah turned bright red.

A conversation Corey'd had with Taran played in his mind. Noah had dyslexia and struggled as much, maybe more than Corey did with reading and that made the teasing remark hit too close.

Corey's stomach sank as he took in Noah's embarrassment. He remembered that feeling well. Noah glanced to the ground, unable to look at Corey even as the adults around them all jumped to his aid. None of the words were helping Noah, and Corey understood. He wanted to say something, but Noah got up and left the room before he could.

His dad, Tristan, pushed to his feet, but Corey held his hand out.

"If you don't mind, I might be able to help."

Tristan's eyes shot to Taran, who nodded.

"Go ahead."

Corey stood and headed down the same hallway Noah had gone, finding him, ironically, in a room full of bookshelves.

Corey banged his knuckle against the door and then waited for Noah.

"It's okay. You don't need to come in and tell me ten things that are supposed to make me feel better." Noah stood, staring out the window into the fields. Corey'd played enough with Noah to know the kid was usually friendly and easy-going, but his hackles were up now. And why wouldn't they be? It was hard to be fifteen and struggle with something most eight-year-olds could do. Hell, it was hard to be over thirty and struggle with stuff eight-year-olds could easily do.

"God only lets us grow until we're perfect. Some of us just don't take as long as others," Corey replied as he walked into what looked like a study.

Noah's head spun toward him. "What?"

"You asked what your aunt's shirt said, right?"

"Oh," Noah chuckled. "Because she's short but thinks she's perfect."

"You know her well," Corey said, and he sat down on the leather sofa.

Noah glanced back out the window. Unlike his aunt, Noah was tall and lanky, but he had the same dark hair and complexion.

"You know I've been here for an hour," Corey said.

"I guess." Noah didn't turn back.

Corey swallowed. The kid needed to hear this, even if Corey hated saying it. "It took me that long to read her shirt. I was nervous when I first got here, which made it hard for my brain to make sense of the words. A lot of people tried to teach me tricks over the years to help me read better."

Noah turned, wide-eyed, to Corey, but he kept going.

"When I'm nervous or tired or even stressed about something, the letters jumble. And the more frustrated I get about it, the harder it gets to do it."

"*You* have dyslexia?"

Corey nodded.

"I never knew that."

"Most people don't. And in some ways, it gets easier. The tricks they teach you, the ways to help you focus on the words, they will help. But I'm not going to pretend that I don't sometimes stare at words all day and never know what they say."

"Me too," Noah admitted. "It's why I like roping better than reading."

"Your aunt tells me you're pretty good at that," Corey said.

"You're good at baseball, so who needs to read."

Corey shook his head. "I do, and so do you. It might be hard, but doing hard things—working for something—that's what builds character."

Noah rolled his eyes.

"I don't text a lot, probably for the same reasons you don't. But I'd like to give you my phone number so if you ever want to talk, you can call me." Corey pulled out his phone. He typed in the number Noah gave and sent off the text. "I sent you something."

"What?" Noah asked.

"Four tickets to tomorrow's game. Bring whoever you want." Corey paused before he qualified. "As long as one of the people you want is your aunt."

"Aunt Teagan's not that into baseball, but I guess I could ask her." Noah smirked.

Corey chuckled. "Oh, you got the jokes, huh?"

"I had to teach him something," Jake said from behind them.

"Sorry, Pops. I know I'm not allowed in here." Noah stood up from beside Corey.

"Extenuating circumstance. I'll give you a pass," Jake said as he moved into the room.

"Want to come with me tomorrow to the Astros game? Your favorite pitcher ever gave me tickets." Noah said.

Corey's eyes widened at the remark.

"I'm not sure I'd say favorite. But I always love to watch the 'Stros win." Jake leaned back against his desk and crossed his arms.

"You've always said he's your favorite. You should have him sign his rookie card. How cool would that be?" Noah rocked onto the balls of his feet and pointed over to the shelf Corey hadn't noticed. "You'd do it, right?"

"*Noah*," Jake's voice warned.

"Sorry, sir," Noah said quickly and headed out the door.

"I'd be happy to sign it for you, sir." Corey stood up and headed for the shelf covered in Astros stuff. His gaze narrowed as he got closer. "Holy shit," he muttered, grabbing the picture of himself off the shelf.

"I wondered about that," Jake said from behind him. "She was finishing up her reign as Miss Teen Texas. If I recall correctly, the world series game was her last official outing. That's her late fiancé with her."

Corey stared at the eight-year-old photo at game seven of the world series. He stood between a young man in Navy dress whites and a younger version of Taran in a red dress, white sash, and crown. He vaguely remembered being pulled off warm-ups for the publicity shot with little miss sunshine. It seemed impossible the bubbly teenager had been Taran.

"She was always the brightest spot in the family; so happy. Had plans to save the world one story at a time."

Corey looked up at Jake's reflective tone. He stood in the same spot, leaning against the desk.

"I probably wouldn't recognize her as the same girl either, and I'm her father. That accident changed her. Pretty quickly, that bright light became a snarky pain in the ass who silently flips the world off one rude T-shirt at a time."

Corey set the photo down. "No disrespect, sir, but that snarky pain in the ass is becoming the best part of my life."

"Since your days with the 'Stros, you've been popular in this family." Jake tilted his chin toward the photo on the shelf. "But my daughter has been through enough. So don't think your standin' with this family won't drop drastically if you hurt her."

"Did you just threaten Corey Matthews?" Taran asked from the doorway.

Jake smirked at his daughter as he pushed his hip from the desk and headed toward her. "*Who* he is isn't as important as *what* he is and how he treats you, kid."

Jake patted his daughter on the shoulder before leaving the room.

"Whatever you said to Noah was perfect. I've never seen him bounce back from his brother's teasing that fast before," Taran said.

"Glad I could help."

"I'm not pushing," Taran paused, and Corey braced for what she might say, "but there are a ton of kids who may benefit from hearing how their hero has battled and overcome their same demons."

Corey swallowed. He got what she was saying. He should talk about it, and helping Noah feel more confident had felt good. Corey knew it would have made a world of difference in his life if someone had spoken to him as a child—told him that it would get better.

"I'll think about it," he promised. Because if there was a person who could tell his story right, it was the woman across the room. But he didn't want to talk about it anymore right now. "You didn't tell me we'd met before, chipmunk." Corey picked up the photo of them.

Taran groaned, but Corey wasn't sure if it was about the nickname or the photo. She scuffed her Converse against the carpet twice before looking up at him. He was still standing by her dad's Astros shelf, and she finally moved toward him to take the picture out of his hands.

"That girl in the crown and the dress? Yeah, you met her. But she's gone." Taran swallowed.

Corey wrapped his arms around her tiny waist, and she melted into him. The warmth of her cheek pressed against his heart.

"She disappeared two years ago, and even though a lot of people wish she would come back. I'm not her anymore."

"I'm sorry for what you went through, Taran." Corey pressed his lips against the crown of her head. "But I'm not sorry that girl is gone. She was a dime a dozen. I barely remember her. But the woman in my arms right now—the one I bumped into in the parking garage three months ago? I can't stop thinking about *her*."

31

"THESE ARE THE best seats we've ever had!" Noah's excitement was contagious, and it had both her dad and her brother smiling.

He'd been glowing since he and Corey talked yesterday. It was a huge step for Corey to admit anything about his dyslexia to Noah. Even more so that he was willing to consider talking about it publicly.

Taran wondered if an article about thriving with dyslexia might be something Corey would be willing to do for the September feature. A story about overcoming something and being successful would do wonders for so many kids struggling with all kinds of things.

"These seats are definitely not something to sneeze at, that's for sure," her father said.

They were two rows back from the corner of the dugout, close enough to home plate that they'd probably hear the umpire's calls.

Tristan smirked. "Seems like they were chosen for a reason."

"What do you mean?" Noah asked his father.

"Corey's right-handed." Her brother adjusted his Astros hat and moved into the seat next to his son. "Watch where he looks between pitches."

Noah still looked lost, but Taran got what Tristan was saying. The seats were in Corey's line of sight.

"Shut up," she mumbled as she moved to the seat in front of him.

"You're really going to sit next to me wearing that shirt?" Her dad frowned.

"I'm surprised you even walked next to her, Pops."

"It's not like it's a jersey. And I'm wearing an Astros hat." Taran glanced down at the oversized white T-shirt. It had the Metros logo on it, but the words were the reason she'd bought it.

"I was told to check my attitude. I did. Still 100 percent New York badass." Noah read the words slowly, but he was trying, and that spoke to just how much talking with Corey had helped his self-esteem.

"You're fifteen, not forty. Watch your mouth, son," Tristan chided.

Taran rolled her eyes. At fifteen, her brother's mouth was a million times worse. When her phone buzzed, she glanced down at it, then stood and headed away from the seats.

"Text me if you want anything to drink," she called over her shoulder.

Once she was in the large open area near the concession stands, she answered the call.

"Hey, Seb."

"T-cup, just calling to see where we're meeting tonight."

Her eyes widened and she pulled the phone away from her ear to look at the date. Uh-oh. It was the fifteenth. For the last two years, they'd had monthly check-in dinners. And she'd canceled on him the last four times. Not the day of the plans though.

"You forgot?" he asked. There was no judgment in his tone, but he sounded concerned.

"Uh, yeah, I'm sorry. I'm down in Katy."

"Oh, tell your parents hello." He paused. "You forgetting a lot or just this one thing?"

Taran's jaw clenched; she knew where he was going with this. It wasn't a lot. Yeah, she'd missed a couple of things, and showed up at the wrong time for events once in a while. She'd messed up and sent the contracts to her boss. And losing track of time like this meant it was going to be really tight getting this month's article done, but she was fine.

"I get that you and the rest of the team have to fight through PTSD every day. I do. The nightmares, the flashbacks, the triggers, the mood swings. But I'm *fine*." Her tone was a bit too biting.

He sighed. "PTSD looks different for everyone. Have you been back to your therapist—"

"Look." He might mean well, and she knew, he felt, as Jeremy's best friend, it was his job to watch out for her now that Jeremey was gone, but she was tired of this. "I don't need a therapist. I don't need to hash this out with you all the time. I'm busy, and life has been stressful for a few weeks." Her voice raised, and her tone cut hard as the tight knot that always sat inside her burned. "I'm fine, and I need you to just back off." She slammed her hand into the garbage can lid beside her, sending it crashing into the wall, paper and cups flying.

Heads turned, and a security guard moved toward her as someone called.

"Hell yeah! New York badass!"

She hung up and slammed the phone into the back pocket of her cutoffs before bending down to help the poor security guard clean up her mess.

"I'm sorry," she said.

The older man gave her a nod. "I sure wouldn't want to cross you."

It took two minutes to finish with the garbage can and get back to her seat.

"So, no drinks?" her brother asked.

"What?" Taran asked.

"Didn't you say text you if we wanted drinks?"

Shoot. She forgot. She clenched her jaw. It was just one small thing. Well, two, if you counted dinner with Seabass. But she wasn't struggling. The tight knot inside burned again, and she swallowed.

"Don't worry. I got it." Tristan stood up and headed up the stairs.

"Everything okay, girlie?" her dad asked, lifting his hand to rub her shoulder. "You look—" He paused to study her face. "Actually, you looked pissed."

The surprise in his voice reminded her of how little emotion she'd shown over the last few years. She sighed, trying to rein in these feelings she didn't even want.

"Hey, you're allowed to be angry. I just asked if everything's okay." His concerned tone was everything she hated about the last few years.

"I'm good, let's just watch the game." Taran turned her attention to the field but her hope for an uneventful evening went out the window pretty quickly.

The first few innings of three batters up and three down didn't really register. Corey was pitching well, and she was happy for him. But it wasn't until after the fifth inning that the mumblings of a no-hitter started. By inning seven, it was becoming clear he was on his way to a perfect game. Not only had Corey not let up a hit, he hadn't walked a batter either.

"Yeah, Corey," Noah cheered loudly from beside her as Corey threw another strike to end the seventh inning. Somewhere along the line, Noah had forgotten he was wearing an Astros jersey and was full-out cheering for the Metros.

Taran clapped too, but the nerves were starting in her stomach. Corey might be on his way to pitching his first perfect game.

Tim Tillerson yanked up the mask covering his face as he jogged to meet Corey halfway to the dugout. The two talked as they headed off the field. Right before Corey stepped into the dugout, his gaze flicked her way. Their eyes met and he winked. She didn't have time to react before he disappeared.

"He does that every time!" Noah elbowed her in the side.

"Told you he chose the seats on purpose," Tristan teased from behind her.

A slight tingle of embarrassment swam with the nerves in her system. Along with something else that pulled at her stomach. It was overwhelming. She clenched her fists and tried to beat it back.

All too soon, Corey was back out on the mound for the bottom of the eighth. Taran wrung her hands together; it was stressful helplessly watching it play out. The first batter went down swinging. She didn't know how Corey did it because he looked calm out on the field, standing on the mound in his dark green jersey.

A snap echoed through the air as the throw from Tillerson hit Corey's glove. Corey bent at the waist and sent Tillerson a nod before he stood up. His windup was clean and elegant. He'd always been touted as a work of art throwing the ball. Taran could see it, the lift of his leg, the pull back, and the snap of his elbow.

The ball cracked against the bat, and Taran yanked her eyes from Corey to see the first baseman easily catch the pop-up. Taran let out her breath. The inning ended with a ground out and another wink that once again flipped her stomach.

Although the game was fast-paced, it still felt like nine innings of torture. She had sat through plenty of perfect games before, and none of them had been this nerve-racking. But it was different this time because it was Corey. She shifted and swallowed the lump in her throat.

The Metros scored another two runs in the top of the ninth, which normally would have had her father spitting mad. But even her dad was rooting for Corey as he struck out batter number one in the ninth.

"I think he's going to do it, Taran," he said.

Corey was officially two outs away from his first perfect game as a major league pitcher. Something he desperately wanted before he hung up his glove.

"Two more batters," Tristan agreed.

But those two had been saying that for the last two innings, while she'd been fighting back nausea. She glanced at Corey again; he stood calmly on the mound with the ball in his mitt. The black number four stood out on the green jersey. In his signature move, he cracked his neck left and then right before he leaned down, watching the catcher for the signal. Corey stood up for the windup, and Taran shut her eyes and held her breath.

"Striiike."

She slowly let out the breath.

"Girl, you're missing the whole inning," her dad said, chuckling at her.

"I hate this game," she huffed. But she wanted this for Corey. She wanted lots of things for Corey. Success, happiness. Love.

Her heart tripped on the word, and she clenched her fists again. She wasn't going there. Not now.

"Striiike," the ump called again.

"Oh God," Taran whispered, still not watching.

"You're so weird, Aunt Taran. Strikes are good," Noah said. "I can't believe we get to watch him pitch a perfect game."

"I've never been at a perfect game before." Her dad squeezed her shoulder. "I'm glad it's Matthews, even if it's against my 'Stros."

She wasn't watching, but she heard the crack of the bat against the ball, and her eyes shot up. Her heart skipped two beats before she saw the ball flying high and long into the outfield. She swallowed. One hit would ruin the entire game. She fisted her hands and finally relaxed as the ball smacked into the center fielder's glove.

Out.

She glanced to Corey to see how he was taking it, and surprisingly, his eyes were on her. Taran sent him a small, encouraging smile, and he shook his head, laughing before the next batter stepped into the box.

"I'm surprised he can concentrate with the way he keeps watching you," Tristan said to her and rumpled the Astros hat on her head. "You got that boy all kinds of twisted up."

"Shut up," she replied and shut her eyes again before hearing the umpire's call of strike.

"Hey, we're all really happy for you. We all thought you'd given up on love," Tristan continued.

"Tristan, I'm about to have a heart attack, so if you want to have a heart to heart, can we please wait until this game is over?" she asked before she heard the crack and shot her head up.

Foul.

The next two pitches were balls. Two strikes, two balls, two outs, and a perfect game on the line.

Taran nibbled on her fingernail as she looked at Corey again. He turned to glance at her, shook his head, laughed, and then snagged the ball Tim tossed at him.

"T, this is history. You have to watch this pitch," her father informed her.

She forced herself to watch, even if she couldn't breathe.

The next minute was a blur. She heard *strike three; you're out*, and she jumped to her feet along with the rest of the ballpark to cheer the man who'd just accomplished the rarest feat in baseball. The team rushed him, and the catcher handed him the ball.

A wave of desire to run to him, hug him, celebrate with him ached deep inside her. But the world was watching. And Corey didn't do public. And for the first time since she'd agree to keep their relationship quiet, Taran wanted something different. Something more, and that yearning twisted the knot inside her. This entire day had been way too much.

Corey pulled away from the group, searching the stands for the only person he really wanted to see. She stood with her family, clapping. All her nerves seemed to have washed away.

She'd been so cute. The nervousness, her inability to watch, her nail-biting anxiety. It had all been what kept him grounded. Knowing she was there, in the crowd, rooting for him while wearing her *damn* Astros hat. It made the game easy. He'd never in his life had so much fun pitching a game. And it was because of her.

It sucked that she wasn't standing next to him. Celebrating with him. Just like she wouldn't be at any of the all-star events next week—because he'd insisted they remain a secret.

A hand grabbed the back of his head and turned it.

"I wouldn't watch her. The world's eyes are on you right now." Daily's low voice was hard to hear over the craziness.

The flash out of the corner of his eye caught his attention. Daily was right; he couldn't stare forever because the press would ask what he was looking at. And he couldn't run over and demand she come down onto the field with him because, although he now was 100 percent sure he wanted this, it was something they had to talk about. He knew it would affect her job—she was still a sports reporter. When she got back from Guatemala, they had to talk about it and figure out the best way to move forward.

It wasn't impossible—athletes dated reporters all the time. But he wanted it spun in the best light. His eyes flicked back to Taran. She had her head tilted to the side, clearly listening to something Noah was saying. She smiled, and his heart lurched in his chest.

"Dude, you hear me?" Daily smacked him hard on the back of the head. "I know this is hashtag life dream, and pitching the perfect game should be about you, but it's *not*. You have to be the Cap'n for the world right now."

Right. He shook his head; time to be Captain-America Corey Matthews. He could be the-guy-falling-in-love Corey Matthews later. He missed his step as the thought hit him.

Damn. He swallowed.

He wasn't falling.

He'd already *fallen*.

It felt like the ground shifted and life had changed, but he glanced around, seeing everything was the same. He had an interview to do, so he swallowed hard, placed himself in front of the dugout, and turned to the reporters. He forced his token smile.

"You guys have ten questions, and then I'll give you a fun fact about chipmunks."

33

"THIS CAMPUS IS almost as big as the original," Taran said as she spun. The grass and buildings that made up this school, which currently took students from third grade through high school, could have been anywhere. But the fact that it was nestled in a small town in one of the more rural areas of Guatemala was impressive.

Taran, Edgar, and two of his security personnel, or as he called them, personal assistants, had made the four-hour drive from Guatemala City to this school together. They'd been here for about an hour and had already finished touring the buildings.

"Just because I keep these satellite schools more private than the original doesn't mean they aren't expanding." Edgar smirked.

The sun beat down on her. Much like in Texas, the summer here was hot, and the back of her shirt was damp with sweat. But the school buildings had fans and even a few portable air conditioning units to keep the temperature inside low so the kids could focus on their studies.

"How hard was it to get the electric and cell towers out here?" Taran asked.

"Wasn't the easiest. That is for certain. And it was costly.

However, it's helped many of the towns around. So, the local governments were cooperative."

What he didn't say but Taran had learned in the past few days as they toured one school and the next was that the man was determined. And his professional athlete status greased lots of wheels to make things happen.

"This is the last one. You've been very quiet all week. Watching, listening, but not much talking." Edgar wiped the sweat off his brow and crossed his arms.

Known in the soccer world for being one of the fiercest defenders of all time, his scowl supported his reputation. He was serious and hyper-focused. But he was also passionate about these schools.

"I'm here to learn about you, not talk." Taran shrugged.

"In every article, you focus on a single point of character. Do you know what you'll be focusing on?" he asked.

There were always two types: the one who didn't worry about her story and let her do her job, and the ones who questioned everything. Until this moment, she thought Edgar was more in the first category, because in the week she'd been with him, he hadn't asked for details about the article at all.

"Most people think it's skill that got you to the top of the soccer world, but I think it was single-minded determination to succeed. It's the same reason you're successful with these charter schools."

The scowl faded to an almost smile, but before he could answer, the bell rang, and kids hurried by them to get to their next classrooms. The school enrolled just over three hundred kids, and most were high school age.

Edgar waved and fist-bumped some kids, praising them for improvements that seemed amazingly detailed for him to know. He scowled at others, reminding them that he was watching their progress, almost as if he was the principal instead of the owner.

Her phone buzzed in her pocket, and she pulled it out, expecting a photo from Corey. Although he didn't text often, he sent pictures of whatever he was doing or sometimes a short video clip. But this time, he was calling.

She moved away from the chaos to pick up.

"Hey, you."

"Chipmunk."

Taran had hated that at first. But every time he dropped the word into post-game interviews and the way his voice took on a soft rumble when he said it had it growing on her.

"How's Cali? Sunny and seventy-five?" Taran asked.

Corey grunted. "It's fine."

Taran's stomach flipped; something was off with him. Her first thought was that he'd found out about the article, but that was impossible. Wayne agreed to let Taran handle it to ensure Corey wouldn't get spooked and cancel.

"What's wrong?" She tried not to sound hesitant.

"Tonight's the all-star dinner, and I've been to eight of these things already." Corey sighed.

"Not in the mood for a media event?" Taran asked.

"I'm never in the mood for a media event, but that's not it. Where are you?"

"I'm at the last school."

"*Fuck*. It's never a good time. We can't catch a break, even on the phone."

It was true. This week, she'd called once when he was in the locker room and left two messages when he was working out. He'd called her in the middle of dinner with Edgar, while she was in the media box at his soccer game, and when she was touring the first school.

"I'm just going to talk, and you can listen because you probably can't say much." He took a breath. "I'm sick of being alone at all these events."

Taran shut her eyes, unsure of what he meant.

"I know I insisted we keep things away from the public eye, and even as I'm saying this, I know this should be a conversation we have in person. But we spend more than half our time apart, so we need to learn to have tough conversations on the phone."

"Okay." Taran's heart pounded a bit in her chest, and she wasn't sure why.

"I want us to be in a place where you can come to an all-star dinner, or I can drag you on the field to celebrate with me after I pitch a perfect game." Frustration laced his tone as he growled into the phone. "I want to figure out a way to make that happen. And I know there are complications that we need to work through. But I need to know if I'm the only one falling—" He stopped.

Her eyes flew open. A fluttering that started in her stomach echoed across her body and down to the tips of every finger. He didn't say the words, but she heard them in his statement.

"Corey," she whispered.

"Tell me I'm not alone in this, chipmunk." That vulnerability in his voice that cut through her every time it came out echoed hard.

"You're not."

He blew out a hard breath, as if a giant weight had lifted off him.

"You get home first, but when my plane lands on Saturday night, I'm coming straight to you. Until then, can you think about the best way to do this? How to handle the media?"

"Me?" she asked and swallowed hard.

He just gave her the perfect reason to suggest she write a story about him. She'd have to tell him the entire situation, but this could mean it wouldn't be so bad if they talked.

"I trust you more than anyone else, and I need help."

She'd never wanted to earn someone's trust so much. And part of her wished she'd already talked to him about the article so she could feel like she deserved it. But she knew it would have ended badly if she'd told him sooner.

"I always want to help you, Corey."

"Taran?" Edgar called.

She glanced around and saw the children had all disappeared into the surrounding buildings. She held up one finger, and he tipped his head toward a gravel path leading to a pond surrounded by trees.

"I hear someone calling you, so I'm sure you need to go, but we're on the same page, right?" Corey asked again.

"Of course," she agreed.

"Good. Kick some article ass or whatever the appropriate 'you've got this' sentiment is," Corey said.

She laughed. "I'll talk to you later."

Taran pocketed the phone and ran her hands over her face, feeling uneasy. She didn't know why though, because Corey had all but given her the green light to write the piece. But the knot inside her tightened. She had to swallow it down and focus on this article now.

She glanced down the path and saw Edgar sitting at a picnic table facing the small pond. She headed his way, locking the tightness inside.

"You've asked for this story for over a year. Do you know why I finally said yes?" he asked as soon as she stood next to him.

"I prefer not to question my *good* luck."

Edgar chuckled. He was only in his mid-thirties and was in great shape. She watched his game in Guatemala City two nights ago, and he'd owned the field. But the more time she spent with him, the older he seemed.

"There has been speculation about why I have missed so many games this year and what it means." He paused, and his dark eyes turned her way. "I'm retiring after this season, and your article will announce it."

"I see," Taran said. Although she gave the athletes she featured the final okay on her pieces, she never let them dictate what the articles said. News of his retirement would be huge, and getting the exclusive on it was a big win, but she wasn't sure what strings this offer came with.

"I want more time to focus on these schools. On raising money to open more satellites. And not just here, but in many countries. I've been focusing my next satellite school in a small town in Colombia." He waved one of his security people over, who handed him a folder.

He placed it on the table and motioned to Taran. The first page grabbed her eye as she recognized the logo before zeroing in on the name. *Schools First.* An organization focused on education around the world.

"Helping Hands." She let her finger drag over the logo.

"Yes, I've been working with the Demodas' charity. They will be my parent organization. But they have focused their time and energy on food, clothes, shelter, and jobs. This off-shoot will focus on schools. Marc and I have been working on the details for over a year."

Taran skimmed over the pages of information, all organized and well thought out. The focus was on determining what an area needed, whether it was buildings, teachers, access to computers and the internet, or basic supplies like books and pencils. The organization even had areas that would focus on the arts, languages, and physical activity. Three pages were dedicated to building programs for children who struggled to learn for any number of reasons. The plan was to create well-balanced, well-run schools around the world.

The entire time she flipped through the information, she felt his gaze on her. Finally, she shut the folder and glanced back up.

"Are the Demodas why you finally said yes to me?" Taran couldn't help but wonder how much Marc and Beth had to do with making this happen.

"The reason I chose you to tell the story is multi-pronged." He glanced back out to the pond. "You've done a few fundraising blogs with Marc Demoda over the last three months."

She nodded. The first had just been Marc donating for views and clicks. But the second two pulled in donations from other major celebrities and even her regular readers.

"I'm sure you'll tell me Marc's name was the draw that made those work," Edgar said. "But it would be naïve of you not to realize that your words, coupled with his status, made it happen."

"Anyone can write the words."

He shook his head. "No, they cannot. You have an amazing ability to cut through bullshit while pulling the reader in and telling them how to feel. *That* is a skill."

It wasn't the first time someone had told Taran this. It had been something she'd heard through high school and college. She had the ability to move people, sway ideas, and change minds with just her words, and that was why she wrote them.

"It's flattering," she said and shrugged. "If you want me to blog a few times about this, I can. I'm not opposed. Especially with you and Marc championing it. That will tie it into the sports world."

"That's not what I want exactly." He cleared his throat. "Schools First needs someone to run *our* blog. To help me, and all the other ambassadors of this cause, with sound bites for speeches and interviews."

She nodded. That made sense. Most charities had someone in that role.

"I want that person to be you."

"*Me*? I'm a sports reporter." She shook her head.

He turned, and his eyes flashed. "I'm well aware of who you are, Ms. Kuppton. I've read everything you've written, including your piece on Syria."

Her mouth fell open. No one had ever connected her to her story about her time with the SEALs.

"I don't go into things blindly. You have a skill set I require, so of course, I looked into you."

"I, uh, I *have*—a job," she stuttered. Honestly, she was barely juggling that and her blog. She had been struggling to keep up. She'd even had to drop weekly two months ago.

"I realize you work for *Sports Illustrated*, and I'm not asking you to quit. I'm asking you to do this too."

Taran stared down at the information on the table. Ideas swirled in her brain, but she shook her head as she shut the information folder. This wasn't something she could do.

"I doubt I'm the right person. You need to find someone who shares your passion."

He pulled up his phone and clicked a few buttons. A grainy video played. Taran winced as she saw her nineteen-year-old self on the screen. Miss Teen USA pageant. It was one of those moments of her life she felt like she'd only been watching, not participating in. Like the girl on the screen was a totally different person.

Taran stood in a deep purple dress with a sash draped over her shoulder, listening to the question directed at her.

"The one thing I'd do to improve the world is ensure every child learns to read and write. Learning opens doors. But the ability to read is not just knowledge. It's entertainment. It's escape. It's enjoyment. And writing isn't just words—it's power. Many things are important. But I say learning first."

She remembered saying those words. And she couldn't claim she didn't believe them now. But she didn't think she could be passionate about them—or *anything*. The knot tightened in her chest. She'd fought that knot, keeping it down, but at the moment, she almost didn't want to fight to keep her feelings away anymore. And that terrified her.

He paused the video.

"That girl seems pretty passionate."

"I'm not that girl."

He nodded. "People change. They grow up."

"No, you don't understand." Her hands fisted on the table. "I can't help you. I can't be passionate. I'll write your article. But that's all I can do."

Taran pushed to her feet.

Edgar gave one clipped nod. "Taran, the person you are today is who I want to hire, but I know that passionate girl is still inside you. And I'd like to work with both."

"I won't change my mind."

"I'll have my driver take you back to the city," he said.

Taran's body relaxed. "Thank you."

"But keep one thing in mind. Your article will talk about my single-minded determination to succeed. And my current goal is to bring you on board."

And the knot inside Taran tightened even more.

34

THIS WAS THE first time Corey walked up to this red door with any level of confidence. Each time he'd come to Taran's place before, he'd been pissed off, confused, or desperate, but this time he knew he and Taran were on the same page. That fact settled every molecule in his body.

Plus, he had a two-week home stretch, and she'd be in Jersey too. She'd even said her next feature didn't require travel, so he'd put in to stay home for the Metros' road trips where he wouldn't be pitching. No one questioned it. His pitching was on fire. If he kept up his pattern through August and September, no one had any doubt that it would be a Cy Young season.

Corey couldn't remember a time he'd felt so settled in himself.

He knocked a second time and had to chuckle. Some things, he guessed, would never change, and Taran answering her door without him having to repeatedly beat on the thing must be one of them.

The door finally swung open, and he smiled, enjoying how her hair was falling out of the messy bun on the top of her head. Her cutoffs and T-shirt assured him she'd be fine with his plan to stay in tonight.

"Is it Saturday already?" she asked and glanced around, almost like she wasn't sure where she was. But she did move back and wave him in, shutting the door behind them. He tucked the black lock hanging in her eye behind her ear.

"Chipmunk, you okay?" he asked and felt another prick of alarm when she didn't react to the nickname; instead, she just leaned into him. He wrapped his arms around her. "What's going on?"

She sighed and shook her head against his T-shirt. He worried that she might not open up.

"It's been a long few days. I have an article I don't know how to write, and I haven't posted a blog this week. And even though I flew home early, I don't know if I'll have Edgar's feature finalized by tomorrow." The words flew out of her mouth so fast he hardly caught them all. So much for his concern that she wouldn't talk. She barely took a breath as she continued her out-of-character word vomit. "It's due for edits tomorrow because they need to know how to format it. And I don't want to do the next month's, but I don't have a choice, and Edgar offered me a job, but I—"

His heart skipped a beat. Taran wasn't telling him she was moving, was she?

"Wait—job? In Guatemala?"

"No. Here, well, I don't know. It could be anywhere I want it, I guess. It's for Schools First."

She continued her rambling about how she couldn't do the job, and he relaxed, having no idea what she was talking about except that she would be in New Jersey.

"Hey." He tipped her chin up to look at him. "Hey. Look at me."

Her eyes were wide, almost panicked.

"You do not have to take a job you don't want."

"I know." Her jaw locked.

He searched her expression, feeling like there was a bigger problem he was missing, but he couldn't get a read on her. Everything about this exchange seemed so out of character for the normally mellow woman.

The need to fix things for her pulsed through his system. "Let me help you. Do you have a draft of the Edgar thing?" he asked, and she nodded. "How about I have Microsoft Word read it to me, and I can give you my thoughts? It's probably better than you think, and I will get an idea about this job offer if I know what Schools First is."

"That would be great." She blinked, and it seemed like a fog cleared, but her entire body tensed. "Wait, did I forget I was supposed to make us dinner? *Shoot.*" She pushed away from him, her whole body tight.

He crossed his arms and rocked back on his heels as she brushed her bangs out of her face.

"I'm sure I can throw something together." She blinked rapidly before looking toward the kitchen and then back at him.

"Taran." Corey tried to keep his voice calm, but he was worried. "We didn't talk about dinner, and you weren't supposed to cook. I thought we'd do takeout."

"Oh good." Taran slumped. "I wasn't sure what I had. But takeout is easy. My computer is over there. I was working on edits, so Edgar's article should already be open. Do you need me to help you set up the read aloud?"

"No, I'm used to it." He searched the room until his eyes landed on her laptop sitting on a small desk. Next to her desk was another one of those tiny cute chairs that made him question his ability to sit on it safely, but as worked up as Taran was, he wasn't going to ask for a different one.

"You feel like anything specific?" Taran asked after he carefully placed his weight in the tiny wooden chair.

"Whatever you want, chipmunk. I'll even pretend I'm a deer and eat leaves if you want that weird place again." His hackles rose even more when she didn't respond to his teasing about the vegan salad restaurant she loved.

She was way off today, and that scared him. There was something almost familiar about her mood, but he couldn't piece together why it seemed that way because she'd never acted like this before.

He shook his head and turned his attention to the computer.

It was on, but he didn't see the document. The only thing open on the screen was a file folder. He moved the mouse to the bar at the bottom and clicked to maximize it. He tried to focus on finding Edgar's last name, but the one jumping out at him was his own. He paused, trying to think of another athlete whose last name was Matthews. It wasn't that uncommon, but the *September* after it meant it must be someone from the New York area since Taran had told him that she wouldn't be traveling this month. No one was coming to mind, and curiosity got the better of him as he clicked open the file.

"I'm feeling pizza. Do you care?" Taran popped her head back into the room.

"I'm fine with anything but mushrooms. I hate mushrooms." She nodded and went back into the kitchen.

He turned back to the computer. Inside the file labeled Matthews were three documents: one labeled *contract*, one labeled *notes*, and one labeled *draft*. He clicked into the draft, but it was blank. That was weird. He went to the contract next, figuring the name had to be on that one. But within seconds of opening it, he regretted the choice—so many words. Why did contracts have to be so wordy?

"Hey, Taran," Corey called, realizing although he didn't care if he had pizza, the team would. "Did you order yet?"

"Putting it in now. Did you want something else?" she called, but she didn't pop her head in this time.

"Yeah, can you add a cobb or antipasto salad? Something protein-heavy so I don't have to lie to the team nutritionist about what I ate today?" He scrolled down to the end of the document.

"They have both, or a chicken Caesar with double chicken?"

The words danced around his head, but his focus was on the signature.

His signature.

No, that couldn't be right. Taran wasn't writing a story on him. Even as the thought flipped through his mind, a heavy lead ball settled deep in his gut. The date said he'd signed it at the end of April, but that *couldn't* be right.

He shut his eyes and took a deep breath. This was not happening. They trusted each other, and he refused to jump to conclusions. His mind was playing tricks on him, forming words that weren't there. He reopened his eyes and focused on the document. But nothing changed. His signature; same date. The same contract that confirmed Taran was writing an article on him.

His hands shook, the dread growing inside him; no way had she tricked him into this. *No way.* He moved the mouse back to the folder to open the notes. His mind worked overtime trying to find any justification, a reason for what he was seeing. Taran never talked about it, but the explanation became harder to find as he scanned the notes. Everything he'd ever told her.

The words on the page swam as a white-hot fist squeezed his heart. He took a breath and looked up.

TARAN PAUSED AND waited after asking a second time which salad he wanted. Why wasn't he answering? She huffed out a breath through her nose, frustrated she couldn't order anything because he wouldn't tell her what he wanted. Her phone buzzed with another text—Edgar was still working to sell her on the job. She fought the knot in her chest, knowing she couldn't take it. Her head swam; too many things were hitting her and she couldn't process them all.

Becoming someone else hadn't been an overnight thing. She hadn't come home from Syria a completely different person. She'd worked to put her old life, the life that had disappeared in a roadside blast, behind her. With every step forward, she pushed the pain away and became a woman that couldn't feel the hurt. Corey had already tested the tight hold on the knot of anguish she kept firmly locked away, and recently, it felt ready to burst free. She didn't want *that* or anything else pushing her. Really, she just wanted this all over because she couldn't handle one more thing.

She sighed, trying to not be irritated that Corey still hadn't answered. Maybe he couldn't hear her since he'd planned to have Word read the article to him. She moved through the doorway to the family room.

"Cor, which salad?"

His gaze slowly shifted from the computer, and the air sucked out of the room. His face said one word—*betrayed.* The undisguised pain in his eyes fed the knot in her chest, causing it to rise, clawing at her throat, almost choking her.

No. He doesn't know. She sucked in a hard breath. How would he know about the article? Her mind whirled. Her file. The random thoughts she'd jotted down.

"You went through my computer?" Her voice had a sharpness she didn't intend, but instead of throwing it back at her, he shook his head, looking lost and alone. She saw the echoes of the child he'd been sitting in her living room, and frustration surged in her system. The last thing she wanted was to hurt him. Why did everything have to get so screwed up? Why did life always go wrong?

His eyes dropped to her hands fisted at her sides before his gaze slowly dragged back to her face.

"Please." His voice died at the end of the word, and he cleared his throat. "*Please* tell me it's not what it looks like. Tell me you're not writing about *me* next month."

"I can't," she croaked. She didn't cry anymore; she hadn't in over two years, but her eyes burned. "But Corey—"

"Sean." Corey's jaw tightened. In the blink of an eye, all the pain and insecurity disappeared. He became the Corey Matthews who spoke to the press. The one who could laugh off a bad game or smile like nothing mattered. "He came to my house; we were playing *Diablo.* That was the first day you got me talking." One harsh laugh cracked out from between his lips. "You're good."

"It wasn't like that." She reached out, but he stood up so fast the chair knocked to the floor. "Corey, trust me."

"Off the record? Or are we on it?" His words cracked like a whip against her skin.

"I would never—"

"Never what?" His voice was eerily calm. "Never trick me to get information? Never use me as a means to an end? Never worm your way into my life for a story?"

"That is not what I did." Her nails dug, cutting into her palms as the knot tightened inside her. Why didn't anyone believe her? They always pushed, trying to get a reaction from her. Trying to make her feel worse.

"No. You got way more than a story. I gave you my heart on a silver platter," he growled as he headed for the door. "Thanks for crushing it, Tinkerbell."

She slammed her arm into her laptop, sending it flying into the vase and causing it to slam into the wall. Something shattered and knocked the lamp off the desk, and onto her bare foot.

"Damn it, you signed the contract, not me. No one tricked you into doing that. If I don't write this story, someone else at *Sports Illustrated* will," she shouted.

He swallowed and shook his head before walking out the door. She kicked the desk, sending it flying into the wall, before crumpling onto the floor.

All her anger deflated, and for the first time in way too long, she cried.

It was hard to know how long she had sat there. It felt like forever, and it felt like thirty seconds. Finally, warm hands carefully touched her arms. She looked up, expecting the two-tone brown eyes she adored to be staring back.

The cold slate gaze was jarring, and she flinched away.

"T-cup," Nick said calmly, holding both palms out. Nothing about his demeanor seemed hostile, so she forced herself to relax.

"What—" But she stopped; she knew.

"Yeah, he reached out. Taran, my family has seen what's happening right now more times than I can count. They've seen me when my anger is out of control, when I've forgotten something I was supposed to do, or when I've lost days or weeks of time. I have a flashback mid-conversation, and everyone but Morgan avoids using words that start with L. Everyone, including Corey, knows what trauma response can look like." He sat next to her on the floor.

Taran glanced around. Her laptop was in two pieces, the screen shattered. Glass from the vase covered the floor, and the desk was at an odd angle, the corner stuck in the sheetrock. Taran groaned and dropped her head into her hands. "I guess I'm more surprised that he cared enough to send you?"

Nick shrugged. "He knows I've never chosen between team family and blood family, so as far as you two go, I'm Switzerland. I don't know what happened, but the fact that he *texted* me made me haul ass."

Taran swallowed the lump in her throat and started at the beginning. Nick listened, but silence stretched out for a long time when she was done.

"Corey knows he's an idiot. Why didn't you just tell him he signed the contract months ago?" Nick asked.

That was the question, wasn't it? She ran her hands over her eyes.

"By the time he signed that stupid contract, I wanted him to trust me enough to do it." She pulled her knees to her chest, trying to hold herself together.

"Why was that so important?" Nick asked.

He probably wanted the answer to be because she cared about Corey, which was true, but that wasn't the only reason. She knew it. She wanted him to trust her because everyone she knew had questioned her at every turn for two years. *Are you okay? Are you sure?* She hated it. But now she saw that everyone asked the questions because they could see what she refused to admit. She wasn't okay.

The front door opened.

"She okay?" The voice wasn't the one Taran wanted to hear.

Seabass moved into the room, taking in the destruction.

"Sorry. I called him." Nick smirked. "I wasn't sure what shape you would be in, and he's better at this shit than me."

Like Nick had done, Seabass ignored the mess and came to sit on the floor beside her.

"Can we say the *T* word now?"

Therapy.

She nodded as she glanced around again. The mess she'd made was just a symbol of the disaster her life had become. "Yeah, I need some help."

35

COREY STOOD IN the locker room with multiple microphones shoved in his face as the cameras rolled. After another Metros win, his smile was planted firmly on his face. Even though inside, he felt like he was slowly dying.

"Coach make the right call pulling you before the eighth?" one reporter shouted.

"Of course," Corey agreed. Although he hadn't let up a run in seven innings, he walked two guys in the seventh. "My arm was getting tight. He and I talked; it's about the win, not how many times I can throw the ball."

"Not everyone would agree," another one tossed out.

"A younger version of myself would have said it was about how many pitches I could throw, so I can't judge too harshly when people are so wrong." Corey forced a laugh.

"Metros are still leading the league. Going into the playoffs at the top slot this year?" The question came from the other direction, so he turned with a smile.

"It's early August. Let's not get ahead of ourselves. A lot can happen in two months," Corey assured. He could fall in love and have his heart crushed.

"But you've got to be happy with how this season is going."

He hated everything right now.

"My pitching is exactly where I need it to be. The rest of the guys are on point, and the bats are on fire. How could I complain?" Corey pointed to the back. "One more, and I'm done, guys."

"Didn't hear any mention of chipmunks today," one of the younger guys who'd been having fun with Corey's fun facts about chipmunks prompted.

Corey's heart imploded, but he kept the smile firmly in place. "I heard they bite, man." He turned and walked away, heading to his locker to grab his shit. He wanted to get out of the locker room, the stadium. Hell, he'd love to leave the country. After getting pulled, he'd gone through the rub-down, ice bath, and shower, so nothing kept him here *right now*. He grabbed his key and pocketed his phone without looking at it.

"You good?" Daily asked from the next locker over.

"Just in the zone," he said and left, skipping beer night to head home. Hopeful he could keep dodging everyone for a while longer.

Nine days later, he couldn't avoid Marc's house anymore.

"What made you decide not to travel with the team this month?" Marc asked as Corey moved back toward him.

Today, Corey had done a complete workout and simulated three innings in Marc's cages. When the Metros had agreed to let him skip the three-day road trip, it had been with the understanding that he'd work out with Marc. So although he didn't want to be here, he had to be.

"Don't fix something that ain't broke," Corey said, but he was itchy to leave. He'd been avoiding everyone so he wouldn't have to talk about Taran. It was easier that way because his heart panged at just the thought of her name.

"Don't pack up your shit. You're coming in," Marc said.

"Not up for it." Corey bent to grab his bag but paused when he felt the hand on his shoulder.

"Not a choice, man." Marc pulled away to cross his arms and glare.

Corey sighed. It absolutely was a choice, but he didn't feel like fighting him. So he walked into Marc's house and slumped onto the leather sectional, noting how many of the Evanses were there. He gritted his teeth. Will, Luke, Joey, Danny, and Nick. Even Grant stood in the corner, which had Corey's eyebrows lifting.

"Yeah, you know it's bad if I leave my house." Grant shook his head.

"I'm chill." Corey flashed his practiced smile.

"Nope," Will said. "Put away *The* Corey Matthews; don't care about him at the moment. But I really need to chat with Corey."

"I'm right here, and like I said, I'm chill." Good wouldn't work. He didn't feel good. Couldn't even say he felt fine. But chill—that summed it up. He wasn't going to lose his shit; he was simply getting through every day.

Will sighed. "You *love* her, Corey. The big, can't control it, makes you all kinds of happy and miserable all rolled into one kind of love."

He loved her.

He missed her.

The last three weeks had given him a lot of time to realize he didn't care about the story. Although she should have told him about it, she was right—he'd signed the contract. It was dumb to do it, but he was used to Sean looking out for him. It never occurred to Corey that Sean would let him make a dumb decision if he didn't represent him. He also couldn't deny the truth of the fact that if she'd had asked him to write an article on him, he wouldn't have hesitated to say yes.

Plus, it became abundantly clear to him when she shattered her computer that she was not okay. Thinking back, he'd seen signs all along that she was struggling, but he hadn't recognized them until she imploded.

"Never said I didn't love her." Corey sighed and shut his eyes.

"So do *something*." The frustrated edge in Will's voice made Corey's hands fist.

"What, Will? Beg her to love me back? I can't help that I fell in love while she was hanging out with me so she could write a story."

Grant cleared his throat loudly and moved from his corner to sit next to Corey. "I remember this feeling, man. A little pissed off and a whole lot hurt."

Corey grunted.

"You led the charge when I needed to get my head out of my ass and not let Trish go, right?" The corner of Grant's mouth turned up in an almost smile. "Because when you can't tell your ass from your elbow, that's what family does—"

"I appreciate what you're trying to do, and I'm glad you guys let me be a part of family stuff—"

"Let you?" Will snapped. "Jesus, Cor." He shook his head.

Nick put his hand on Will's shoulder.

"He's not going to hear this from you, Will. You're his best friend. He expects you to say it." Nick stepped toward the sofa and glared down at Corey. "Listen to me, though. We don't *let* you be a part of anything. You *are* a part of this family, and you have been for more than twenty years. You," Nick pointed his finger at Corey, "are as much my brother as the asshole sitting next to you."

The echoes of "same" from all the brothers around the room formed a lump in Corey's throat. He looked from Nick to Grant, then Will, Luke, Danny, and Joey. Finally, his eyes fell on Marc, who gave him a firm nod. Corey had spent a lifetime looking for a family when he'd been a part of one the entire time. He'd always thought of them as his family—his brothers, and he needed to stop letting his self-doubt keep him on the outside. He could see in each of these guys' expressions that they meant it. He'd long ago become an Evans.

He cleared his throat. "Thanks."

"Oh, I'm *not* done," Nick demanded, and Corey's eyes shot back to the intense slate gaze boring into him. "What did you tell me when I didn't know what was going on with Morgan?"

Corey couldn't hold Nick's eyes, and he stared at the stone coffee table.

"Not going to answer? Fine, I'll remind you." His voice was steel. "You told me to talk to her, because if I didn't admit how I felt and figure shit out, I'd be watching her with someone else. Is that what you want?"

Corey swallowed hard.

"I've said this a few times now, but if you want this to work, you have to stop being the one to walk away, Corey," Marc said from across the room.

"I saw her the other day," Danny said.

Corey's entire body locked. Where the hell had Danny seen her? What was he doing with her? But suddenly, a calm washed over him. He relaxed into the leather sectional behind him. Danny wasn't going after Taran any more than Corey would go after Danny's girl. He trusted him.

"How is she?" he croaked.

"It was just in passing. I was on my way to get checked out after the fire last week." Danny shrugged.

"You good?" Nick asked.

"Yeah, just procedural because the entire family died. They like to make sure we're handling our feelings on it." Danny frowned. "But anyway, I saw her in the parking lot. She looked sad, Cor."

Corey gritted his teeth. "I get that you all mean well. And I hate hearing she's upset." He cracked his neck. "But here's the thing; *I'm* not the one who can fix this."

He heard the soft sound of a throat clearing, and he glanced behind him toward the entrance to the foyer.

Beth stood next to Sean. His eyes flitted around the room before he looked to his feet. His former agent rocked back on his heels, looking uncomfortable, a few sheets of paper in his hand.

"Sean's looking for approval for the article," Beth said.

"I've left a few messages, but you aren't returning calls. I figured I'd try Beth and Marc." Sean scanned the room again.

Corey looked at Beth, and she inclined her head just slightly, saying she'd read it. He swallowed, remembering the notes on Taran's computer. A part of him was desperate to see what she'd said about him. Another piece, though, was terrified at the idea. Never had he opened himself up to a person like he had to Taran.

"Give it to me." Will stepped forward, and Sean handed him two white pieces of paper. A million times faster than Corey ever could, Will scanned the article. He glanced up at Corey twice as he read.

Corey's stomach sank. He thought he'd prepared himself for anything she'd written. But as Will sat next to him. Corey's heart lodged in his throat.

"Can I read it to you?" Will asked.

Corey nodded, shut his eyes, and braced himself.

"Fame makes people larger than life, more an idol than a person. Corey Matthews has lived most of his life as a possession of the American people. Someone everyone felt they had the right to know. Myself included. We create beliefs and expectations based on what we claim is the truth we've heard. I've met dozens of athletes who have surprised me over the years. But never one who not only completely changed my perception and beliefs about them—but also about myself.

"When I walked into Corey Matthews's apartment, I expected to see collections, art, and photographs of his significant accomplishments, all the things we dream of in a house. I didn't expect that the wall over his sofa would be framed works of art by his nieces and nephews. I had no idea that his priceless collection would consist of bottle caps from family nights. That the pictures he framed would be of his godchildren's christenings and snapshots of Christmas mornings. I expected grand, but what I found was better. I didn't walk into a house; I walked into a home. And that sums up Corey Matthews perfectly. You expect grand, but once you get to know him, you find something much better."

"Wait." Corey stopped him as his heart raced in his chest. "This sounds good."

Will smiled. "I think a part of you knew it would be."

Corey smiled as Will continued to read. Taran explained that Corey was a person who wanted boundaries and wasn't unwilling to share and be open but had learned after a lifetime in the limelight that he had to share on his terms. She highlighted his hope that he could share more in the future and, in turn, the media would respect his boundaries. It was almost like she put forth a reasonable argument that the public could get behind and support him.

It was what Corey had been hoping to do when he asked her to think about helping him change his stance with the media.

He swallowed hard. As poorly as Taran had handled everything about this—as much as he wished they could go back in time and she'd talk to him—the article itself was perfect.

"On a *personal* note."

Corey's eyes shot to Will's, and hope surged in his heart like a shot of adrenaline.

"I owe Corey an apology. For the last few months, I've been after something from him. He believes it was a story, but it was more than a story. I was after his trust. And although I didn't earn it, he gave it to me openly and without hesitation. He deserves everything he's wished for, and I hope it's not too late for me to have a part in it.

"So in case you didn't know, America, the man has a huge heart, and if you give him some time and space, he'll share it with you. And trust me, it'll be worth it."

His mind whirled. Maybe this was fixable. He glanced around the room. Maybe it was all fixable. But to do that, he had to stop running away when things got hard. And not just from Taran.

"Sean." Corey stood up and walked over to the man who watched him warily.

Sean pulled his shoulders back as if he was bracing himself. Corey stopped directly in front of him and stared down, seeing Sean swallow. Corey smirked. It was nice to know he still intimidated the man, but that wasn't his intention. He held his hand out.

"I owe you an apology."

"What?" Sean's eyes widened, and he looked from Corey's hand to his face and back again.

"I don't pay you to be my friend. You aren't supposed to approve of all my choices, and you're the guy I want to say, 'whoa, whoa, think this through.' I shouldn't have fired you on a whim, and I clearly remember how miserable you were when I signed the contract for Taran's article without reading it." Corey watched the tension drop from Sean's shoulders, and he took a breath. "I don't deserve your help, but I'd love it if you were willing to represent me again."

Sean crossed his arms over his chest. "I'm upping my fee."

Corey laughed. "Of course you are. That's fine." He still held his hand out, and finally, Sean shook it.

36

"HOW ARE YOU doing?"

Usually, it put Taran's teeth on edge, but that question was why she was here. Bruce sat back in his chair, crossing his ankle over his knee, and waited. The man, with his buzzed hair, T-shirts, and tattoos, looked nothing like she'd picture a therapist would. But the former army officer Seabass had recommended was a godsend.

"I'm feeling less like I'm standing in quicksand." Taran shook her head. "I put my notice in at *Sports Illustrated*. Wayne was actually disappointed I was leaving. Ironic, huh?"

"You're good at your job. Sarcasm and snark don't change that fact. And I know you realize how much the magazine will miss you." Bruce's eye bored into her. "And how do you feel about the new position?"

"The good kind of stress. I'm excited about working with Schools First. There are moments when I feel that tight ball of pain, but I'm trying to let it go. My life is different from how I'd planned it to be, but I realize that different can still be good. I can keep some of the things I wanted without letting it break me."

Letting part of her old self back in meant allowing the hurt of all she lost back in as well. It was a struggle to let the ache in her chest stay. But like Bruce said, when she faced the deep cuts, she gave them the chance to start to heal. That's what she wanted and what she was beginning to do.

"Now, the biggest gaping hole in my heart isn't the loss of my old life. It's the loss of my new one."

Bruce cleared his throat.

"I know my life is more than Corey Matthews." She rolled her eyes. "I'm working on being dramatic."

He chuckled. "You still haven't heard from him?"

"I didn't write the article so he would call me. But I'd hoped he might. So it was disappointing." Taran tucked her bangs behind her ear and switched from sitting crisscross on the sofa to tucking one leg under her. "The positive thing to come out of him not calling is that I got to feel disappointment."

"And?"

"It sucked," Taran said, receiving a full-out laugh in response. "I know that wasn't what you meant. I worked through it. It hurts, but I hurt *him,* and I can't expect him to forgive me just because I wrote a good story."

"Have you thought more about reaching out to him?"

Taran warred with herself over that. She wanted to more than she wanted to do anything else. But it didn't feel fair. He was in the home stretch of the season. The Metros were leading the league, and he was doing well. The drama would mess with that. She needed to put him first.

"If I don't hear from him once the Metros are done for the year, I'll reach out."

She spent another twenty minutes chatting before she headed out. It was ridiculous to think back at all the effort she'd put into pretending to be fine and refusing to deal with her issues for the last two years, because Bruce was good. Therapy was good. The best part was that she felt better. Last weekend was her parents' fiftieth wedding anniversary, and when she teared up at the slideshow, her sister and mother practically tackle hugged her. In those ways, it was nice to feel normal again.

The worst part was how much she missed Corey. She continued to torture herself by watching his games and interviews. A silly part of her heart held on to the hope that he'd drop a chipmunk comment into them again, although he hadn't since claiming they bite. It was hard to believe that she used to hate hearing that word out of his mouth.

The drive home was automatic, like she was on autopilot. She had one more article to do before she was officially finished with *Sports Illustrated*, and she was hoping to get the last name off Wayne's big five list. Finishing his list of impossibles before she left would be the way to go out. The basketball star had been on a media hiatus, but she'd reached out to his agent, hoping that he'd change his mind before the start of the season.

She scooped up a manilla envelope from her front steps, but it wasn't until she dropped it on her kitchen counter that she saw the name. Her heart lurched.

Chipmunk.

In the blink of an eye, she had it ripped open.

Trust is a two-way street, especially because I want more than just that.

The contract was so familiar because she'd seen tons of them from Sean. Corey must have rehired him. And although she knew what she was looking at, she couldn't believe the words. She didn't consciously decide to go to Corey's, but she was pounding on his apartment door with the envelope in her hand fifteen minutes later.

When it opened and she was hit with the smell of Obsession for Men, her stomach bottomed out. It seemed impossible that it had been over a month since she'd seen Corey. Because standing there seeing him in his typical jeans and white T-shirt, it felt like no time had passed.

His eyes slowly roamed over her like a caress before landing back on hers. The air felt like it was sucked out of the hallway, and everything seemed to disappear as they stared at each other.

"Hey," he said finally.

"Hey." She swallowed.

Corey stepped back and let her in. The second she was inside, she was wrapped in the warm hominess that was his apartment. When she turned back to him, he hadn't moved more than two steps from the door. His stance was wide, with arms crossed like he was bracing himself. When she didn't say anything, he cracked his neck. Unsure of where to start, Taran lifted the contract toward him.

"You need a co-writer for your autobiography?" Taran couldn't hide her shock.

"I need *you* to be my co-writer," he corrected.

"How did this even happen?" Taran asked.

The corner of his mouth turned up. "My agent; he's a re-sourceful guy."

"Hot Shots." She held his two-tone eyes, remembering the conversation. "Hate them."

"Reporters." He swallowed. "Used to hate them, but then I met this woman, and she turned everything upside down."

"I know the feeling." She paused again. This was so hard, but she needed to say these words. "Corey, I'm sorry. I should have told you about the article."

He searched her face for a long moment before he nodded.

"Yeah, you should have. I think there were a few things you should have told me."

"Yeah," she agreed.

"Want to sit down and tell me any of them now?" The hesitance laid heavy in his voice, almost as if he wasn't sure she'd say yes. But also, the undertone of longing sounded like he was desperate for her to open up. And that longing and the contract in her hand gave her confidence.

She moved wordlessly to the sofa, and he sat a cushion away, the space between them a metaphor for the current gap in their relationship. But maybe if she could open up and talk to him, they could close that chasm.

"After the roadside bomb, I was in so much pain. Not physical; physically, I was fine." She tossed the contract onto the table and tucked her hair behind her ear as she turned to face him.

His gaze locked on her.

"But emotionally, it hurt to think about it. It hurt to remember Jeremy. It hurt to find meaning in my life. It hurt when people asked if I was okay. I hated it."

Taran shut her eyes and took a breath. The couch shifted, and she felt a warm hand on her leg. She forced herself to look at him. In his face, she saw sadness for what she'd gone through, but also adoration. She kept going because he needed to hear these words.

"It was easier to lock the pain away. But when I did, I shut a part of myself down. I was sleep walking through life, not feeling anything, but it was easier than hurting." Tentatively, she placed her hand over his.

He turned his hand palm up and laced their fingers together. "I get that sometimes running away from things is easier than dealing with them. I've spent too much time walking away when shit got hard. But I don't want to do that anymore." He shifted closer. "Not with you." The husky words sent a fluttering through her chest.

"I've never been able to hide from my feelings for you. The first time you kissed me, I started to wake up."

His eyes danced, and he almost smiled. "Like sleeping beauty."

She chuckled. "I guess. But you made me feel more than awake. You made me feel alive and loved. And I wanted to hold on to that so bad that I didn't want to say anything that would wreck it."

"Not saying hard things doesn't make them go away." He raised his eyebrows.

"I know, and I'm so sorry, but I was so afraid of admitting so many things, especially how I felt about you."

He sucked in a breath. "And now?"

She looked into his two-tone eyes. "I love you, Corey."

He wrapped his arm around her, pulling her over to straddle his lap. He tucked her tightly against his chest and buried his face in her neck.

His arms shook as he hugged her. "I love you too," he whispered. "I've missed you so fucking much."

The top of his hair tickled her jaw as he held her. Warmth washed over her, along with a wave of contentment. The ache in her chest was there, but she felt whole for the first time in a very long time.

Taran ran her palm along the rough hair of his beard as she tipped his face up to hers. His breath danced across her lips, and she longed to press her mouth to his, but she had more to say.

"Corey, from now on, no more hiding. About anything. I'll feel the hard things. I'll say the hard things, even when I know you might not want to hear them."

"And I promise I'm not going anywhere. We deal with the hard shit together."

Her heart swelled with his words, and she pressed her lips to his, sealing the pledge with a kiss.

37

COREY GLANCED NEXT to him. It probably wasn't the time or the place, but his girl's silky smooth skin was calling him. He dropped his head, pressing his lips against the soft hollow where Taran's neck and shoulder met.

"Mmm," she hummed, which was evil because it enticed him to do something that he shouldn't do here.

"How do you feel about beard burn on the red carpet?" Even as he asked the question, his lips moved along the smooth skin.

She pushed him back with a chuckle. "Bad, I feel *bad* about that."

He groaned. "You just look so fucking hot, chipmunk."

Her gown was off the shoulders, and her hair was pinned up so her satin skin was on full display. He traced her collarbone and dipped into the sweetheart neckline of her dress. She shivered, and that constant pull of desire that Taran brought out surged deep in his gut.

"And your legs in those heels." He groaned, loving how the blue fabric parted, showing off legs he wanted to uncross and wrap around his waist. "You're killing me."

"We can leave as soon as you accept your mother's lifetime achievement award, and I promise to make it worth the wait." Her mint-green eyes sparkled with dirty promise.

"God, I love you," he said.

It had been two weeks since she came to his apartment with the contract he'd sent her. Taran had agreed to help him write the book and find the balance of letting the public in and keeping his boundaries. He had complete faith in her.

Unfortunately, Hot Shots felt very strongly that if he was telling his story and wanted it to come off in the right light, he needed to step up and accept his mother's lifetime achievement award at the Tonys. But he wasn't doing it without Taran beside him.

"I love you too. But we're going to shock the press and probably most of the world when we step out of the limo together. Let's not make it worse by looking like we were fooling around on the drive over." Her eyebrow shot up.

"Fine," he pouted and sat back against the leather seat, but he rested his hand on her bare thigh. There was something about the grounding assurance he felt when she was right there with him that gave him the strength he needed to push through this night. And the warmth of her against his palm did that. It kept him grounded in this moment with her.

"We're officially on deck." The driver's voice came through the intercom.

"You're sure about this, right, Cor?" Taran asked.

"No, I absolutely don't want to accept this award, but Sean says I have to." Corey cracked his neck.

"No." The concern in her voice had him turning even as the car moved forward. "I meant about bringing me. Are you ready for this story?"

He shifted to face her, resting his palm around her jaw. As he stared into her green eyes, he saw his whole world. "Chipmunk, it's more than a story. It's the start of our life together, and I'm a hundred percent sure of us."

Her smile set his heart on fire, and the door beside him opened. Corey stepped out, turning back to grab her hand. Because with Taran beside him, the flashing lights and calling questions didn't matter.

Epilogue

BRIGHT LIGHT POINTED in his direction as multiple voices gave last-minute instructions, but Corey searched for one face. It didn't take him long to find Taran standing off to the side, out of the chaos. He had wanted her sitting next to him—after all, this was a joint project—but it wasn't about just him anymore.

She gave him a soft, encouraging smile and a firm *you got this* head nod, and he turned his attention to the camera as the morning show host, Andrea, introduced him.

"So much has happened in your life lately I'm not sure where we should start." Andrea shifted on her stool to address Corey.

"Since I'm here for a specific reason"—Corey flashed his token smile and gestured to the table between them—"how about we start with *The Hard Way*?"

Andrea nodded. "I feel like I've been hearing about this book forever and yet I was shocked when it released in two formats."

His publisher had been gung ho about promoting his book before Taran had even written the first draft. And at first, the company wasn't thrilled with the idea of writing one version for middle grades and one for new adults, but once Sean and Taran tag teamed them, the publisher got on board.

He spun the titanium band on his ring finger and spoke the words Taran had helped him put together.

"As soon as my wife and I started the actual writing process, I realized that although adults would be curious about my story, having watched me since I was born, it was the strugglingly twelve-year-olds I wanted to hear my story the most. The kids out there having a hard time, whether they're like me with dyslexia, or maybe ADHD or ADD, depression, or getting over trauma or any number of struggles; I wanted them to know that someone else had been through it. It's a million times easier not to do it alone."

"You shocked the world two years ago when you started talking about your dyslexia."

Although he'd been doing this for a while now, it was still odd to him to talk about his struggles with reading. But he was no longer afraid to do it.

"My nephew, Noah, was the catalyst for that. He and I bonded over our shared struggle, and he admitted knowing someone else had been through it and turned out successful gave him a lot of confidence."

"And now you've done almost two hundred assemblies in schools all over."

Corey nodded. "With an organization called Schools First, and they do a fabulous job helping me talk to kids all over. Between that and the book, I hope that no child who is struggling ever feels as alone as I did."

"Yes, *The Hard Way*. I read the middle grade version, and I have to say you did an amazing job."

"That's all my incredible wife, Taran."

Corey's gaze automatically moved from the camera to the beautiful woman in question.

"She has been an endless support for me, through the book and my retirement from baseball after this last season." He chuckled as Taran's eyebrow cocked. "She's even getting used to me being home way too much."

Andrea laughed. "I'm sure she's loving the extra set of hands this last month. Do we want to talk about the other big thing that happened?"

Taran gave him another nod.

"I'd love to talk about my son."

"I'm going to start by saying that I was lucky enough to get to hold the little man before we came out here and he's adorable."

"He is, if I do say so myself. And I know everyone has been somewhat patiently waiting for us to introduce him. Taran and I really appreciate the time we've had to just be a family of three this past month."

"Can we bring him out?" Andrea asked.

Corey nodded to Taran as he stood off the stool making room for her to sit. He took his son out of her arms and settled him into the crook of his elbow. His heart still exploded every time this little boy blinked at him. Corey carefully tilted him for the camera to zoom in.

"Isn't this little man the cutest thing ever?" Andrea gushed like the overly-caffeinated morning show host she was. "So let's talk about his name because as soon as I heard it, I knew it meant something."

Taran shifted on the stool next to him. "It was actually Corey who suggested it, but as soon as he said it, I knew that was our son's name. We had some important people we wanted to honor, ones who took care of both Corey and me."

Corey turned to the camera. "So, everyone, I'd like you to meet our son, Evan Jeremy Matthews."

Dear Reader,

First, let me just say a massive THANK YOU! Thank you for reading More Than a Story. Thank you for supporting me. It's only because readers exist that writers get to live out their dreams.

So, I loved this book. Probably way too much. You can laugh or roll your eyes at that. But from the moment he came into More than the Game, Corey Matthews called to me. And I'm so happy to be able to give him a happily ever after. I actually had to tell my editors that I loved this story so much that I'm way too close to see it clearly, so they'd have to push me to fix it. I hope it ended up in a place that you all can love Taran and Corey as much as I do.

If you want more of Corey and Taran check out my website www.Jennibara.com for bonus epilogues, as well as my reading group on Facebook Jenni's World.

If you love a baseball bad boy, check out my novella for the Silver Lining series, coming out in fall of 2022. Ryan Daily might have to stop giving Corey a hard time long enough to figure his own love life out!

If you just love the Evanses, check out my website for Pre-order for More Than Myself a Holiday release coming November 2022. Which brother will be next? That's always the question, isn't it? Don't worry I promise to get to them all in due time!

Finally, remember: Live in your world, fall in love in mine.

Jenni
www.jennibara.com

Acknowledgments

Thank you, my wonderful readers, for reading my work and loving the Evan family as much as I do. Thank you to my street and ARC teams for all your sharing, your reviews, your support. You are all amazing!

A big thank you to my patient husband, who has to deal with me living in another world half the time. You are there with me planning time that we don't have into our schedules with bring these characters story to life. I couldn't do this without you and all your support. All of me loves you! To my kids who have to hear, "Hold on a second, mom is writing."—it takes a lot for you all to deal with my writing, but you all are awesome about it.

Haley, thank you so much for all your help. I don't think I have to the words to express what you do. I give you random projects, or big ideas, and then you have to figure out how to do them. But you always do! I mean look at TikTok! (SIDE NOTE: do you follow @jennibara because Haley has so much bringing the Evans men to life there) You manage all my stuff so I can just focus on the next story and I'm so thankful for that. You are the best.

Amy, thank you for dealing with me. I'm not the easiest but you manage to just say Oh Lord and keep going. Thank you for the endless phone calls so I don't need to drive alone, and helping me fix every little issue beta readers find. And thank you for keeping me on topic when I can't focus on it. ALSO, I can't wait to be supporting you this fall when Always Yours releases!

Erica thank you for all you do for me, helping me with blurbs, giving me tips on what works, and showing me how determination makes things happen.

All my author friends thank you for being supportive and inspiring writers. Brittanee Nicole, AJ Ranney, Amanda Zook, Bonnie Poirier, JL Reed, Garry Michaels, Kat Long, Jane Poller, Annie Charms, Daphne Elliot, Lizzie Stanley, Lydia Chelsea, Blye Donovan, and so many many more.

Thank you to my parents, who support me in all I do all the time. I couldn't get through life without you guys. Being able to count on you both all the time for help or support, or encouragement, is the best gift. Thank you for being examples I can stride to be with my kids and being the best grandparents ever.

Beth, thank you for being so flexible and understanding with this book. For being amazing with your edits and proofreads and checking everything twice! Your communication is wonderful keeping me in the loop. You are always a joy to work with, even if I can't figure out who vs. that and I want inanimate objects to be able to do things!

Stephanie, I love the interiors, you are awesome. And the fact that you deal with my million emails to make sure we are on track with patience is amazing. Thank you for all you do.

Kari, your cover is incredible, and your patience with me asking for changes was unending. I sing your praises to everyone.

Jeff, thank you for being the final nit-picky check to make sure everything is perfect. Becoming a romance reader wasn't on your to do list, but I'm grateful you did it anyway!

And big thank you to the rest of my friends and family who have helped me with encouragement and feedback. I love you all and am so thankful for your support.

About the Author

Jenni Bara lives in New Jersey, working as a paralegal in family law, writing real-life unhappily ever-afters every day. In turn, she spends her free time with anything that keeps her laughing, including life with four kids, or five, if you count her husband. She is just starting her career as a romance author writing books with an outstanding balance of life, love, and laughter.